The Slingshot Guy

L.J.Parsons

First edition published 2020

Editors   Robyn Bennett and
Bob Boze

Cover Designer: Daonza.com

Formatter: (Tapioca Press)
ISBN: 978-0-473-53081-5 paperback)
ISBN 978-0-473-53084-6 (eBook)

Contents

Chapter 1

2007

'Hang in there, Mitch,' Cameron Owen muttered. In anguish, he watched Mitch trying to get over the fence while the cop's sausage sized fingers rose to reach his legs. Cameron's heart pounded as he hid behind the graffiti-covered walls one hundred yards from Rivera Street in Encanto, San Diego, California.

The cop in a blue uniform was trying to pull twelve-year-old Mitch Ryan down from the wall. He growled, 'Gotcha! Where do you think you're going?' His paws gripped Mitch's legs, dragging him down.

Oh no, this is the end of me, that's it I'm done, Mitch thought as he held tight to the wall while trembling. He tried to regrasp the wall but the backpack hanging from his shoulder was throwing him off balance. As he turned his head, a glimpse of hope came when he spotted Cameron off in the distance.

Cameron paused as beads of sweat trickled from his forehead, then down his face and neck, as he motioned Mitch to be quiet by touching his finger over his lips.

The cop had chased Mitch for twenty minutes before he'd grabbed him, trying to get over the wall. 'Please Cameron do it... now,' Mitch whispered, sweat running down his face.

Seventeen-year-old Cameron's electric blue eyes squinted in the faint light of a nearby lamppost. While he waited for the last car to pass, he told himself, *you've done this before; you can do this again.* Then, with one hand, Cameron yanked out the slingshot from its ankle holster, and with the other he pulled a handful of stones from his pocket. Adrenalin surging, his eyes narrowed. Cameron aimed as if his existence depended on it. He stretched the rubber band of the slingshot as far back as it would go. A split second later the stone left the slingshot, striking the cop on his lower leg. A second later a second stone struck his other leg. Screaming in hellish pain, the cop crashed to the ground. Mitch shot Cameron a look, thanking him as he climbed over the wall, the cop lying on the ground, cussing Mitch.

'Cheers mate,' Cameron yelled as he too fled.

Chapter 2

Relief flooded Cameron's face as he ran past the unkempt lawns and houses with peeling paint in the typical crime-infested neighbourhood. A few minutes later he entered the hectic city centre and went into the mall. He pulled the hood of his jumper off his head. His clean-shaven, fair-skinned complexion, chiselled nose, square jaw, and the thin line scarred bottom lip, blended him in well with the crowd. While he pretended be shopping, he texted the time and meeting place to Mitch. Cameron's features, and his humble puppy eyes, would make sure no one took him for a drug dealer.

They met with Anton Miller, the president of the Red Serpent Gang, where Cameron and Mitch collected their 25 percent from the $5,000 drug deal. Hungry and exhausted, they headed for Karim Kebabs, a dingy looking place with ancient tables. They sat across from each other on the rickety chairs in a distant corner, across from the food display case. The scent of the roast beef was too tempting as Mitch licked his lips and breathed deeply. Cameron asked for a large lamb kebab and a root beer, while Mitch ordered a large beef kebab and a Fanta.

'Why didn't you strike him as soon as he chased me? Mitch asked. His straight blonde hair hiding his hazel eyes as they wandered around.

'He was running, not quite an easy target. I could've but there were bloody people everywhere,' Cameron replied with his deep voice as he ran his fingers through his light brown wavy shoulder-length hair.

'You know, Anton has no idea that it's your slingshot that saves the day all the time. And why won't you tell him?'

'I'll tell him one day. Let him think that I've been using the gun for protection. But in the meantime, let's keep it a secret.'

Mitch carried on talking while stuffing food into his mouth. 'You're a kick-ass with a slingshot, man. Did you feel awesome when cops gave you an award for bravery?'

'No not really, I was just at the right place at the right time. Anyone would have done the same given the circumstances, but I'm pleased it was what lead to the arrest of that psychopath.'

'That's so cool huh, your name was in the headlines: 'Cameron the sling shot guy saves girl from a serial rapist.'

'But who told you? That was two years ago,' Cameron asked, his eyebrows raising.

'A girl in my class. Her name is Madison. She always tells everyone how thankful she is and how the slingshot guy saved her.' Mitch answered.

'Hmm... Chatting her up, eh? Is she your girlfriend?'

'I wished, but her old man is a cop so that's the end of my love story; thank you very much. You and Hollie Ok?' he added.

'Yeah. Why, what is wrong with Hollie?' Cameron asked.

'I don't know, she's been acting weird lately. She's your girlfriend, why don't you ask her?'

'But she's your sister, you know her better than I do.'

'Stop being a pussy; ask her what's going on.'

'Don't think I haven't. I did. It's obviously something she needs to sort out herself.'

'But it's been a while now, she's been off on another planet man, I think it's because she's not taking any drugs.'

Cameron's phone dinged.

'I just got a text from Hollie, she's home already,' Cameron said.

'It's not like her to be home at this time,' Mitch said.

'Well, she just asked me to bring her something,' Cameron said. I'll order her a beef kebab and a diet coke.

They took a taxi and passed the city centre. Although it was quite normal to hear the whoop, whoop sound of a siren in the city, the sound still made Cameron and Mitch uneasy.

Noticing Cameron's nervousness, Mitch tried to reassure him. 'They can't see us. Look, there's a truck on the left, a van on the right and a bus following us,' he whispered. Waving his hand, Cameron motioned for Mitch to be silent.

As he took a deep breath Cameron suddenly realized the pungent smell of engine exhaust and gasoline was giving him a headache. He closed his eyes. He'd put up with the headache as he knew he had something to look forward to as he thought about Hollie the love of his life.

Three months ago, Cameron had met Hollie at the gay bar where he worked as a dancer. Cameron would never forget when he first saw 18 years old Hollie, as if she was looking for someone and in fact, she was looking for his gay friend.

Cameron asked her, 'Are you looking for someone?'

'Yes, but now I've found you. Sorry, just kidding. Is Marcus around? He works here.' They were both high, so neither was sure if it was lust or love at first sight. Apart from Hollie's swimsuit model figure, her passionate deep-set brown eyes with curly eyelashes attracted Cameron the most.

Later, when Hollie took Cameron home with her that night, Cameron had passed out during their first kiss: too much drugs and Jack Daniels. But Hollie was not disheartened by their not making love the first night they met.

The following morning Cameron woke with Holly naked, beside him. He scanned her bedroom, noticing roaches of weed filling the ashtray on the bedside table. On the floor were a pair of black stiletto shoes. Over a chair nearby were a glittery beaded bra and matching panties that looked like a stripper's dancing costume. The smell of stale alcohol and weed remained in the air and made Cameron sneeze. He was pleased to see his backpack by the bed side, knowing he could change his clothes and brush his teeth later. He thought of having a shower then but changed his mind. On the bed side table, he left a note for her.

Walking into the kitchen, he found a stack of dirty dishes on the bench and decided to head off to buy takeaway for breakfast at a nearby McDonald's. Passing a florist on the way back, he compulsively grabbed a bouquet of red roses.

Hollie woke, expecting Cameron to be just another guy, sleep with her and then gone the next morning. As she sat up, she remembered Cameron saying, "I'll be back soon." Then kissing her. He'd made her heart flutter but this has to be a joke, she thought. Instinctively, she pulled her laptop out and looked at Cameron's profile on Facebook. She was surprised when she found he was from the other side of the town, the rich area of Chula Vista where influential and affluent people lived in houses valued at 2-3 million dollars. How had he ended up working as a dancer in the gay bar and why was he now living in Encanto, where gang related crime was rampant? She got up, tidied up her bedroom and the kitchen, did the dishes, then went to take a shower.

Cameron arrived and was impressed, noticing the place had been transformed, the bedroom tidy and no dishes on the kitchen bench. He heard someone in the shower and assumed it was Hollie, so he waited in the kitchen. The sound of flowing water in the shower stopped and a few minutes later, Hollie emerged wearing an oversize yellow jumper and black leggings, with a towel wrapped around her wet hair. Instantly the scent of Hollies vanilla skin lotion filled the air. Her eyes widened, amazed at seeing Cameron with the bouquet in his hand.

Without mascara and fake eyelashes, Cameron stood staring, captivated by Hollie's deep-set brown eyes with natural curly eyelashes. Her flawless light brown skin, and a small dimple on her cheek, made her look younger than 18. Cameron gazed at the floor, trying not to make his intense attraction to her obvious. Although Cameron looked tired and rough, as well as sweaty, in his black hoody and black low waste jeans, he still made Hollies heart melt with those electric blue eyes of his.

Cameron put the McDonald breakfast packs of pancakes, bacon and sausages on the table, then handed her the flowers. Hollie turned her back to get a glass of water to put the flowers in as the smell of roses wafted in the air when she took the decorative cellophane wrapping off. She closed her eyes as she inhaled the scent of the roses and turned, but before she could say a word, Cameron surprised as he pulled her into his arms and kissed her.

'Hi, thank you for such a lovely surprise, and you didn't have to buy breakfast. You could've helped yourself in the pantry; there's spam and eggs. Hollie couldn't resist Cameron's body heat, the scent of his sweat mixed with his musk deodorant. Her body went on autopilot as she reached over and pulled him in for another kiss. A minute later, she had hauled him back into the bedroom, ripped both of their clothes off and they were in bed, making mad passionate love.

Afterward, Hollie grabbed her bag and rummage through it for a cigarette. 'Do you want one?' she offered.

Finally catching his breath, Cameron took a cigarette and they both laid next to each other, smoking in complete silence.

Cameron stared at Hollie, trying to think of something sweet to say but decided she'd probably heard it all, so he said nothing. Finishing his cigarette, he asked, 'Can I use the shower.'

'Help yourself.' She rolled her eyes. He's different for sure, she thought, as he grabbed his backpack, then went to the bathroom.

After a quick shower he found Hollie sitting on a chair in the kitchen, smoking another cigarette. She waved to Cameron to sit across from her.

Cameron sat and opened the McDonald's bag, taking out the breakfast packs one at a time. To start a conversation, he asked the first thing that came to his mind, 'Are you a dancer?' He immediately thought it was a harsh question and felt dumb for asking.

Hollie squashed the cigarette butt in the ashtray. She thought about how to answer and decided it was best to tell the truth and see if Cameron would still be interested in her.

'Yes, I work at Hot Spot.' She paused. 'I know you'll ask why next. It was the only job I could find after I left home to escape from my stepfather who was sexually abusing me and physically abusing my brother. Our mom is a cracked addict and she manipulated us to stay so she could use us to feed her habit. She sold me to men to sleep with so she could have money to buy drugs and used my little brother to sell what she didn't use herself. Dancing at Hot Spot was the only job that gave me enough money to get an apartment to buy food for me and my brother.

Now that she'd been up front with him, she asked, 'So what about you? What's your story? Why are you dancing at The Third Eye, a gay bar?' Hesitating, she added, 'I must say you're pretty good at it.'

Cameron was concerned Hollie would reject him, like his classmates at school had. But she had been up front with him and deserved to know the truth. He took a long. deep breath.

'Like you to survive,' he finally said.

'Well I looked you up on Facebook. Do you still live in Chula Vista?' Hollie took a bite of her pancake.

'No, I left home. To start with, my dad is a New Zealander. He joined the U.S. Navy after he married Lora, my mom. Recently he was accused of being a paedophile but the charges against him were dropped since there were no evidence. But shortly after, he was kicked out of the Navy because of his ongoing drug use, but the rumours spread that it was because he was a paedophile. And soon my school heard about it. After that mom and dad's wealthy friends wanted nothing to do with us.'

'I get it that people would think your dad was dishonourably discharged because of being a paedophile. And let's face it, even if he isn't guilty, people will always doubt it. But it's awful that you would be accused of it because of him. And what about your mom?' Hollie asked.

'Mom was charged with embezzlement. They accused her of stealing a lot of money from people's retirement funds to support her gambling habit. She lost her job and she's almost bankrupt, even though she's stopped gambling.'

'Do you have any brothers or sisters?'

'Only a brother. He's older than me,' Cameron told her. 'James is 18, he still lives with mom and he's a high school dropout like me. Because of the bullying, and mom and dad's scandals, all our friends ditched us and we left school.'

'Same here I drop out of high school too so welcome to the club. So, what's James up too then?' Hollie asked.

'I think He's helping mom to sell anything they can at the swap meet. I don't know what else they could sell, they already sold the boat, my aquarium, and everything else from the house. He's looking for a job and he wants to go to college.'

'Is James good looking like you?' she asked.

Hollies comment warmed Cameron's heart and he stared at Hollie for a moment. 'James is taller, 6'-2", so 2 inches taller then me. I'm more stocky. He has a longer nose, oval face and blond hair. So, we look different.'

There was silence while they ate, both trying to absorb the pieces of their life they had shared with one another.

'I take it you left home because of your parent's scandal.'

'Not really,' Cameron answered. 'One-night Dad was drunk and for the first time, I heard him verbally abuse mom, telling her she was a whore and accusing her of having an affair. I hated him for saying that. So, to hurt him, I told him I wished he wasn't my dad and he told me not to worry because I wasn't his son and told me to leave, so I left.'

'I take it your dad is a alcoholic and a druggie so don't feel bad about leaving. Just be thankful that he's out of your life.'

'What really hurt is that I couldn't accept that he's not my dad. I felt he always loved me the same as my brother James. I think he even loved me more. We would go out fishing and he was always interested in whatever I was interested in. He would spend hours with me playing with my slingshot and when I had this huge aquarium, we'd go looking for tropical fish and he'd hang out with me in the pet shop for hours. While he spent time with James, he always complained that making miniature boats was boring. And I remember when we were in New Zealand, and our dingy sunk in the middle of the ocean when we were fishing, he saved me first.'

'Sounds like he might be a good dad after all. You're lucky. My dad died of crack overdose.' Hollie swallowed hard. 'I won't tell you what he was like. I don't wanna go there.' She stared at Cameron, then asked, 'Would you search for your biological father one day?'

'Nah, as far as I'm concern, whoever he is he rejected me, and I still love my dad. He's the only dad I know.' Cameron blinked, trying to control tears.

They continued to talk about their favourite music, movies, sports. Cameron confessed that he was just 17 and his friend Marcus had hooked him up with a fake ID so he could work at the gay bar. They both agreed that they didn't like dancing, but the money was good. They also shared their dreams. Cameron wanted to be a marine biologist and Hollie a nurse.

Since they didn't have to be at work until 8, they decided to go to the movies. On their way-out Mitch turned up, and Cameron couldn't help but notice how affectionately Hollie treated him. She roughed up Mitch's hair. 'This is Cameron were going out to the movies, you want to come?'

At 5'6" tall, Mitch barely met eyes with Hollie. 'Nah, thanks,' Mitch shrugged. 'Can we go to San Diego Zoo instead?'

'Sure, we can go there instead,' Cameron told him.

***

Over the next two weeks, Cameron and Hollie couldn't get enough of each other. They also realized that they only had each other and decided to move in together. All they knew was they was they were deeply in love, they trusted and protected each other and that made them inseparable.

Within three months, Cameron became close to Mitch. He became the younger brother Cameron had wished for and Cameron became the older brother that Mitch would do anything for. It didn't take long for the three of them, Cameron, Hollie and Mitch to bond. And Mitch, who was being groomed by the gang, to drag Cameron into pushing drugs. They quickly became a team: Mitch delivered, while Cameron was the lookout and the protector.

But more often than not, Cameron's mind was on the one he could not wait to see, Hollie.

Chapter 3

Hollie opened the door as soon as she heard his now familiar footsteps.

Cameron stared in amazement. 'Wow, this old linoleum floor looks so shiny when it's clean… and what happen to the cobwebs on the ceiling?'

'Did you spend a mega-buck on air freshener?' Mitch asked, as his nose wrinkled.

'Babe you're home early, anything exciting happen?' Cameron asked, then gave her a peck on the cheek and hugged her, easily lifting her 5-foot 4-inch frame up against his chest.

'I quit my job,' Hollie said, her brown eyes glistening.

'Why?' Cameron and Mitch asked in unison, their eyebrows furrowed.

'I've accepted God into my heart. I'm a Christian now. I realized my job goes against what I believe in.'

Mitch looked down at her as he realized it would not be easy for him to get his next fix. 'What do you mean? You were an atheist before you went to work. Now you've come home a Christian?' he said, sounding sarcastic and waving his hand around. With a heavy step, Mitch turned, climbed the worn-out wooden steps and went upstairs.

Hollie raised her eyebrows. 'Trust me on this, we're moving out. I've found a new place,' she said, pulling her long dark brown curly hair into a bun as she sat on the scruffy grey-colored couch.

After snorting cocaine up in his bedroom, Mitch went back down. His eyes were dilated, and a tinge of powder sat round his nostrils when he sat beside them. His mood had changed after the drugs took hold and just when he was about to object to moving, he realized he could get drugs anywhere. 'Oh cool finally, we're leaving this seedy joint.'

'What job?' Cameron asked her as he rose to his feet and picked up the remote control for the TV. But Mitch snatched the remote control, set it down and turned on his Xbox instead.

Hollie's eyes gleamed. 'As a nurse assistant, it won't be as much as what I get dancing at Hot Shots but...'

Cameron gave her a hug before she could utter another word. Mitch, eyes glued to his game, not hearing a word they said.

Cameron blinked. 'That's awesome, I wish I could spoil you. Damn I'm useless. I don't even have a proper job.' He opened his backpack. 'Here, this is to pay for the rent and groceries. And, since I love you, I go where you go,' he added as he stroked her back.

'Doing drugs and dealing has to stop. And, I'm sorry, but we can't have sex until we get married, and you become a Christian.'
Cameron thought Hollie was not serious about not having sex. He stood and put his hand on his head.

'No hugging, kissing at all...?' Cameron asked, raising his hand in protest.

'Hugging and kissing are fine. Are you willing to do that?' Hollie asked him.

Even in her grey track suit with no makeup, Hollie still looked ravishing. Cameron seemed to stare into her soul, his overflowing love for her undeniable. 'It won't be easy. But I'll do whatever it takes.'

Hollie glanced at Cameron loving every bit of him. 'It won't be easy for me too. I love you Cameron, that's why I'm doing this. You and Mitch are the only things that matters in my life.'

Cameron's face flushed. 'I have no job. There's nothing around, how can we manage?'

'I've got it all figured out. My doctor told me I had cancer so; I saved money for the surgery. But, when I got a second opinion, they said I didn't have cancer.'

Cameron shook his head. 'But why… why didn't you tell me?'

'I didn't, because you'd worry and do something impulsive like robbing a bank to pay for my surgery. But God is so good, he gave me this wakeup call.'

Feeling powerless and shameful that Hollie would think of him that way. Cameron hugged her again. 'Thank God for that. Oh, babe it must have been hard for you.'

'And so, the money after suing the doctor should be enough. We can start a new life. The doctor's lawyer said no harm was done so he did not pay as much of what I expected. But it's still enough for a down payment for the house and to survive for a few months while you look for a job that doesn't involve selling drugs.

'I want you and Mitch to stop now, before it's too late. Anton wants you both hooked on drugs, so you'll do what they want, that's how they operate. We must trust God on this. Anton won't find us easily in a gated community as he's such a moron he will never think we could afford to live there.' Hollie had convinced herself, that with her faith in God, she was sure this would work.

Cameron could see her reasoning and with his love for Hollie, there was no need to convince him further. 'So, when do we move?' he asked.

'Tonight, I already told the landlord and today's our final day.'

Cameron cocked his head. 'Where are we going?'

'Alta Vista,' Hollie said.

Mitch put the Xbox remote down on the coffee table. 'That's a gated community, how could we afford that?' he asked.

'Never you mind my little brother, all you have to do is go to school and do your homework. I'll take care of everything else,' Hollie replied.

That same night Cameron, Hollie and Mitch packed everything up and took off. One of the Christian members of the church had offered Hollie the house, a house that had been in foreclosure and was left fully furnished. She had also rented it to Hollie at a mate's rate.

Chapter 4

A few weeks later Cameron found a job at Alta-Vista Dynamic Gym, not far from where they were now living. Hollie budgeted their household finances. No more buying signature clothing, shoes, no drugs, and no dining out. That would save them a lot. It pleased them to see the interest on their saving account accumulate too. To make Hollie happy, Cameron went to church with her. Mitch continued to refuse to go to church though. Fishing and going for a walk were their weekend routines. Deeper in love, Cameron and Hollie were happy.

It was now over a year since Cameron left home and quit school; rebelling because of his parents' scandal. Spending Christmas with Mitch and Hollie was the best Christmas he could remember. Still, Mitch continued to use and do small drug deals but Anton had left Cameron alone. Neither of them noticed as Mitch continued to sneak out every time they went to church. He made excuses about playing at sports with his school friends. Hollie and Cameron trusted him. Mitch continued to use and sell drugs for Anton until he was hopelessly hooked and in debt to Anton.

After another full day plus overtime – every penny being saved for their wedding and honeymoon - Cameron cooked dinner, following a recipe from the internet. 'Babe, dinner is ready.' He took off his apron over his grey jersey.

From the huge lounge off the kitchen, Hollie yelled, 'Won't be long sweetheart I'm almost finished filling out this application form. And, before I forget, I've got the EpiPen you asked me to get from the drug store.' Then added, 'Yum I can smell the coriander from here.'

After rechecking and putting the application form in the envelope, she straightened her leggings and oversize jersey and went into the kitchen.

'Thanks for getting my Epi-pen.'

'I'm just thankful you noticed it had expired, otherwise if you'd been bitten by bees you could've died.' Hollie shut her eyes briefly trying not to imagine what could have happened.

'It's alright. I've never used it the last seven years but having it with me all the time lets me know I'm safe if I do get stung.' Then he added, 'Guess what?'

'What,' Hollie answered.

'I got promoted today. I'm the new assistant manager.'

Hollies eyes widened. 'Congratulation my darling! You deserve that promotion,' she added, as she hugged and kissed him.

'It's no big deal I just kept putting my hand up for any extra work, even if it was cleaning toilets or running errands for the boss. And I've learned a lot too; like how to properly use the wet vax. I love you,' he added.

'Love you too. For me, it's a big deal that my fiancée is now the assistant manager of the city fitness center.' She paused. 'Are you sure it's the extra work that got you promoted or was it that toned butt of yours ... along with that cute smile?'

Cameron beamed but didn't reply. Even though he was thinking about how he was always catching his female boss looking at his buttocks and the fact that she was constantly commenting on his smile.

'I think we have enough money for the wedding, and now we can save for the honeymoon,' Cameron said, rubbing her chin, kissing her then pulling her into a tight hug. 'I reckon a wedding in Fiji is a bloody good idea.'

Hollie let out a chuckle. 'You still sound funny when you talk. A little like an Aussie, but you're from New Zealand – although you were born here in the US, right?'

'I suppose. That's how my dad talked, and I guess I picked up his kiwi accent.'

'Anyway, what you told me about when you were young, seeing this awesome wedding in Fiji, gave me the idea to plan our wedding there. And bugger it, I sound like you now. But Fiji will give me a good excuse not to invite my mom as I don't want her at my wedding,' Hollie said.

'Now, now, that's not very Christian. I thought you'd forgiven her.'

'Yes, I've forgiven her for my own peace of mind. But I don't need to associate with her.'

'But I thought you were okay, going out, having cuppas with her. She cleaned up her act and found a good guy after her rehab.'

'Sorry, I didn't tell you about the last time I saw her because it hurt so much just talking about it.' Hollie paused and drew in a quick painful breath. 'After I was diagnosed with cancer, I saw mom at the mall, I waved at her, but she walked away. I followed her, but she totally ignored me. So, I gave up. Then later I saw her with her new boyfriend and his family driving away from the mall. I felt like she was ashamed of me, so I got wasted. That and my skimpy clothes, I must have looked like a hooker. But all I wanted to do was to tell her I had cancer.' Hollie's face grimaced in sadness as she tried to hold back the tears.

'I understand, But I hate to see you upset,' he said.

'I know you do. You're lucky; you've had a good start in life. Not like me where my dad died as a crack addict and my mom used me and Mitch so she could feed her cocaine addiction.'

'Babe, stop. You have no idea how much it hurts when the parent you love and put on a pedestal, only to find out...' Cameron paused, looking down so she wouldn't see his pain. 'At least you knew what your parents were like from the very start. Let's forget our parents for a moment, huh.' After a long-drawn out sigh, Cameron gazed at her and his face lit up. 'I can imagine you in a white wedding dress walking on the beach, holding a white umbrella.'

Hollie closed her eyes trying to imagine what Cameron was describing. When she opened her eyes, they sparkled with optimism. 'How about a honeymoon in New Zealand? That's my wildest dream. It's a shame your grannies died. I would've loved to have met them. But I look forward to meeting your auntie and cousins,' she added

Cameron broke eye contact at the mere mention of his cousins and he quickly changed the subject. 'Let's eat I'm starving … and where is Mitch?' Cameron noticed concern flick across her face the minute he mentioned Mitch.

'You're concerned about Mitch, aye? We can postpone the wedding. Mitch is more important. We can use that money to send him to the boy's ranch. To keep him out of jail.'

'I thought, taking him out of that environment would do him a world of good,' Hollie said, 'but I was wrong.'

'Don't blame yourself. We were too busy to watch him every minute. Besides, it's Kevin that's been real bad company since he's been hanging around him,' Cameron said.

'You wonder why a rich privileged boy would want to steal when his parents can give him anything he wants. On his sixteenth birthday, they bought him the latest BMW, for goodness sake,' Hollie said, angrily.

'Just as well someone told you in church what they've been doing. Luckily, the old couple in your church who caught them stealing their jewellery didn't press charges,' Cameron said.

'Yes, but I still need to search and see if Mitch is hiding any other stolen goods and report him to the police if he is. And now it's made me think that Mitch was the one who stole the ten thousand dollars from Anton's apartment,' she said, clawing her fingers through her hair in frustration. But still, she was pleased for Cameron's support.

Cameron took a deep breath. 'Just as well we found all the jewellery, shoes, games and other stuff. Goodness knows how long he's been robbing people. We have no choice but to report the stolen items to the police. It would only have been a matter of time before he was caught,' Cameron said. He dished the food onto each plate and set them on the table.

While eating, they went over their plan to talk to Mitch, to warn him that if he carried on with drugs, they would be forced to put him in a boy's home.

The next day Cameron reported the stolen goods to the authorities.

Chapter 5

Cameron texted Hollie and told her not to cook dinner. He'd stop and buy Subway sandwiches; tuna, her-favourite, for her and chicken teriyaki for him. Later, still in his black and orange, nylon polo shirt uniform, he sat in the lounge and phoned Hollie to give her a heads up to order a pizza for Mitch.

Mitch came home after school, parked on the couch and played games on his Xbox. Expecting the cops to arrive at any time to arrest Mitch for the stolen goods, Cameron hoped it would go smoothly. He insisted that Hollie not be present, so she didn't have to witness her brother being arrested.

'I've asked Hollie to order a pizza for you. Why are your eyes so red?' Cameron paused. 'I can smell weed on you. You didn't go to school today either, did you?'

Mitch tilted his head and leaned aggressively towards Cameron. 'Whatever. And what if I didn't go to school? What are you going to do about it? I'm not your side kick . I can do what I want.'

There was a knock on the door.

'That's your pizza. Go answer the door, please,' Cameron told him.

'If you say so,' Mitch sarcastically tossed back, opening the door.

A female police officer with dark brown hair, wearing a blue uniform, stepped in.

Mitch fought hard to stay calm. He stood in terror, knowing he had just made a drug deal, less than two hours ago.

'I'm Officer Rowena Cruz. Are Cameron Owen and Mitch Ryan here?' she asked in a calm, gentle voice.

After identifying themselves, Mitch shot Cameron a questioning - what- is- this- for? – look. He frowned.

The cop stared at Mitch and Cameron. Her eyes narrowed and she cleared her throat. 'Sit down, please. Cameron. You too, Mitch. Our inquiry is still early. Cameron, can you please tell me, does Hollie have a tattoo on her back? Two love hearts linked together, with Cameron and Mitch written in them?'

Once they were seated, she went on. 'I'm sorry, Hollie is dead. The police found her body this morning in the Bay View Hotel. The assailant set the room on fire, but the firefighters were able to save Hollie's body from being burned in the fire.'

The policewoman took a deep breath.

Cameron and Mitch could not believe what she'd just told them. Shock and disbelief stormed into their faces as they both sat speechless. Tears welled up in their eyes and they trembled.

She reached out and touched Cameron's arm softly, a sign of sympathy.

Cameron could not believe – didn't want to believe - what she was telling them.

'Yes, that's her tattoo,' he said, squeezing his eyes shut.

'And, was she wearing a blue uniform?'

Cameron nodded. 'Yes.'

'Can you please come to the morgue to identify Hollie's body?'

Mitch stiffened, as if he was about to have a convulsion and collapsed on the floor. He roared. 'Nooo! Not my sister! You're wrong. It's not Hollie... It can't be!' His voice echoed throughout the room.

In shock, a sudden emptiness hit Cameron. He tried to be the rock, to support Mitch as he pulled him in. He hugged him as tight as he could and they both crumbled onto the couch, huddled together, tears overflowing.

There was another knock on the door. This time it was the pizza delivery. Cameron quickly paid him and left the pizza on the coffee table.

As soon as the policewoman left, Cameron made a phone call.

Chapter 6

Hollie's funeral was held at her church. Her favourite music, "Hero" by Mariah Carey, played while the congregation argued about their opinion of Hollie. Some said she was a hypocrite, living in sin with Cameron. Others sympathized with her, saying they believed that Hollie had changed and had become a true Christian. Her mom was not at the funeral but Steven Owen, Cameron's dad, Lora his mom and James his brother, were.

Lora's feelings were in conflict. She was pleased that Cameron initiated contact over a year after he had run away from home. It appeased to her that Cameron had rung her in his time of grief. But informing her that his girlfriend was dead was still devastating for her.

The investigation of Hollie's death confirmed she had been raped and then murdered. Cameron had a solid alibi and was not a suspect.

After her murder, he felt he had nothing to live for. His job at the city fitness center ended when he didn't turn up for work and failed to call in. Soon, Cameron couldn't afford to pay the bills, so he turned back to Anton and dealing drugs. This time Cameron's clients were the rich who lived in the affluent neighbourhood that he lived in. Anton was ecstatic to have Cameron back as a part of his drug operations; his sales were triple that of drug pushers dealing in the city center.

Posing as a rich college student, he blended in, selling drugs to the rich adolescents, and their friends. Cameron's good looks proved to be a lure, pulling young women in and getting them hooked on drugs. Anton also gave him a full paid membership to the gym where he used to work so that he could maintain his clients and develop a second market for selling drugs. Mitch continued to hang out with Cameron in the gym, both of them selling drugs in the locker room on a routine basis.

Lost in an ocean of grief, to numb his pain, he started smoking weed, drinking alcohol and taking meth again. Anything to numb his pain. All the money he made from dealing, and what was left of their savings, was quickly used up buying drugs, shoes, top label clothing and anything else to look the part of a rich kid. He bought himself a Corvette Stingray, thinking it would help make him happy, but it didn't.

Two months later after Hollie's death, as Cameron's grief deepened, he felt like giving up on himself.

For Anton, it was the best time for him to take advantage of enticing Cameron into more gang criminal activity. One day during one of the gang parties where gang members were high on drugs, women with revealing clothes, which showed their tattoos and body piercings, laid all over the couches and the floor. The scent of alcohol, weed, meth, and body odour hung in the air. In the distance, Anton noticed Cameron seemed sober enough to have a chat. Anton waved Cameron over to the bar. Wet patches of spilt alcohol on the floor made Cameron slip as he staggered towards Anton. Anton turned down the thumping bass sound of Eminem's 'Slim Lady" so he could hear Cameron talk.

From the collection of alcohol at the bar, Anton handed a shot of Johnny Walker to Cameron.

'After being jumped last week you must be pleased with yourself tonight. Sorry, don't take it personally. It's just a part of our induction, but you must be chuffed smoking out your payback earlier this evening in the games fight. You've got few bruises, huh.'

'Yes, but you should see the other guy,' Cameron said, feeling proud.

'Those taekwondo kick-ass moves you made, I'm sure the gang got the message: Don't mess with me. I wonder where you learnt those moves?'

Cameron struggled to forget the thought of his dad who put him and his brother James into Tae Kwando. 'Does it matter where I learnt it from?'

'No, not really, but just to remind you for your initiation I have to see you tomorrow at six after our meeting. Be sure to attend.'

With the weed affecting his judgement, Cameron didn't think twice and agreed to meet him the next day at the headquarters.

On the day of the meeting, at 6 pm Cameron sat quietly as he tried to get used to the sight of the cigarette-stained walls and the smell of unpleasant body odour. The photos of dead gang members all over the wall gave him the creeps. As he listened, deep inside, all of what they had discussed, Cameron thought was all wrong. Apart from the senseless beating of some rival gang members. And in particular the financial support to the cops and other authorities, although $5000, his share of drug dealing money for a week was great but Cameron thought it was unjust as the cops and the authority got more of a share than the one who actually was doing the job. *I suppose it's the same anywhere; the manager sits on their ass while the workers work their guts out,* he thought.

After the meeting, Cameron stayed. As usual, Anton was at the head of the table smoking. 'I'm thrilled to give you this job as I know you will get this right.' He paused briefly and squashed the cigarette butt in the ashtray. 'Just to give you a heads up. Jake Duncan of The Sons of Kane gang, our rival, was the witness of the cop Mike Mahoney who killed another cop. He's our informant. As you know, he's one of the cops on our payroll.'

'How do you know it's Jake Duncan? The news said no there were no witness to this drug bust gone wrong?'

'From Mike himself. Jake Duncan is the one who got away.'

'Yup. I got it. So if they found out it's Mike who killed this cop, we're all in dire straits as all our drug distribution is protected by him and his mates.'

Anton cocked his head on the side. 'So, I want you to whack him. This would be a drive-by shooting of one of the gang's. This is the address and the time. It'll be the last initiation for us to welcome you into our brotherhood. Tanner Sheldon will be with you'

Cameron was aware that the tall and skinny African–American meth addict, Tanner Sheldon, who was born into the gang, wouldn't be there to save him but to make sure the job was done. As the weed and alcohol had worn off, Cameron felt intimidated and felt he had no choice but to do what Anton commanded.

On Saturday at 8 pm, the day of his assignment, Cameron felt unsettled. Grief engulfed him. He couldn't care less if he lived or died. Then he received a phone call from Anton; the plan had changed. There would be no drive-by shooting. 'We've received a tip that there will be no gang party. Jake will be coming home with his girlfriend, who is our informant, so you must wait in the car. His girlfriend will leave the back door open for you. Once she's gone then you know what to do.'

However, Cameron followed his gut feeling. He thought, *I must make a plan as I want to get away in one piece and to save Jake Duncan instead of killing him.* He planned to offer Jake $5,000 to convince him to leave town. But he had to take fake dead photos of him first to show Anton.

The time for the killing of Jake was midnight, but Cameron left to study the place at 8:30 at Del Castro Street, Mission Valley where Jake Duncan would be. It was a dark and cold evening with only a few cars on the road. The smell of trash hung in the air. There were few people around who were walking their dogs, plus young ones with backpacks and wearing headphones. Cameron parked his Corvette Stingray outside. *It's pretty dark. That's good. I could hide against the side of that tree.* He strode towards the tree. It was quiet. He had been told no one would be home. He scanned the house and noticed a closed garage, a wooden deck at the back-door balcony and a Pitbull on a long leash who started barking. Since the dog was about to attack him, he raced to the car. 'Oops. I hope no one sees me,' he muttered. He drove around to familiarise himself with all the narrow streets and short cuts in case anything went wrong, so he could get away easily.

At midnight, Tanner turned up at his place. As usual he was high on drugs. Cameron had a piece of meat to entice the dog. He inserted his slingshot into his holster, and the 9 mm pistol into its ankle holster.

They hopped in the car and headed to Jake Duncan's place. Cameron offered Tanner more drugs.

'You won't tell Anton about this,' Tanner said hesitating.

'No. Why would I tell him? It's just to keep you cool while we wait. It could take a while. It looks like you need your fix now, huh?'

Convinced that Cameron would not tell Anton and desperate for the next fix, he grabbed the baggie of meth, took his pipe and inhaled it for a few minutes. Tanner was spaced out. *Thanks. You stay like that until I'm done*, Cameron thought.

After half an hour, Jake's girlfriend left. He rushed out of the car while Tanner remained spaced out.

A dog barked. *Was there someone there?* Promptly he threw the meat to the dog. The dog snapped at it.

A guy appeared. Cameron hid under the wooden deck. His heart raced as he peeped between the gap in the wooden deck floor. He was sure the guy didn't fit Jake's description as this guy was taller and larger. When the security light came on, he recognized the guy. It was the cop, Mike Mahoney. Cameron went inside. Jake Duncan was not in the first room. He checked the second room and found Jake, who appeared dead. Instantly he thought it was a setup. In shock, he was about to leave but then he heard a rattle of breath from Jake. He noticed a cell phone on the bedside table and dialled 911. He told the dispatcher the address and said he was dying. He wiped the phone with the bed sheet to erase his fingerprint, then he put it in Jake's hand.

Cameron jumped in the car. As he drove away, he noticed a cop car pulling up. He concluded that he was being set up. But the cop car cruised by. Cameron turned into a narrow street and made a quick short cut to the main street.

When he arrived home, Tanner was still catatonic. Cameron dragged him out of the car and laid him on the couch. He phoned Anton to inform him that Jake was already dead when he got there.

"Great, but you've still passed your initiation as you've proven that you would do this for the brotherhood,' Anton replied.

Although Cameron was welcomed by the gang, he was still on guard. If Jake regained consciousness there would be a question of his loyalty to the brotherhood.

An investigation soon followed. Cameron's alibi was that he was with Tanner the entire evening, which dismissed him as a suspect. Tanner had no choice but to agree to Cameron's alibi. If Anton found out he was on drugs during the operation that would be the end of him.

To escape memories of the brutal way Hollie had died, he began having sex with as many women as he could. Young, middle aged, old, it made no difference; nor did he care about his or their feelings.

Mitch was caught again dealing and went to the juvenile detention center but was soon released. The judge weighed his circumstances as a victim of child abuse, his mental state and the death of his only sibling, Hollie. But he still had to undertake community service and attend counselling. Although Mitch was returned to a foster home, he remained in contact with Cameron and hung out with him at the gym.

Cameron stopped paying the mortgage and soon their house went into foreclosure. Missing Hollie, Cameron realized he didn't want to lose his parents or James, and he started visiting them every chance he got.

Three months later the police found out who was responsible for Hollie's death. It was a young college student from an affluent family. And he was out on bail.

Once Cameron found out, his life's goal was to avenge Hollie's death.

His vengeance intensified when he received a letter for Hollie – her application for nursing school had been accepted. He would not stop until the person responsible for Hollie's death was brought to justice – his definition of justice.

A month after Hollie's death, Lora came home to the house on Sunny Side Avenue, an affluent area in Chula Vista. It was a cold and windy evening. Lora was exhausted, her blue eyes bloodshot and her legs heavy after working as a cleaner at the five-star Sandy Bay Hotel at the Marina all day. Five feet, four inches and well-proportioned with a medium build, Lora sat down sagging on the chair beside the grey granite kitchen bench.

A year ago, after hitting rock bottom and being terminated due to her embezzlement case, their two-million-dollar house was appraised at $800,000. Due to the recession, and the poor condition of the house, it was in the process of foreclosure because she couldn't make the payments. But what hit her hardest was Cameron leaving home because of her gambling and her affair. That was when Lora turned to God and became a Christian. Riddled with guilt, she felt praying helped her cope. She now prayed anytime and anywhere.

Still sitting on the chair, Lora shut her eyes, bowed her head and began to pray. 'Thank you, God, for forgiving me and for the strength you give me every day, preventing me from gambling. Please help me to get Cameron back in my life. I pray for James, and hope that he's got the job he applied for today. Keep my sons safe. Thank you Lord, in Jesus' name.'

She prepared dinner. One of her treasured routines was to have dinner with James. *Fried chicken, mashed potato and gravy. A quick and easy dinner tonight,* Lora thought. While peeling the potatoes, her cell phone rang. It was Steven. It had been a year since their separation. Steven had given up drinking and drugs, and as Lora's temper had calmed since she'd become a Christian, they had begun to talk to each other again.

'Hello,' Lora said.

'Can I see you today? I need to talk to you. I don't want to talk on the phone.'

'Why? Is there something wrong?'

'No. I'll tell you when I get there.'

'Okay. What time?'

'I'll be there in less than a hour.'

Within forty-five minutes, Lora had finished cooking. She put the fried chicken and mashed potatoes in the warming drawer. The aroma of the fried chicken wafted in the air. While waiting for Steven, she pondered over the first time they'd met. It was during the early eighties. Steve Owen was born and raised in New Zealand. At twenty-years-old he went touring around the US.

Nineteen-year-old Lora Mace was a sale assistant at a prominent jewellery shop. It still made Lora smile each time she remembered the first time she met Steven. Six feet tall with an athletic build, Steven looked down at the glass display cabinet. He wore a black beanie over his head and a Koru-designed green pendant on a black string. A heavy backpack hung over his shoulder.

'Hi. Can I help you, sir? What are you looking for?'

Steven's hazel eyes met Lora's deep blue eyes. Steven seemed to be drawn to her at once.

'Actually, I'm not looking for a watch but I am looking for a date. Would you go out with me?'

'You're kidding me. Right?'

'Seriously, no, I'm not kidding.' Steven gazed into her eyes. 'Has anyone told you that you have the most beautiful blue eyes? And…. '

Lora cut him off. 'Get out of here. I've heard that pickup line before.' She looked at the clock on the wall.

'Well, I'll be here at 5 pm if that's your closing time, if no one is picking you up.'

Her heart melted but Steven sounded like an Australian tourist and she felt he was putting her on, Lora quickly thought of a white lie. 'Well, I've got someone picking me up so which watch do you want?'

Steven pointed to a watch, paid for it and left.
When Lora finished work, she saw Steven across the street walking towards her. 'It's my lucky day it looks like your boyfriend stood you up so can I take you out for dinner?' he asked.

After many dates, they fell in love and got married within six months. Steven joined the US Navy. For the last nineteen years he had been stationed at San Diego, California, where he and his family had lived, and James and Cameron were born. Their life was ordinary at first. Lora waited for Steven while he was deployed. Apart from the busy life of being a mom, Lora studied business management, which gave her a chance to work at the Phoenix Holding Investment Group. Later when her sons became teenagers she was promoted to consulting manager, handling only multimillion-dollar investments.

When Steven returned from deployment he told her, 'Dad's lawyer informed me of my inheritance when mom and dad passed away last year. I'm very surprised that the estate was left to only me. I'm going back home I'd like you and the kids to come with me. We could start all over again. I don't want my sons to miss out on my inheritance.' He took a quick breath. 'It's over a year now. I've missed you so much. This is my only wish to have you and the kids back.'

The thought of having a place to live in a quiet little town in New Zealand where no one knew about her scandal appealed to her, along with the hope that no one would bully their sons. Lora agreed to Steven's plan.

'Okay, but what about your sister Beth? She could contest the will.'

'Yes, she could. But I'm happy to share it with her. Even then there will still be more than enough. My parents' properties and the compounding interest of their savings are worth over five million New Zealand dollars now. Dad's attorney confirmed this, but I can't touch any of it until the settlement with Beth is finalized. I'm surprised as Mom and Dad never led on to me how much they had and I've never seen them spend much apart from spoiling our sons.' He paused, taking a deep breath as he realized that he had been oblivious to his parents' account because of his alcohol and drug addictions. Steven continued as he sipped the coffee. 'But knowing Beth she will want to have it all as she was left to look after them so she thought she deserved it all. She accused me of not caring much about them, so I don't deserve any of my folks' inheritance.'

'Oh, that ungrateful sister of yours. She didn't even thank us after taking her in when her abusive husband tried to kill her and their children. We hid them for months. We've never heard from her since.'

'Let's not talk about her for now. What's more important for me is how could we save enough money for the plane tickets and some pocket money to settle while I work on the case.'

Thinking how poor they were, Lora recalled how much she'd lost gambling. Lora struggled to shake off her guilt. 'Oh, how could I let these things happen? The kids are the ones that suffered the most, especially Cameron. I'm their mom. I should've been there when they needed me.'

'Lora, let's stop blaming ourselves. I'm done with the booze and drugs. I'm sorry I blamed everything on your affair. I needed the booze as an excuse to forget you were cheating.

Lora would normally have snapped, but this time she was unruffled. 'I'd like to move on, but just to remind you: I did not cheat on you. Seventeen years ago we were separated. I left when I found out you were having an affair with a girl on your ship, so in rebound I slept with a guy from my high school reunion. And…'

Steven raised his hands in surrender. 'Okay. I messed up and I failed you but please stop right there. This is not going to work if we keep blaming each other. And stop blaming yourself, you can't turn back time. I thought you learned all about forgiving yourself with your Christian faith now. I'm over arguing about why Cameron is rebelling. You blamed me because of my drinking and I blame it on your gambling. All I know is Cameron is getting in deeper with his gang. The sooner we take him out of that environment, the better. And just to remind you, yes, you made some mistakes, but you gave them the best childhood.'

Deep inside Lora agreed and recalled the birthday parties, toys, music lessons, the fishing boat, involving them in tae kwon do, sports and overseas holidays.

Steven continued on. 'And you're smart getting a degree so you can handle multi-million dollar investments as a project consultant manager. I was so proud of you, until you met Bianca, and she coerced you into gambling.'

'Please. How many times have I told you, yes, she introduced me to it but I carried it too far.' Suddenly, Lora realized she had been blaming herself and had forgotten what the Bible said about forgiveness. She tried to snap out of it, thinking of her sons.

'This will be a challenge for us. How can we convince Cameron to join us? James will be fine, I hope. And I have to start saving now but, God, it's good you see. I got a phone call from my foreclosure lawyer two months ago advising that I don't have to pay the mortgage while we are settling the case. I've started saving for the deposit on an apartment so I won't be homeless if they foreclose. Now, I'll use it for the trip instead and I should have the money within three months.'

'When do we leave?'

'In three months. Sorry I can't help much as I just got laid off from a concreting job. I'm useless at the moment as I just have enough to pay my rent. There was this job at a car wash I've applied for so I hope I get it.'

Lora felt sorry for Steven as she knew that Steven normally lost his job when his employer followed up on rumours.

Lora's phone rang. It was James. 'Mom, I met up with Cameron and Mitch in town and we had dinner so don't worry about cooking. Cameron will be coming home with me. I will be home in half an hour.'

She hung up and turned to Steven. 'The kids will be here in half an hour. Sorry, you know Cameron will not come in if he knows you're here.'

'Okay. I can't blame him. I'm sorry that I hurt him.'

Lora didn't answer but asked him to leave.

As she waited for the kids, she couldn't help but think of that night when Cameron and Steven had argued and Cameron found out he wasn't Steven's son. This is why Cameron wouldn't talk to Steven. Although this was the second separation within seventeen years, she took him back because she was still in love with him. But this time it would only be for her sons' sake and made Steven aware of that. Could she trust Steven again with his drinking? The last years' events kept popping into her head, particularly being caught up in an alleged embezzlement charge that led to her eventually losing her job. She had worked as a cleaner to survive. But after Steven's proposal she was thankful there were no charges laid against her. She'd had an affair with the CEO he cleared her of the embezzlement charges, which meant she could go to New Zealand.

Within an hour Cameron, James and Mitch arrived. Mitch handed a box of Dunkin' Donuts to Lora.

Noticing James's depressed look, Lora asked, 'What's wrong son?'

'Well, I did not get the job at the boatyard as a handyman. The manager said I was too young, had no experience and no work references. Stupid people. How could I have experience if no one will give me a chance?'

Although Lora could smell weed on them, she was happy to see her sons and knew that giving them a big lecture about drugs at this time would not make any difference. But it worried her a lot. She felt helpless especially with Cameron. She assumed Cameron was deeper into drugs and she knew James only smoked weed when he was with Cameron. Lora prayed, *Oh God I surrender these problems to you.*

'Hi, Cameron. What's up, son? How are you, Mitch? This is a lovely surprise.' Lora opened the box of donuts and placed it on the table. 'Do you want some dinner?'

'Nah, we're alright. We just had something at Denny's,' James told her.

As usual, when James and Cameron bonded they liked to play chess. Cameron took the chess board from the kitchen cabinet. Cameron set down the expensive chess pieces made of marble. As usual, Cameron liked to be on the defence so he set his black piece on the chess board then set a white piece for James. Mitch watched, eating the chocolate glazed donut, and expecting to have a turn with whoever lost the game.

With Mitch around, Lora didn't mention anything about Steven's proposal. While Lora watched, she thought to ask Cameron again if he would like to meet his biological father. She had recently got hold of Cameron's biological father's address. She went upstairs and took an envelope from her handbag. She put it in her jean's pocket and walked back to the table.

Cameron lost the game. 'I don't lose twice, you know. I'll get you next time,' Cameron said as he winked at Mitch, teasing him.

'Whatever. I'd easily beat you twice in a row,' James said.

Then it was Mitch's turn to play James.

While Lora watched, she thought this might be a good time to talk to Cameron. 'Cameron, while you're waiting for your turn again, can I speak to you upstairs?'

Lora chose to talk to Cameron in her bedroom. She didn't want him to be reminded of the aquarium he used to love, spending hours looking at and feeding the fish. Nora had sold it to help pay the mortgage, plus she couldn't maintain the upkeep of the aquarium. She took the envelope from her pocket and handed it to Cameron. 'This is your biological father's name and address.'

Before she could say another word, Cameron went berserk. He grabbed the sheet, tore it up, and threw it in Lora's face. 'What's wrong with you, Mom? I already told you. I don't want to know him and don't ask me again.'

Cameron ran downstairs. ' We're out out of here, Mitch.'

Mitch scurried after Cameron, as he slammed the front door.

James stared in empathy at Lora who was in tears, as she slumped into a chair.

Hurting for his mom, James sat closer and stroked her arm. 'What did you and Cameron talk about, Mom?'

'I tried to give Cameron his biological father's address, but he tore it up and threw it in my face. I knew I shouldn't ask him again. I knew he was high and it wasn't the right time, but I wanted to make sure that he doesn't really want to meet his biological father. But there is no right time for Cameron. Re-member last month? What he did to you today is quite mild compared to the last time he visited us.' Lora reminded James of what had happened. A month ago, when she had asked Cameron to tie his shoelaces so wouldn't trip over them he snapped. 'Why you're always on my case? I wish you were dead,' he'd yelled.

Guilt overcame her again as she blamed herself as to why Cameron was acting this way. 'But he came back the next day and he was very apologetic. Will he come back again? Tell me, as you're the only one who can talk to him.'

'Yes, he'll come back. Cameron has not been himself for a long time now what with the drugs, his girlfriend dying and the pressure of the gang. You've got to understand that.'

'Yes, I understand. Oh, sweetheart thanks for reminding me. Although I hate to hear it is that why Cameron called you Dr Phil, because you have all the answers? I Love you and I'm glad you're here. What would I do without you?'

James thought it was funny Cameron always called him Dr Phil when he gave him advice. He smiled thinking that his mom always maintained her sense of humour, even in the middle of a drama.

They sat quietly for a while, then Lora told James about his dad's offer of going to New Zealand. James was ecstatic about the plan and agreed with it. Lora thought, *If James persuaded Cameron to join us, his brother would agree,* she thought. Then wondered, could Cameron really be persuaded to agree with this plan?

Three months later, after working two jobs as a cleaner and a super-market bagger and not paying the mortgage, Lora managed to buy plane tickets. Lora was now set to leave New Zealand. And, Cameron had visited her a number of times.

Chapter 7

Encanto, San Diego, California, 24 January 2008, 6 pm. The day and time Cameron had arranged to meet with Anton Miller.

Along the footpath leading to the headquarters of the Red Serpent Gang, Cameron strode toward the meeting place. Wearing a grey gym T-shirt, shorts and Adidas running shoes, he looked like a rich kid out for a run. With only vengeance on his mind he was oblivious to the cold wind, and the nauseating stink of diesel fuel as he passed the dusty cars parked along the driveway.

Three gang members guarded the front of the mechanics shop that housed the gangs meeting room. Each was dressed in a leather vest with a red serpent logo on the chest and back. The one with a snake tattoo on his arm gave Cameron a thumbs-up to let him know it was okay to come in.

Cameron knocked on the wooden part of the red leather upholstered door; justice for Hollie's death the only thing on his mind. Grief-stricken, but not fearing for his life, he would do whatever it took to make someone pay for her death.

Anton opened the door. He cocked his head and raised as eyebrow. 'I know why you're here but revenge won't bring Hollie back.' Then he motioned Cameron to come in and sit down.

Cameron sat, looking up at Anton, as he added, 'But to let him get away with it won't bring her life back either,' his eyes filled with angry retribution. 'I have a guy who will take care of him for you,' he continued. 'All you have to do is pull off a major drug deal I have lined up in exchange. I'm pretty sure you can do this without a problem.'

'No, I want to kill him myself.'

Anton understood how Cameron felt. Staring at him, Anton felt sorry for him; knew how naïve he was and that he had no idea of the odds against him. Cameron sat nervously combing his fingers through his hair. Anton sat facing Cameron, the smell of stale cigarette smoke lingered in the room. The faint light reflected the yellow cigarette smoke-stained ceiling of the gang's head-quarters. Next to Cameron was a glass cabinet with a black leather vest with the gang's name and a snake logo in it. Across the room, the wall had an extensive list of gang members who had been killed.

'This buy is three hundred thousand dollars worth of cocaine,' Anton told him. 'I'm sure it'll go off smoothly. You're only seventeen but you're already a valued asset to us, Cameron. How you got away with some of the buys beats me.' Anton blew a ringlet of smoke in the air. 'You're hardcore man! That's why I don't want you knocking this asshole off. You have a golden future here and I don't want you being implicated in a murder and thrown in jail.'

Inhaling another drag, he held it briefly, before continuing. 'The authorities will make you their prime suspect at once. My plan is to have you out of town when we whack him. You'll have a rock solid alibi, if you know what I mean.' He smiled and stroked his straggly dark brown beard, obviously loving his plan.

Cameron knew there was no way out of this deal. He tilted his head and shrugged, taking a cigarette Anton offered. 'The logic of your plan just regis-tered. Andrew Hamilton comes from an affluent and privileged family. He'll buy his way out of prison. Not to mention, my plan to plead insanity after I whacked him, would never have worked.'

'Now you're making sense. We'll take care of him. Deal?'

Cameron smiled, they shook hands, and he left the room.

Chapter 8

At 7 pm they prepared to make the drug deal. On the coffee table Cameron and Mitch snorted lines of cocaine through a rolled dollar bill. Inhaling the last bit of the powder, Cameron took a long deep breath.

'This is my dad's address in New Zealand, and mom's phone number. Give them to the police if anything happens to me - and the time and place where I should be if you don't hear from me by the agreed time.'

Mitch grabbed the remote control for the Xbox and snorted another other line of cocaine. 'Why? You think something will happen? You give me the creeps, man. But, okay, I got it. Just put it on the table. You're really freaking me out,' he said, his hand on the game control but his eyes fixed on Cameron.

Before leaving, Cameron grabbed two pictures of him and Hollie but left another of Mitch and Hollie. He shoved them into the gray leather backpack Mitch had given him last Christmas, then left; turning on his way out to watch Mitch, who was now glued to his Xbox game.

Fifteen minutes later, someone knocked on the door. Surprised, Mitch found James at the door. 'What's up buddy?' Mitch asked, rubbing his hands together nervously.

James stuttered, 'I.. I... mu... must see Cameron. It's real important. He's got my passport and plane ticket.'

Consumed with his own game-playing agenda, and trusting James, he handed the note with Cameron's whereabouts to him. 'You can find him here at...'

But James took off before he could finish.

***

7.15 pm: Alta -Vista Dynamic Fitness Center.

There were two cars parked in front of the gym near the front door. Along the footpath, box hedges and rubbish bins blocked the light of the gym from reaching the front yard or the sides of the building.

'Great. He's here ahead of time,' Cameron muttered to himself, as he stared at the green Jeep Commander .

Cameron still had the code to the gym's digital door lock, and punched it in. He knew the layout of the gym well and had done multiple drug deals here before and felt at ease.

He put the bright yellow 'Wet floor - Cleaning in progress' cone in front of the door to the men's toilet so no one would enter; then sprayed some cleaning fluid in the air.

The drug buyer, dressed in a Nike gym shirt and shorts, entered the gym. High and confident from the cocaine, Cameron guided him into the restroom. Cameron pulled the 1.5 kg package of pure cocaine from his backpack, while the buyer took $300,000 in cash from a red and black gym bag.

The exchange took place, they each checked their take, and when they both were satisfied, they left.

Cameron smiled to himself at how smooth the transaction had gone. Looking like ordinary gym patrons, using the toilet, they both walked out the front door of the gym.

***

As soon as James left, Mitch changed clothes and left the apartment at 7:30 pm.

Mitch had been watching Andrew Hamilton since he'd been charged and released on bail for Hollie's death. He knew where Andrew would be and planned to kill him tonight.

Armed with dutch courage and confidence from his high, he was driven to avenge his sister. He took a cab to the San Diego Marina, arriving at 8:30 pm.

Most people were paying little to no attention as they worked on their boats, listened to music, or dined in the restaurants nearby.

With his fair complexion, golden-blond hair and straight nose, Mitch's surfer look allowed him to easily blend in with the crowd: Just another rich kid, son of a boat owner, hanging around the marina. His white, and navy blue striped woolen jersey and NY baseball cap, with his blond fringe showing, just added to the desired image.

Watching Andrew as he stepped out of his car, Mitch was careful to keep a few steps away from the sidewalk. He quietly followed behind him down the narrow wooden dock until there was no one else around. He reached out and grabbed Andrew by his collar, catching him completely by surprise. His rage of revenge and adrenalin surged as he dug a knife into Andrew's abdomen, then quickly shoved him into the water. A few people turned their heads at the splashing, but he was barely noticed as he clamly walked away from the marina.

He took a cab to the mall and headed to the arcade to play video games.

Suddenly, he remembered the notebook.

***

At 7:30 pm Cameron made his way back to his car.

Suddenly he heard a siren. Four meters away, he watched his drug buyer in his car,being chased by the police. As he came by, he threw the gym bag full of drugs onto the trunk of Cameron's car, then raced off in his Jeep Commander.

Before he realized it, a cop on foot had come up behind him and was pointing his gun at Cameron. 'Stop and lay on the ground or I'll shoot.'

Without thinking, Cameron jumped over the row of trash bins and hedges next to him.

While the cop requested backup, Cameron moved down the line of trash bins, putting a little distance between them. The cop started searching the area. Cameron watched him as he pulled out him slingshot from his ankle holster. He aimed it at one of the blue rubbish bins down the row so the cop would hear it and go the other way.

The stone hit the rubbish bin and a split second later a bunch of rats jumped out. Watching the rats coming towards him, the cop looked like he had seen a ghost. He shuffled his feet, trying to avoid the rats. He tripped over his own feet, dropping his gun on the ground, as he curled into a fetal position to shield himself from the rats. Seeing the cop lying in a fetal position, Cameron was tempted to take another shot at him, but his conscience voted against it. 'Cheers mate,' he yelled, as he headed in the opposite direction.

After taking a cab home, Cameron dashed into his apartment and hid half of the money under the kitchen sink. Then he headed back out the door.

***

Cameron went to a condemned house down the street and into the back yard that was surrounded by a tall corrugated panel fence. It was the arranged hiding place for the money. As he pulled the paper bag with the remaining cash out of his backpack, he spotted two passports and plane tickets sticking out of the top of the bag.

He looked at the passports and then the tickets. They were in his and James's names. Cameron's heart pounded and he ground his teeth. 'What a dickhead you are. James, why on earth did you do this?' he muttered.

After putting the money in the location shown on the map, he covered it with dirt. Then he texted James, telling him to meet him at the Starbucks café close to the airport. Although there was a shortcut to the main street, Cameron followed the directions he had been given by Anton and took the alleyways out to the street.

***

Cameron followed the alleyway along the back of the stained walled apartment buildings, passed huge numbers of overflowing foul-smelling rubbish bins, and headed out to the main street. He covered his nose with the cowl of his grey hoody to fend off the odor. He stepped over the wet patches that he was sure were sewage leaks. All he knew was that he needed to return James's passport.

When he saw a car's headlights flash across the alleyway, he backed away. He saw a cop arresting a guy, and heard a familiar voice. Watching from across the street, he saw his older brother James pleading with the cops as he hid between two large rubbish bins. 'What the heck? This is it, I'm stuffed. What the hell is James doing here?' Cameron muttered to himself.

'Th… that w… was not mine. I…I didn't know that was inside the bag. I picked it up down the street out of curiosity,' James stuttered.

'I've heard it all before,' the cop said sarcastically as he handcuffed James's hands behind his back.

Cameron realized that James must have followed him and picked up the gym bag from the top of his car while the cop was chasing him. Without hesitation, he pulled the slingshot out of his ankle holster and aimed it at the cop's head. Suddenly, a swarm of bees flew out from the rubbish cans. Cameron thought they were coming to attack him and ran. Two steps later he tripped, tumbled and landed on his face. He landed on the wet ground soaking his face and saturating his clothing with wet sewage matter. Worse yet, he'd dropped his slingshot and now found himself in front of the African American police officer; his dark blue uniform stretched tight across his podgy belly.

As the cocaine wore off, the reality of things hit Cameron like a ton of bricks. His confidence went out the window, and was quickly replaced with shock after the encounter with the bees. If he had been stung, he could've died, and he didn't have his Epi pen with him. His eyes darted between James and the cop while he tried to catch his breath.

'That bag of cocaine is mine. My brother is telling the truth. Please let him go officer.' Cameron's voice trembled as he waved his hand toward the open red and black gym bag; plastic bags of cocaine lying beside it on top of the cop car.

'Put your hands on your head and lay on the ground,' the cop ordered. He handcuffed Cameron, then pulled him up, grabbing the backpack from his shoulder.'Okay, your brother may have a chance of clearing himself but you both have to make a statement and then it's up to the judge to make a decision.'

Cameron and James stood at the side of the cop car, hoping the judge would be lienient.

Staring at James, the thought of his brother going to prison crushed him. Cameron's brain was going full speed trying to figure out how to get them out of this mess. Suddenly he realized the cop had not read them their Miranda rights nor did he check their ID's. He only seemed to be interested in searching for deadly weapons. Maybe it had been deliberate. Maybe the cop was crooked, leaving the door open for Cameron to make a deal.

'Can we sort this out?' he asked the cop. 'Apart from the one-and-a-half kilos of cocaine, there's fifty thousand dollars in my backpack and I can give you one-hundred-and-fifty thousand dollars on top of that. All you need to do is let us go.'

The cop unzipped the backpack and stared at the rolls of money, the rubber bands straining to hold each roll from springing open.

'You'll have that plus the one-hundred-and-fifty thousand dollars,' Cameron said again. 'Please let us go,' he begged.

The cop swallowed hard, and his eyes widened. 'That's good. One-and-a-half kilos of cocaine, the cash and bribing a police officer. That's more than enough to put you two behind bars for fifteen years, minimum,' he said, as he shoved them into the car.

Something about Cameron's voice had been nagging him. Suddenly he realized what it was. Was it possible? Was this the guy that had saved his daughter?

Chapter 9

Cameron and James sat squeezed next to each other in the back of the police car. As the cop started the car, Cameron's mind raced, determined to find a way to get out of this situation. All he wanted to do was save his brother so he could have a future.

'Can I please ring my mom?' he pleaded.

'Okay, you can.' The cop turned the ignition off and stepped out of the car and opened the back door.

'Is this your phone?' the cop asked, holding the only phone he'd confiscated during his search of them.

Cameron gestured yes. The cop punched 'mom' on speed dial and handed him the phone.

'Mom, it's Cameron. I'm sorry, I messed up. James and I got busted for dealing drugs. Can you come pick James up at the police station? I'm going to jail,' Cameron said, tears streaming down his face.

'Are you okay?' she asked.

'I'm fine. James is a little shook up. He's worried about you leaving him here.'

'Whatever happens we're not going to New Zealand without both of you, no matter what. Hang in there. Love you. We'll be there soon,' his mom said.

From the time Lora had informed Cameron that she was taking him to New Zealand to get him out of the environment he was in, Cameron had refused. *Lora is in denial; she doesn't want to hear that I'm not going with them to New Zealand*, he thought. But now, Cameron knew he had to agree to go. He knew it would calm her after the news that he'd been caught dealing drugs. 'I love you, mom, so much,' Cameron said, as his lips quivered.

The cop got back into the car, drove out of the alley and turned left onto 5th Avenue.

In desparation, Cameron begged the police officer again. 'Pleaese ,please, let us go. We'll both learn from this; just take the money and my stash. And I'll give you the map where the other one-hundred-and-fifty thousand dollars is hidden. Use it help your kids go to college, pay your mortgage, or have a vacation.' Without a reply from the cop, Cameron continued relentlessly, trying to persuade him. 'Our flight is in three hours. If you put me in jail, when I get out I'll carry on dealing drugs to survive and what good would that do? Please drop us at the airport, our passport and tickets are in the pocket of my backpack. And the map of where the money is is in the bottom with my socks in the back pocket. No one would know about this. We'll be out of San Diego for good. Can't you see there will be no loose ends?'

'You commit a crime, you do the time, boy,' the cop answered, drumming his fingers on the steering wheel.

Feeling very stupid and guilty of stealing the gym bag from the top of Cameron's car, James said, 'Cameron, I'm sorry.'

'Cameron Owen?... Is that you?' the cop asked. *It was him*, he thought as he slowed to a steady 35 miles per hour.

'Yes, sir,' Cameron replied, holding his breath.

'Craig Pearson. I'm Madison's dad. Remember?'

Why the hell didn't I recognise him? Cameron thought. 'I thought that was you.' Cameron said, trying to recover as he shuffled back and forth in his seat.

'I can't thank you enough for saving my daughter, from that psycho. I get furious just thinking about him. I'll never forget what you did. But that doesn't mean that I will let you get away with this. You look so different. That's why I didn't recognise you at first,' he said.

James decided to add his two cents worth to help Cameron. 'Yes, officer. Cameron hit that bloody psycho far up his ass with his slingshot. Now he's in jail and can't hurt anyone else.'

'Cameron, how did you end up in this mess? Dealing drugs. You were a model student.' He paused and sniffed the air. 'Now, you stink like hell and what's that on your face?' the cop asked, staring at him. 'I was saddened when Madison told me about your friends turning against you because of your dad. But for the record, your dad was not guilty of molesting those girls. He was cleared of that charge. It was an utter lie made by their mom who just wanted to destroy him and label him a pedophile. That must be tough for you guys, man.'

Unexpectedly, the cop made a snap decision. 'Okay, you guys deserve a chance at life but don't screw this up, man.' He made a quick U-turn onto Route 75. 'We should be at the airport within ten minutes if the traffic stays moderate.'

The cop pulled the car over. He put the money in the gym bag with the cocaine then handed it to Cameron along with his backpack.

Cameron's eyebrow furrowed.

'Here's some pocket money for you guys.' He handed five rolls of $1000 each to Cameron. 'Give me the map,' he said as he uncuffed both of them them and Cameron handed the map to him. Two minutes later, they turned into the airport. The cop pulled up to the front of Terminal Two at San Diego International Airport.

'Thank you so much officer, Pearson,' Cameron and James said in unison. An expression of gratitude and relief written all over their faces.

He didn't answer and just waved goodbye as he pulled away.

Within minutes they entered the terminal and walked up to the check-in desk.

Once they were checked in, James rang Lora. 'Don't go to the police station,' he told her. 'We're at the airport, mom. Meet us there as soon as you can and we'll explain everything. We're fine.'

'Oh okay. Thank God. Love you, James,' Lora replied

'Love you too, mom,' he answered, then put his phone back in his pocket.

Chapter 10

9 pm. As soon as James and Cameron passed through the automatic sliding doors at the airport, the K-9 drug sniffing dog loped towards Cameron. The security guy requested Cameron accompany him to a cubicle nearby, then escorted Cameron as they weaved past the airline check-in counters, baggage scales, monitors, self check-in machines, travelers holding tickets and passports and snake-like queues filled with passengers and their luggage.

In fear of what was about to happen, Cameron was oblivious to the PA announcements calling out passenger names, flight arrivals, departures and delays. But when he heard his name being called, it caught his attention. 'Paging passenger Cameron Owen. Please proceed to the gate of hell as that is where you're going to be if you don't get your act together.' *What the hell is that? Am I going nuts?* Cameron thought.

The security agent searched Cameron's body and clothes and found nothing. But after rummaging throrough his backpack, he found the $5,000 and a pink notebook that looked like a diary.

The security agent's eyes narrowed. 'Your diary?'

Cameron blinked in confusion. *Could it be Hollie's?* Holding his hand loosely behind his back Cameron answered, 'Yes.'

Although the security agent wasn't convinced it was Cameron's diary, he had no evidence it was stolen so he gave the diary back to Cameron. 'Hmm, you own a pink-colored diary? And where did you get the money?' the guy asked, as he handed it back.

'My savings for our trip. I've beein saving it for years.'

The security agent seemed convinced, but then suddenly he sniffed the air. 'Why do you smell so bad?'

'I fell in a puddle of sewage on my way here. I was in a hurry so I wouldn't miss the flight.'

'So you're travelling with your family and that is your brother with you?'

'Yes, sir.'

'How come you only have a backpack to travel to New Zealand with?'

'My mom and dad have the rest. They'll be here soon.'

'And I have to say you look nothing like your brother.'

'When people ask why my brother and I look so different my dad's answer is always that mom slept with the milkman.' When that didn't even get a smile, he added, 'Just kidding.'

Cameron gave the security guy his parents details and after he checked the computer screen, he told him, 'Okay, you're cleared. Wash yourself and change your clothes. I don't think they'll let you on the plane with that freaking smell.'

Pale with gleaming beads of sweat over his forehead, Cameron left the room looking for James.

***

As he left security, Cameron's heart sank. James's green-emerald eyes were red, as if he had been crying, as his oval face turned toward Cameron. 'T-Thank G- God...' James stutterered as he clawed his fingers through his hair.

Before James could finish, Cameron gestured him to stop. It was painful for Cameron to hear his brother stuttering; he did not want to remember painful memories of a young stuttering James. 'Let's sit down for a minute.' Cameron waved his hand toward the waiting area with a rows of chairs. They sat beside each other as he shared his brother's stress, along with his own.

Cameron stroked James's arm. 'Take a long deep breath, slowly, bro. We're okay. Don't worry.'

After a few deep breaths, James calmed down and leaned back in the chair. He clasped his hands at the back of his head thinking of their narrow escape from being thrown in prison.

'Just as well Mom and I planned to put the passport with the plane ticket in your bag, otherwise it would have been a catastrophe . She has huge trust in you; that you won't let me down. She was sure that if you found it you'd look for me. Then mom asked me to beg you to come with us at the last minute.' James heart pounded as he thought about what could've happened if they hadn't been able to talk their way out of things after they'd been caught.

'The only reason I came with you is I don't want you to miss out on a new life and a shot of going to college in New Zealand that dad promised us. But you've screwed up my plan,' Cameron said, slowly shaking his head.

James cocked his head and raised his eyebrows. 'Screwed up your plan? You're pathetic. Mom and I just saved your ass. We're got off the hook because of the passports, and the tickets. The cop wouldn't have been talked out of it if we hadn't had the passports and tickets.'

Cameron's face tightened in anger. 'I... saved your ass; I could've left when I saw you being arrested.'

James raised his hand in surrender, suddenly realizing his his brother too had played a part in getting them out of this mess. 'Thanks bro, but actually it waqs mom that saved our asses. And just to let you know, if you didn't come, none of us would be going to New Zealand cos mom was not leaving without you, or me. She took a big risk when she bought the bloody plane tickets, even though you said no. And not to mention that she busted her butt to save for this, God damnit.'

Cameron felt a hint of guilt as he rested his head on his hand. 'You're right.'

James couldn't believe what had happened to his once happy and caring little brother. He dreaded what Cameron could be capable of doing. He missed his laughter and even the pranks he'd played on him. He leaned back on the chair. 'You've doublecrossed the gang. They will hunt you down. You had a lucky escape today. What were you thinking? Did you take the cop for a ride as well so we could get away? I hope not.'

'No, I didn't. The cop will get the money if he follows the map correctly.'

'I don't get it. Why would you rip the gang off? You know you won't get away with this; they'll kill you,' James said, rubbing his neck.

'Because the gang wanted to kill me first.'

James eyes blinked, the fear in them apparent. Since Cameron had joined the gang, James had been too scared to ask him why, and he feared the truth. But he asked him anyway. 'Bloody hell. You're really in deep shit, huh? How did you find out that they wanted to kill you? And how did you get into this hellhole?'

Cameron's face grimaced, confused as to which question to answer first. 'With the drug deal last time, I almost got shot. Since then, I've had this gut feeling that Anton had set me up. I bugged the headquarters one night during a raving gang party, when all of them were spaced out on drugs. That's how I found out that Anton was going to kill me after this last drug deal. But little does he know, I planned ahead of him. Anton probably thinks I'm now dead. Sucker. He doesn't know I got away from the cops and I'm on my way out of the country.

'Did you have to kill someone to be initiated into the gang?

'I haven't killed anyone yet, I was assigned to kill Jake Duncan as an initiation. But when I found him someone else got to him before I did and fighting for his life. I couldn't finish it. Instead I called 911 using his phone.'

James felt reassured in knowing Cameron had not killed anyone. Breathing rapidly he said, 'Jake Duncan was in my class. He was the eyewitness for the murder of this rich dude. On the news last night they said that he had come out of his coma and is in stable condition. The cops are looking for the suspect. Why don't we tell the police? Let's report it.'

Cameron rubbed his hands and leaned forward. 'No, I can't because I don't know who tried to kill him and besides, the police and the gang are in it together. As well as Andrew's dad. Plus, now they all want me dead.'

'Good thinking, planting that bug,' James said, taking a breath. 'But you've must have done something else for Anton to want you dead.'

'Anton felt that I'd been disloyal to the brotherhood when they found out that I didn't kill Jake. They thought I was a witness to his attempted murder. Also, they kniow I found out Andrew's dad provides financial support to the gang. He pays them for protection. Once the gang knew my plan to kill Andrew, his dad ordered them to kill me. So the drug deal was to look like I was killed during a drug bust.'

'Is there anything else you're not telling me?' James asked, jiggling his leg.

Cameron rubbed his shoulder as he continued. 'I still have one-hundred-thousand dollars at my place. I've hidden the money in different places to buy time... If I have the money with me, the cops and the gang will kill me as soon as they find all the cash.

'But, the cop gave me back five thousand dollars when I tried to bribe him so, here's two-and-a-half thousand for you.'

James hesitated and felt guilty knowing it was blood money but took it anyway. 'Thanks,' James told him.

While handing the money to James, Cameron's phone rang. After listening he told James, 'Mom and dad are in line in the security check and they'll be a while.' Cameron and James shot each other a look of relief; in a few minutes their family would be boarding their flight out of the country. Cameron wasn't looking forward to seeing his dad. Although he missed him, he had mix feeling of hate and love.

'Will you be okay with dad? I know he really hurt you when he got drunk and said you weren't his son,' James said.

James didn't push the issue about their dad. He realized this was not the time. 'You haven't told me about why you smell like sewage,' James said, wrinkling his nose.

'Cos I fell in sewage. I know, I reek. I've got to get rid of these clothes.

This is oumeetingplace, aye. I'll see you in half an hour or so.' 'Yip. I'll see you later,' James replied

'I'll text you. I won't be long,' Cameron said.

Their meeting place was across from the duty free shop, by Gucci and Prada. James watched people passing by, comparing himself to those wearing elegant jewellery and signature clothing. With his old beat up shoes, tattered brown T-shirt and trousers, James felt out of place. Putting his finger in his pocket reminded him of the $2,500 and it gave him an adrenalin rush. *Jeez, I can afford to buy those expesive label clothes and jewelry at the duty free shop* , he thought. Minutes later he came out with a set of new clothes and headed for the toilet to change.

Cameron too bought clothes, shoes, a new backpack and soap. Since the airport had no public shower facility, he went to the disabled toilet and scrubbed the bottom half of himself with soap and wet paper towels. Donning new underwear, black jeans and shoes, he finished the top half of himself at one of the sinks. He sprayed Lynx deodorant under his arms and caught sight of himself in the mirror, noticing the Celtic cross tattoo on the right side of his chest. It reminded him of Hollie. It had been her birthday present to him to *show his faith in God, and at that time Cameron had felt God was giving him a chance for a decent life with Hollie. It also corresponded with the love heart tattoo she had on her back.* He sighed as he slipped on a Calvin Klein white shirt, followed by a new grey hoodie. Exhausted, grief grabbed him and without warning, his legs weakened. He went back into the toilet stall and sat down. He life felt empty and he longed for Hollie. He leaned back, his eyes heavy with fatigue as he dropped off to sleep.

He woke with a start. Glancing at his watch, he'd only been asleep for ten minutes. He slipped his new backpack inside the old backpack. As his hands rested on the pink diary, He paused. *Should I read it?* he thought. And then his phone rang.

Chapter 11

Mitch thought that Andrew got what he deserved. Killing him had given him a jolt of pleasure. But as he stared at the photo on top of the TV of Hollie and Cameron at the San Diego Zoo, eating ice cream, his world crumbled and he burst into tears.

Out of the blue he realized that Cameron was not yet home. After exploring the house, Mitch figured that Cameron had the backpack and he realized that Hollie's diary must be in it. To stop his hands from shaking, he smoked a joint and turned the stereo to full volume, playing the *Big Yellow Taxi* by Counting Crows.

While Mitch swayed hypnotically to the music, Anton kicked the door open, jolting Mitch out of his daze. Following behind Anton was Kevin and Tanner. Tanner had a tight hold on Kevin's collar and had a knife pointed at his neck.

'He'll slit his throat if you don't tell me where the notebook is that you've stolen from me. And where Cameron is with my money! Kevin told me about you and him raiding my apartment and taking the notebook,' Anton shouted.

Mitch glared at Kevin who let out a violent wail. His heart reached out for Kevin. He knew Anton wouldn't hesitate to have Tanner kill Kevin. 'It's with Cameron. I put it in his backpack and I don't know where he is.'

Anton signalled to Tanner to let Kevin go. Kevin yelped and ran out the door.

'Turn this place inside out,' Anton ordered.

Tanner did as told, emptying drawers, wiping contents off shelves and throwing stuff on the floor. He'd found the money, 'I found one-hundred-thousand dollars.'

Anton's nostrils flared, and the muscles and veins in his face strained. 'That's two-hundred-thousand dollars short. He's taken off with the rest, the bastard. Tie Mitch up," he said, told Tanner. Mitch was relieved to see that they didn't find the pocketknife Cameron kept hidden under the towels in the bathroom cabinet. Mitch was thinking about how he could get away. If they let me use the toilet I'll have a chance, he thought.

Tanner bound Mitch's hands in front of him with plastic ties.

Anton scribbled something on a piece of paper. He pulled his cell phone out of his pocket and dialled Cameron's number. With the phone against Mitch's jaw, Anton pointed the knife into his neck. 'Read this note,' Anton exclaimed as saliva splattered on Mitch's face.

Mitch's voice trembled as he read. 'Cameron, Anton will kill me if you don't give him the rest of the money and the notebook.'

After searching Mitch's pockets, Tanner said, 'I got an address and a phone number. It's for Lora Owen.'

Anton examined the crumpled note assuming the number was Cameron's mom. 'I'll ring this number and you ask where Cameron is,' Anton said gruffly. He shot Mitch a look that clearly said if you tell her what's happening, you're dead.

Mitch forced himself to follow Anton's direction. He swallowed hard. His voice trembled. 'Hi, Mrs. Owen, it's Mitch here. Do you know where Cameron is? We were supposed to go fishing?'

'Cameron isn't here. I'll tell him you rang if I see him,' Lora said, her voice coming over clear on speaker phone.

'Thanks, Mrs. Owen.'

Anton informed him of what he was about to do. 'Fine, I'll find Lora and use her as ransom to get my book and t money back.' Then he left Tanner to watch Mitch.

Mitch felt devastated that he'd given Lora's address to Anton and planned his escape. He knew Tanner was a meth addict and he still had some supply he could offered him. 'Hey Tanner. Can I use the bathroom. I'm busting.'

Tanner was sitting on the couch, he rubbed his hands together. 'You can do it in your pants for all I care.'

'But… I need my fix too. I have it here. I'll tell where it is. You can have it all if you let me use the toilet.'

Tanner scratch his head. 'Tell me where your stash is first, then I'll let you use the toilet'

'Okay, it's in pantry, in the old Nestle Quick container on the top shelf.'

Tanner went and found the meth immdiately. He went back and released Mitch's hands so he could use the toilet. 'Don't mess with me and don't even think about escaping.'

Tanner took a 45 pistol out and waved it at Mitch. 'Hurry up I don't have all day,' he told him, as he filled the pipe lying on the coffee table, lit it and inhaled.

His heart racing, Mitch flew to the bathroom, took the pocket knife from the cabinet, stuffed it in his pocket and climbed out the bathroom window.

While Anton was on his way to locate Lora he got a phone call from Tanner. Mitch had escaped.

Then Tanner took off to find Mitch, before Anton found Tanner and made him pay for letting Mitch escape.

***

Cameron's phone rang; it was Mitch. 'Anton is after you're mom. He'll kidnap her in exchange for the notebook and money. '

'Mitch, listen. We're here at the airport. We're about to board a flight to New Zealand so we're safe. It's a long story.'

'Cameron, you need to know, I killed Andrew Hamilton,' he said, with a sense of pride in his tone.

Cameron gasped, and his heart raced. 'When? And where are you?' He rose to his feet.

'An hour ago, I'm here in the cleaners' room at the gym. I escaped from Anton. He kidnapped me looking for the notebook and the money'.

'The pink notebook?' Cameron asked.

Mitch explained how he killed Andrew, how he hid the notebook in the bag that Cameron was carrying.

'And how did you get away?'

'I gave Tanner my stash and when he got high, the idiot let me use the toilet. I grabbed the knife hidden in the bathroom cabinet and escaped out the toilet window..'

'Anton just sent me the video of you tied up, threatening to kill you if I don't meet him, the scumbag.'

'Yupp and he doesn't know stuff about you leaving. I hope things will work out for you In NZ... I'm turning myself in.'

'It's good that you didn't tell me you're going to New Zealand, they might have gotten it out of me if I hadn't escaped. I wish I could come with you,' Mitch added.

Cameron was about to explain why he was going, but he heard a loud voice in the background of Mitch's phone call.

'Open the door and surrender otherwise will kick the door in.'

The line went dead.

Chapter 12

James returned to their meeting place. He wore a black Ralph Lauren T-shirt, blue jeans and tan varsity jacket. When James saw Cameron in the distance, he hardly recognized him. He merged in well with the sophisticated-looking tourists walking beside him.

James had been careful about what he said to Cameron, respecting his feelings since Hollie died. 'You've washed up well. You look like you had a bit of a beauty sleep.'

'So, why do you have to always be on my case?' Cameron asked, giving James a glassy stare.

James backed off. *Maybe he's just dying to have a smoke, or to take the next hit,* he thought. Not sure what else to say, he added, 'How about we get something to eat?'

Cameron shrugged, and as they walked he noticed James slowing down to admire himself in the windows reflection.

'Hurry up then. Why are you walking so slow? And stop looking at yourself. Okay, you look fantastic in your new outfit. Get over yourself,' Cameron snarled, turning into the food court.

Normally, James would have returned his brother's retort with a smart answer, but after today's escape he decided he'd just be quiet for now.

Cameron thought of Mitch. He was concerned about what would happen to him. He regretted that he hadn't been able to say goodbye and tell him that he cared and loved him like a brother. Thinking of what to do with the notebook, his mind battled as to whether to tell his family. If he told his family they could inform the authorities, so he decided he couldn't trust anyone. Even the cops and the gang were in it together. So, for their safety, he vowed not to tell his family. He also wondered why he couldn't feel any satisfaction now that Andrew was dead. Instead, his longing for Hollie just intensified more.

When they entered the food court, the smell of cake and cinnamon filled the air when they passed a bakery. It didn't make Cameron hungry; all he wanted was the next hit, but he feared the gang would find him if he went outside to the smioking area.

After paying for their food, James cocked his head and stared at Cameron's overloaded tray. He commented, 'Cameron people are looking.'

'Who cares? I haven't eaten since yesterday.' The tray almost tipped over as he sat at a table.

'Are you sure you can eat all that?' James frowned.

'Watch me.' Cameron picked up a large slice of pizza. That was followed by a big bowl of salad, a cinnamon roll, a blueberry muffin and a large chocolate milkshake.

James had a hamburger and a slice of cheesecake. 'You ate like a caveman,' James said.

'Look at me, do I look like I care? We haven't eaten together like this since I left home almost a year ago and that's all you can say?' Cameron replied.

James let the comment go.

Cameron blamed James for ruining his plans to collect all the money and then forcing him to go to New Zealand. He couldn't see why James was so happy after everything that had gone on and their narrow escape.

He'd take care of James's good mood. After few minutes, Cameron bought another milk shake. As soon as he finished it, he let out a deafening burp to piss off James. One that made the custumers near them turn.

James realized what Cameron was trying to do and it made his blood boil. Within seconds Cameron's, stomach growled again and he got up and went to the toilet.

James waited for Cameron.

As the craving for cigarettes and drugs wore off, Cameron's mind began to clear.

Chapter 13

In the security line, like a gambler expecting to flip the winning card, Lora was full of anticipation to see her sons. Exhausted, she tilted her head back and closed her eyes, then muttered, 'I'm glad that's over.' Once more she looked at their tickets and passports, noticing it was her birthday but thinking nothing of it.

Anxious about their sons, Lora and Steven were heedless of the announcement being called over the intercom of departure delays.

Walking along with Steve, he asked, 'Lora, can we talk over there?' He pointed to a vacant row of white vinyl chairs in the departure lounge. 'Please don't text the kids to meet us just yet.'

'Okay,' Lora answered, sighing heavily.

Steven took in a laboured deep breath and rubbed his eyes. 'We have plenty of time before we take-off.'

'Steven, God is opening a new door for us, and the kids have been through enough. Cameron especially.' But she was already starting to feel herself give in. 'Alright, let's find somewhere to have a drink,' she said, her eyes scanning the shops for a bar or café with a quiet place to talk.

They found a table in a quiet location where they could also watch for Cameron and James. Although Lora was hungry, she didn't feel like ordering anything. The stress she felt when she thought about her sons was getting to her. Her sons were in deep. Yes, they managed to avoid imprisonment, but there was still the inevitable problem of gang payback. That's the part that made Lora and Steven's stomachs churn.

The aroma of percolated coffee surrounded them. The display case of mouth-watering, passionfruit cheesecakes, carrot cakes, and doughnuts filled with nuts and chocolate still wasn't enticing enough to snap them out of their misery. In the end, they settled on two cappuccinos.

Steven gestured for Lora to sit down.

'Steven, I don't think there is much to talk about. I just hope this time you keep off the booze and weed,' she told him.

'Thank you so much for taking me back. I screwed up, and promise to make it up to you and the kids,' He said, stroking the grey hair on his left temple.

Lora stared across the table at him. He was still the New Zealander of Scottish descent; the one with the athletic-build, six-feet-tall, with fair skin, and hazel eyes that she had fallen in love with.

'I'm sorry. I wish I could take it back. I'm done with drugs and booze. No way, bloody hell, not after being kicked out from the navy because of it. I know I'm responsible and It broke my heart to see Cameron acting up. He was a good kid until... he thought I'd got kicked out of the navy because I molested those girls. Then, like a fool, I got drunk and told him he wasn't my son.'

Lora blinked trying to hold back the tears. 'Yeah, the way you told him caused more harm than good. We'd agreed after he turn 18 we would sit down and tell him in the most loving way that he wasn't your son. He thought the world of you. That boy adored you. And I held my self-responsible too for him leaving. He hated me for gambling and then finding out about my affair. How can we possibly blame him for how he turned out?

'Do you think he'll ever forgive me?' Steven asked. 'And do you believe I could've molested those girls?'

'I never did but, sadly, even though you were cleared, people think you did it. You were dishonourably discharged, not for the drugs offences, but for molesting them.' Lora paused, and swallowed hard. 'And with Cameron, I don't think this is the right time for you to try and talk to him.' Her voice was raspy. She shook her head and avoided making eye contact. She took a sip of coffee then crossed her arms. 'We have to move on and focus on the kids now, put our differences behind us. What you told Cameron hurt him so much.' Lora glared at Steven with a mixture of resentment and hope.

Steven's shoulders were slumped, and his head was lowered as they sat in silence, thinking of the future for their sons.

Because of their father's scandal, Cameron and James left school as their trusted friends, one by one, turned against them and then bullied them. Lora hoped that Cameron and James would go back to high school. In the future she imagined her sons graduating, then going to university.

Lora's phone buzzed. It was Cameron. 'Mom, we're at the Baker Delight Café. Close to our gate.'

***

Cameron came back to the cafeteria after using the toilet. He rang Lora to let them know where they were, while James finished eating.

'We've clear through the security check but we stopped in the café for a something to drink,' Lora told Cameron.

'Okay, we're going to go to the duty-free shop,' Cameron answered.

The duty-free shop wasn't very busy, the sales assistant behind the display counter bored, with a smile plastered on her face. They browsed the jewellery display cabinet, then bought a sports watch, neck cushions, chocolates, and presents for their parents. They avoided the alcohol displays as it was a painful reminder.

They went back to the gate where they waited for Lora and Steven.

The airport reminded Cameron of the trip he had taken with his mom to the Bali and the Caribbean. Also the holiday when he was six when his grandparents (pop Glen and nana Mollie) took James and Cameron to Italy. It was in Italy where he started sleepwalking. They had been staying in the Via Milazzo Hotel in Rome. Cameron remembered waking from a sleep-walk in a haze, standing in the elevator in his PJs. Fortunately, he had left the door ajar and as soon as he was back in the room, he woke his nana and told her about his excursion.

'Oh no. Thank God you're safe. What happened, darling?' Mollie asked, as she hugged him and changed him out of his soiled PJs. "Let's get you in the shower, my dearest one." After the shower, Nana Mollie wrapped Cameron in a big fluffy towel and set him in her lap.

'I woke up feeling lost. I went back where you took me. To the place where the sculpture of King David was. The statue came alive.'

'Oh, you poor bubba. Then what happened, love,' Mollie asked as she hugged Cameron tighter.

'I was scared. Then he took my hand and we went for ride. We sat at the top of an up and down bus. Then he told me all about himself, like how he killed this giant Goliath and how he practiced with the slingshot. It's a long, long story as we went around and round in the two-story bus. Then we stopped at many places to eat pizza and gelato. I'm sorry I wet myself, nana. He gave me a sling shot and told me to use it for my protection.'

Nana Mollie frowned in disbelief.

'Don't you believe me, nana?' Cameron asked.

'I believe you but promise me you won't tell anyone about this.'

Cameron was brought out of his reminiscing when he noticed a giant figure through a glass window, that looked like Anton. The figure said, 'I will kill you *Cameron*,' then ran his hand across his neck.' Without a beat, Cameron gave the figure the finger and watched it disappear. *Jeez, what is that all about? Is it a figment of my imagination? Am I hallucinating? A flashback from the ecstasy I took last night?* he thought. His mind went to his parents being kidnapped. Panic-stricken, he sent another message to his mom: *I'm at the café. I'll see you soon.* After a few minutes, his parents came into view and he breathed a sigh of relief.

Lora walked ahead with a backpack slung on her shoulder and Steven followed behind holding a duffel bag. Spotting their sons, they rushed to them and hugged them like they were war heroes arriving home.

Lora drew a quick breath. 'Thank God. Are you guys okay?' Lora asked.

'We're fine mom,' James replied.

***

They all agreed to have some refreshments at the café just outside their gate and took seats around a table after ordering drinks and snacks.

Amid the anguish, Lora felt at peace, knowing her sons were safe, as she asked, 'Tell me what happened, son.'

The noises from the café with people laughing and talking made it difficult for Cameron to hear his mom's soft voice. He also couldn't help be a little envious of the people around them as they seemed genuinely happy, and fearless. Trusting his mom would understand Cameron told his side of the story. Lora listened painstakingly, rubbing Cameron's shoulder.

Anxious to hear about Mitch, she asked wondering about his phone call. 'How's Mitch, love?' her voice deep and raspy. She sipped her soda, then added, 'You know Mitch phoned me. I didn't tell him where you were, as I felt that something wasn't quite right. His voice was quivering and he called me Mrs Owens. He never calls me Mrs. Owens. So, I didn't tell him that you're here at the airport and that you're okay.' As she stared at Cameron, her heart ached for him, and the vacant look in his eyes; like someone had stolen his soul. *What happened to my sweet little boy?* she thought. Breathing heavily, Lora prayed deep inside. Please, God. Help me to help heal Cameron's broken spirit, and I pray for both of my sons to succeed in their new life in New Zealand. Keep them safe always. Thank you, Lord that you gave them a chance to start a new beginning and me another chance to be with them again.

Suddenly, Cameron realized the gang could trace Lora's phone.

As if on cue, her phone rang. Without thinking, Cameron grabbed her cell phone and dropped it into a glass of water before she could answer it. They all looked at each other apprehensively. Cameron was speechless and chewed his bottom lip. 'Mom, I'll buy you a new phone in New Zealand. I just don't want anyone tracing this one and knowing where we're at.' He plucked the phone out of the glass and wiped it with serviettes before putting it in his pocket.

'Thank you very much, son, but you don't have to.'

After hearing his son's ordeal, Steven seemed ashamed. Rather than being around for his sons, Steven had been selfish and focused only on Lora's affair. He had turned to alcohol.

A woman approached the family. 'Wow! It's so awesome to see you guys here. Where are you going?' Bianca asked, balancing a tray of coffee and a vegetables with chicken; a Louis Vuitton bag draped over one arm and her shoulder-length straight blond hair setting off her black and white Gucci suit.

'Hi, Auntie Bianca. We're going to New Zealand. Cameron and I will go to high school there,' James said, beaming.

Cameron glare at James.

'Splendid, my darlings. Cameron don't look so sad. What's wrong, my dear. What happened to that cute smile?' Bianca asked.

Cameron grinned. 'I'm alright. Why are you here auntie? You're looking good.' Cameron fought hard to hide his feelings. He clutched his backpack, stroking the compartment with the notebook in it.

'She's not your bloody auntie as far as I'm concerned. She led your mom to drink and gamble… and more,' Steven said, slamming down his coffee cup.

Ignoring Steven, Bianca said, 'I'm on my way to St. James in the Caribbean, for a few days of relaxation. And, a bit of gaming, perhaps.'

Lora tried to hide her embarrassment as she stared at Bianca, speechless. Feeling nauseous she pressed her hands against her stomach. 'Stop it,

Steven, Bianca had nothing to do with my gambling. And, this is not a subject for in front of the boys, please.'

Bianca turned red, embarrassed for Lora. She took a slow deep breath, and thought, *Just as well he didn't mention Lora's having an affair. I would've poured this coffee on his groin.*

'There is nothing to hide, mom.' James said, leaning back in his chair.

Cameron peered at Bianca. 'Excuse me. But Auntie Bianca is the only friend who has stuck by mom when the all gone a hoo fan. Mom, you're lucky to have a friend like her. And you dad… you have uncle Terry, he's your best mate dad not like us. We've been ditched by everyone.'

'Yip, uncle Terry he's a funny guy. Of course he's dad best mate since dad saved his life,' James threw in.

Steven's heart warmed, recalling how he had saved Terry's life in a bar fight when they were in Florida.

James's lips curled. The same people who had befriended their mom and dad, suddenly had forgotten about Cameron and James.

Something nipped at Lora's heart as she watched her sone. She never forgot when the school called her to come in to see the principal.

Cameron noticed his mom's pale face and her squinting eyes, 'Are you okay, mom?'

'Oh, sorry. My eyes are dry so shut them for a second.'

Bianca remained standing by their table, staring at Lora. 'Are you sure? You look sick. We could go to the drugstore if you need something. Eyedrops, perhaps?'

'No, you're not taking her to any drugstore. Leave Lora alone.' Steven's nostrils flared.

'Please guys, I'm fine. I've got some Tylenol, and eye drops, in my bag.'

'Alright then… now that I've got you are all together… ' Bianca said in a soothing voice. She put her tray on the table and rummaged in her bag pulling out a digital camera '… Can I take a picture of you guys?'

Without hesitation Lora said, 'Yes, please.'

Bianca noticed the tension written all over their faces. 'Smile, you're on candid camera.' She pressed the camera button. 'It's just so cool to see you guys together. The boys, oh Lora, they look so smart in their clothes. To be honest, I'm jealous.' She smiled and added, since I'm not sure when I'll see or hear from you again, I'll let you have this camera. I am mad at you though, for not telling me you were moving to New Zealand.' Bianca added, handing the camera to Lora.

Lora cleared her throat. 'I'm sorry, Bianca. I didn't have time to tell you, you know how it is juggling two jobs.'

Steven's eyes narrowed further as he glared at Bianca. 'Quite frankly I asked her not to tell you because I didn't want you following us to New Zealand.'

Bianca drew in a sharp breath then let it out slowly. 'Thanks for letting me know, Steven. You just make me want to come and visit Lora more in New Zealand; now you've told me my presence wouldn't be welcomed.'

Cameron tried to change the subject, trying to avoid the heated argument that was about to spark. 'Thank you very much, auntie, for the camera.'

'You're welcome, Cameron. Oh, you remind me of someone I know with that smile.' She turned to Steven and glared at him with acute dislike, serving notice that Steven was not Cameron's biological dad. Then she added another jab: 'Keep off the booze, Steven… bye for now,' she said, turning and waving goodbye.

The queue was long at departure gate 33 as they joined it, eventually handing over their boarding passes and walking down the boarding ramp.

Their United Airlines Express flight to San Francisco, with a connection to Air New Zealand into Auckland, departed on time at 11 pm.

Chapter 14

At 9 pm on January 24, after a thirteen-hour flight from San Francisco, then a connecting flight from Auckland to Nelson, they reached their destination. All the passengers began to disembark. Cameron unclicked his seatbelt and took his backpack from the overhead. He clutched the outside of the backpack to ensure the notebook was still there. He couldn't locate it and for a moment and fought down a sense of panic. Rummaging around inside, he breathed a sigh of relief when he found it wedged against his hoody. Behind him was a line of impatient-looking passengers. 'Excuse me.' He apologized and blew out a quick breath. 'What the hell. Jeez, if looks could kill,' Cameron muttered.

Lora had given Cameron a Tylenol as he had had a thumping headache during their flight, but it had a little effect and the craving for drugs made the beating in his head intensify.

The flight attendant, with perfect white teeth, beamed farewells to the passengers as they stepped down the narrow stairway. 'Thank you. Enjoy your time in Nelson.'

It was summer in New Zealand and coming out of the dim light of the airplane, Cameron and James instinctively shielded their eyes with their hands from the glaring sun as they disembarked.

Cameron yawned and rubbed his eyes with his knuckles. 'Thank goodness we've landed. I didn't get any sleep.'

'Me neither,' James answered.

Cameron hiked his backpack strap closer to his neck. 'Did you notice the flight attendant with short blond hair?'

'Yip, blondie. She's cute,' James replied.

'Blondie kept putting the blanket on top of me each time I nodded off, which kept me awake. When I fell asleep, I dreamed a swarm of bees was chasing me. Blondie threw a blanket on me to prevent the bees from stinging me, but a freakish looking witch took it off and I woke up, coughing and choking. It scared the crap out of me. That was the end of my dream, thank goodness. Am I going crazy?'

'Yip. I think you're going nuts, and the ecstasy you've been taking lately has made it worse.' James shrugged.

Cameron didn't answer. He couldn't remember much since Hollie had died he had saturated his brain with drugs or booze; nor could he remember how many females he had slept with.

They walked through the arrivals gate. People were excited to see their friends and relatives, hugging and kissing each other as they passed on their way to the baggage claim area to get their luggage. Once their luggage was collected, they returned inside the main terminal area to wait for Beth. Steven's sister. Their flight was the last arrival for the day. Both Lora and Cameron had bought new phones at the Auckland airport and they sat in the waiting area exploring the new features and functions.

James and Steven sat across from Lora and Cameron, all of them yawning.

Steven wondered where Beth was.

'Does anybody want some food?' James asked.

Cameron put his cell phone in his pocket. 'I'm starving too. Let's get something.'

Lora took her wallet out of her backpack and started to give James some money.

James gestured her to stop. 'I got this, mom. Can I get you and Dad something?' He cocked his head to one side, then continued, 'Oh, I know. You both like ginger beer.'

'Yes, please, James. You'll need to hurry as I think they're about to close.' Lora pointed to the empty cafeteria. She yawned. Stiff from sitting so long, she stood up from the couch giving her body a good stretch, then took off her grey pullover and wrapped it around her tiny waist.

James and Cameron returned from the cafeteria empty-handed as it was closed and nothing else was open.

After an hour of waiting, Lora began pacing. 'Steven, Beth should have been here a long time ago. Are you sure let her know what time our flight was due in?'

Steven frowned showing Lora the text message he sent to Beth. 'Yes of course.'

Lora read the message, which confirmed that she would be picking them up. She frowned. 'Maybe she forgot.'

'Should I try to ring Auntie Beth, Dad? 'James asked as he ran his fingers through his hair.

Steven was sweating, as he handed the cell phone to James. 'Here, have a go, I already programmed her number in.'

James took his phone and pressed the number. After listening to the recorded message he said, 'Nope, Dad. Just a recording saying the number is invalid or inactive. Are you sure you entered it right?'

'Oh great!' Cameron said, cracking his knuckles. 'I'm starving, and we need to do something as we can't sleep here.'

'Cameron, can you find a Nelson taxi?' Steven asked, through gritted teeth.

Cameron Googled the taxi service on his phone. 'It's 03-547770, Dad.' Cameron dialled the number then gave the phone to Steven.

Steven ordered a taxi. 'Okay, guys. The taxi will be here in five minutes. I ordered a van so there would be enough room for all of us and our luggage.' A minute later, Cameron looked outside as the van pulled up. Ten minutes later, they were on their way to Honimoki.

***

The van drove along the coastal road. Cameron poked his head out of the open window, gazing at the countless stars covering the black sky. It blew Cameron away to see the full moon playing hide and seek among the grey clouds as its reflection glistened onto the sea. 'Wow, this is so amazing,' Cameron said. Feeling euphoric, he suddenly realised his headache was gone. Taking a deep breath and he felt the ocean breeze blowing on his cheeks. Even his craving for drugs and a cigarette had disappeared. A wave of calmness passed over him and he settled his head on Lora's shoulder.

During the drive they had the taxi stop at a cafe, where they had to wake Cameron and James from their nap. It only took a few minutes for each of them to grab a mince pie, cakes and muffins. Cameron added his favourite ice cream, hokey-pokey. To his disappointment his craving for a cigarette had surfaced. He gave in to the temptation and with his fake ID, asked the shop assistant for a pack of Marlborough.

With the hokey pokey one hand, Cameron licked the ice cream, closing his eyes as the refreshing creamy-sweet taste registered. As he started to pay for the cigarettes, he shrugged, saying, 'I've changed my mind about the cigarettes. Thank you, sir.' It seemed like the hokey- pokey eliminated his craving for a cigarette.

The taxi driver started the van, then drove along the motorway, past Richmond town.

'What's the latest news in Honi?' Steven asked the taxi driver, taking his first bite of mince pie.

While the taxi driver focused on the road and drummed his fingers on the steering wheel he replied, 'Honi was in the national news last week. A tourist found a body in someone's garden on Wiremu Street. It was the third murder in town this month. The young'uns call the town Honi-morekill now. It's distressed the church-going people in town. So, they're up in arms praying for a hero come along and save the town. They believe that if they pray a lot, a hero will come. They think the cops are not doing much.'

'I never heard of any murders happening around here when I was young,' Steven said, adding a big yawn.

Cameron fought off sleep as he chewed the last crunchy toffee bit in the ice-cream. 'And that's where we're going to live? Thanks, Dad, I'm thrilled.'

'Huh, Honi-morekill. Cool, I can't wait to live here,' James blurted out sarcastically.

Steven stared out the window, still fuming. 'I still can't believe that Beth didn't turn up, or answer her phone. Who would do that, leave their family and not even try to get in touch? What is bloody wrong with her? After what I've done to help her and her family, this is how she repays me?'

'We'll find out once we get there. I hope she has a damn good reason as to why she didn't turn up,' Lora said, her voice calm.

***

The taxi turned into Marika Street then pulled up to a house with a con-crete walkway leading to an ornate iron gate.

Getting out of the taxi Steven's anger with Beth boiled. 'She'll pay for this. I'll get even.' He leaned against the open window of the taxi. 'Oh, sorry. How much do I owe you?'

The taxi driver looked at the meter, 'One-hundred-and-fifty dollars, please.'

Steven took his wallet out and handed him $150 in cash. 'Thanks, mate.'

'Can't we give him a tip? He accommodates us at this late at night and drove us this far,' Lora said.

'You're in New Zealand now, sweetheart, that doesn't matter,' Steven said, patting her on the back.

'Don't worry. I've got this.' Cameron pulled out one hundred and fifty American dollars from his pocket and handed it to the taxi driver.

'Thank you very much, sir,' the taxi driver said as his eyes widened.

James shook his head. 'That's seems like a lot of money for a tip,' he said, thinking that they normally don't tip in New Zealand.

'Hey, the guy did us a big favour. I don't think many taxi drivers would do that in New Zealand. I think he earned it,' Cameron said, thinking it wasn't really his money and he could easily spend more than that on drugs or shoes.

The house was totally dark so, James and Cameron turned the torches of their cell phones on, then led the way to the veranda.

Steven was familiar with this house since this was where he grew up. 'Hey, guys. Help me find the key. It's under one of these potted plants.'

They searched for the keys. 'The key isn't here, dad,' James said, slapping the dirt off of his hands.

'It's not here,' Cameron added, shrugging.

Lora stood, waiting patiently. 'Cameron, can you remember where Nana Mollie hid her house keys?' Lora asked. Cameron just shook his head.

'We can get in through the bathroom window at the back. It's never locked,' Steven replied. 'Watch your step,' Steven added, as they walked on the uneven surface of damp lawn. They had their cell phone torches on to help guide their way to the back of the house. When they reached the back, and with the help of their luggage, Cameron climbed up to the window frame and slipped inside of the bathroom.

'I'll open the front door,' Cameron yelled.

Steven, Lori and James picked up their luggage and made their way back to the front door.

As Cameron walked through the living room, memories came flooding back; particularly of a pig hunting trip with Pop Glenn. 'Cameron got this one in one strike,' Pop Glenn had said, dropping a dead wild boar onto the front porch.

'He is gifted, you know,' Nana Mollie had said, taking the freshly baked scones from the oven.

Lora took the raspberry jam out of the wooden cupboard and said, 'He's like his grandfather on my side. In Ohio they called my dad the *Slingshot Man*. I wish he were still alive to see his grandson carry on his tradition.'

'Yip, shame he didn't meet his lovely grandchildren,' Pop Glenn said.

Cameron cherished the fading memory. Paintings lined the hall wall and he stopped to stare at the portrait of Beth's twin son and daughter, Brice and Azoma, his cousins from Scotland, before making his way to the front door.

As he opened the front door, two policemen pulled up. Steven walked out to greet them and after several minutes of discussion, they pulled away.

'What was that all about?' Cameron asked as he stepped out of the house.

'Oh, just my pain in the ass sister reporting us for breaking into the house.'

Lora, Steven and James made their way back up to the veranda, just a red BMW driven by a young man wearing a beanie pulled into the driveway.

Chapter 15

Beth and Azoma stepped out of the car. In black leather pants, a crimson halter top and high heels, Beth wobbled toward the front door. Azoma staggered a step behind, her face radiating hatred, as she lit a cigarette. 'I'd hoped the cops had taken you and your family to the police station by now,' Beth seethed, then turned on the security light by the gate as the driver in the BMW pulled away, tooting.

Despite Steven's anger with Beth, he was delighted now that he could see the two-story, white one-hundred-year-old Victorian house, with its sky blue tinted window frames, in excellent condition.

Beth's heavy-boned body struggled to stay upright as she walked towards Steven and his family. She tilted her wrinkled face with its small chin and long nose. 'Hi, little brother. Though you're not really my brother, no, not by blood. I was the one that was adopted,' Beth stuttered through her sarcasm. 'I contested the will. You don't have the right to live in this house … until your lawyer provides evidence that you own it, you can't kick us out.'

Wearing skin-tight black jeans, which emphasized her bony back side, and a red top that exposed her navel, Azoma drew on her cigarette then blew the smoke into Steven's face. 'You're not welcome here,' she snarled. 'Go back where you belong. And don't even think that you can have this house.' She flicked the cigarette butt on the veranda floor squashing it with the toe of her stiletto.

In an effort to hold his anger, Steven clenched his teeth, then turned and glared at Beth.

'You're zonked out. What's got into you? You're crazy. I didn't ask our father to leave his estate solely in my name.'

'Zonked out? You have a short memory. Have you forgotten the times you were so drunk you slept at any stranger's house? Our poor parents had to go to weekly Alcoholic Anonymous meetings so they could cope with your drinking. Mom and Dad's *Golden boy*. My petition to the court is still open and it will prove that the whole estate was left to me.' Beth searched inside her handbag for her house keys.

Frustrated, Cameron listened as Beth and his dad argued. 'This house isn't worth it. Let's get out of here.'

'And what the hell were you doing inside my house?' Beth asked.

Cameron's stomached churned at the sight of Beth. 'Excuse me but this is dad's home. It was left to him.'

Beth raised her hand in protest. 'It's so typical of you, Steven. You must've been drunk when I told you that you can't have the house. We have the right to live in it until my petition is approved.'

'After what I've done to save you and your family? We've let you stay in our house for a year to hide you and your children from that abusive husband of yours. This is how you repay us?' Steven said.

'Well, I didn't ask you to help me. You offered,' replied Beth

'Oh, you are one ungrateful swine ,' Steven said.

'Let's get inside, Azoma darling, Beth said as she went inside. 'Lock the door behind you,' she added.

Before shutting the door, Azoma blurted out, 'Hey, Cameron. Just to let you know, so you won't forget; that scar on your lip? I did that on purpose when we were fishing. I threw the fishhook at your eye, but I missed.'

Cameron licked his scarred bottom lip. 'Thanks, Azoma. I appreciate your honesty. Just so you know, I peed in the Cool Aid I gave to you each time you had breakfast when you guys stayed with us.' He beamed as Azoma's face took on a look of horror.

James laughed loudly and Steven smirked

Disgusted, Azoma slammed the door behind her.

Steven could feel his blood pressure spiking but tried to keep his cool. 'James, can you ring Honimoki taxis, please?'

'Ok, Dad.' James rubbed his eyes, then pressed in the number for the taxi service just as the veranda light went out and it began to rain. 'There's no answer at the taxi service dad,' James said.

Everyone was soaked by the time they reached the gate, dragging their luggage down the driveway.

Cameron realized what Beth said about her owning the house could be true, but this was not the time to start blaming his dad. *Don't even go there,* he thought.

Steven looked at his phone 'It's about a thirty-minute walk to town, but I have a Plan B.' He phoned his best friend Terry. 'Hi Terry. Steven here.'

'Steve how are you mate? What time is it over there?'

'No, I'm here in Honi,' Steven replied. He told Terry that they desperately needed a ride and briefly recounted the clash between him, his sister and his niece.

'Sorry, mate. I can't drive. I had a hip surgery three weeks ago. But my wife can. Where are you?'

'We're in front of my house at Marika road.'

'Okay, I'll tell my wife.'

'Thanks, mate.' He hung up. 'Okay, guys. Terry's wife Ruth is going to pick us up. She'll be here in 10 minutes,' Steven said.

Sopping wet, exhausted and hungry, ten minutes seemed like an eternity. Finally, a beat-up white Mitsubishi Galant pulled up at the curb. A woman in her forties stepped out of the car with a welcoming grin. She had auburn hair roughly plaited and wore a light green, tie-dyed flimsy dress.

Ruth left the headlights on, opened the passenger door and popped the boot open. Shivering, she and James put their luggage in the boot.

'Hi, Steven, and you must be Lora,' Ruth said.

'Nice to meet you, these are our sons, James and Cameron. Thanks so much for rescuing us,' Lora told her, as they all got into the car.

***

As soon as the car pulled away, the security light went back on at the Victorian house. Beth and Azoma had changed into black dresses for their tri-monthly Wicked Gathering where members of the Faithful Satan Cult would be arriving. Glancing outside, they watched as members parked their Porsches, BMWs, Mercedes-Benz, Rolls Royce, Jaguars and Alfa Romeos on the street. The women wore backless, black dresses with matching lavish jewellery, and the men tuxedos, paired with signature shoes. The sound of their shoes reverberated into the night as they followed the S-shaped path that led to the underground rooms that were installed when Beth had renovated the house.

At almost six foot, Brice got out of his black BMW, his black suit and white shirt straining against his muscular chest. With poise Shantell, Brice's companion, slid out from the passenger's side. Her little black dress stretched and hugged her full figure, showing off her cleavage. Giving each other a sexy grin, they followed the others.

Shantell cocked her head to the side; her moss green eyes scanned the property. 'Security guards with guns, why?'

'They're Cedric's men. They're here to protect my mom's estate.'

As the members approached, Beth opened the door. She looked sober after having been binge drinking the whole day. A flush of elation crept over her face. 'Good evening, hail Papa Satan!' Announced Beth, the crow's feet around her eyes wrinkling. She smirked at the cult members as they stood at the door.

To please his mother, Brice said, 'Good evening, mother.' His velvety brown eyes glistened as he walked through the door.

Beth sighed affectionately at her son. 'Good evening son. Don't forget, Azoma will guide Shantell through her initiation this evening.'

Reaching for Shantell's hand he said, 'Relax, you'll be alright. Don't forget, this is your choice. You can bugger off if you don't want be here.'

When Azoma appeared, he released Shantell's hand, as she and the other cult members followed Azoma.

Azoma guided them down the cobblestone steps and into the huge underground cellar; an ideal, out of sight place for their meetings. Several huge crimson candles lit the surface of the walls. The smell of the hot candle wax penetrated the air. In the huge hall, two long rectangular tables were set out, each wrapped in a silvery sheet. An oval-shaped table was placed between them. Above, the ceiling had an intricate painted design of fierce dragons and wicked goats with tall, twisted horns. Along the wall surfaces, were smooth cabinets in elegant mahogany, holding cases of wine, port, bourbon, champagne and a variety of glasses. All of the exits were draped with red velvet curtains. The group, accustomed to the ceremony, surrounded the first table.

Standing at the head of the oval table was Beth, the host, along with Azoma and Brice, her co-hosts.

As Beth opened the meeting, she gave the audience a sparkling grin. 'Good evening and welcome to our wicked gathering. Please accept our new recruit Shantell Higgins.' She waved her hand, signalling Azoma to continue with the presentation.

Azoma, with her 5' 6" slim frame and shoulder-length wavy fine light brown hair, was the model for the girl next door look as she carried on with the introduction. 'This is Shantell. She slept with her tutor and his wife found out. They got a divorce.'

'Hmm,' the flock murmured in unison.

Bridgit Grant, a nurse with orange-dyed hair, raised her hand, 'Not so evil, hmm.' She blinked her long, fake eyelashes.

Azoma smiled. 'Get this everybody. Shantell can falsify any signature, and she slowly poisoned her stepmother to death.' As she turned around stepping from the platform, Azoma's backless gown was cut almost to her backside, which drew the eye of every man there..

'But we want to hear more about what evil this girl can do,' someone shouted.

Beth raised her hand. 'Please, let's give the girl a chance. Shantell, can you give them an example on how you could forge a signature?'

Beth looked around for Dr. Arsenio and Shantell nodded when Beth and the doctor made eye contact.

Someone gave a pen and some paper to Dr Arsenio. After taking the paper with her signature on it, the lawyer examined the doctor's signature.

With a confident grin, Shantel glanced at it, then copied it.

Azoma showed the copy, alongside the original and the members were stunned.

One member, a police detective, marvelled at the signatures. 'Well, doc. your signature looks like chicken scratch, typical of a doctor's handwriting. No wonder nurses get their orders wrong.' He looked at it again and shook his head in amazement. 'And you forged it perfectly, Shantell. Get out of here! How did you do that? I can't tell the difference'

As the group stared at Shantell, what seemed like neon laser light rays darted around her. The lights swirled as their spell penetrated Shantell and the group marvelled at their new member.

Beth went back to the platform. The spell had weakened, but she waited for the next hit to intensify. She struggled to stop her shaking hands, but no one noticed.

'Without further ado, let's start with our first challenge,' Beth ordered.

Brice stood beside her with a timer in his hand.

Shantell creeped closer to Azoma.

With a slight frown, Shantell pressed her lips together. 'I've seen that doctor and the nurse before, they work at Nelson Central Private Hospital, don't they? They are real baddies, aye?'

Azoma smiled with pride at the mention of the doctor's and nurse's evil achievements. 'Yip. They are kick-ass dodgy. Dr Arsenio has got away with thirty slip-ups in her operations. In fact, she's been responsible for the disability of fifteen patients and twenty deaths, but no one has suspected anything. And Bridgit, the nurse, tortures her patients and bullies her workmates. One of her co-workers committed suicide.'

Shantell's green eyes blinked rapidly then stopped in a wide stare. 'I remember that nurse when I visited a girlfriend whom I was jealous of. Of course, I only want to see her to pretend my concern, but more so to see her suffering.'

'Why was the girl in hospital?' Azoma asked.

'She was sent back to hospital because Dr. Arsenio was incompetent. She had poked and prodded tubes into her guts to examine her.' Shantell paused for a second to clear her throat. 'Well, this girl was out of bed and tried to get back under the covers, but she was in agony, in tears, and her face was blue. Bridgit said in a harsh bullying tone, "If you can get out of bed, you're not in pain. You can get back in yourself.'

Impressed Azoma blinked with delight and said, 'That's not too bad. Did it make you happy?'

'Yes, I was thrilled to see this girl get verbally abused. Brigit left the room, and the girl gripped the bed and pulled herself in. I noticed blood on the sheets, but I kept quiet, so I used the top sheet to cover her, but the pain was too much for her. I pushed the call bell. Brigit came back, told us off and said not to ring the call bell again. She left without giving her pain relief. She passed out. I don't know what happened to her. Who cares?'

Azoma giggled. 'Well done.'

Beth snapped her fingers to gain the group's attention.

Shantell and Azoma stopped talking.

'Let's start the first competition,' Beth commanded.

Spontaneously the accountant with a mischievous grin, rolled the sheet off the first table.

Shantell's eyes popped at the sight of the table full of alluring alcoholic drinks: vodka, rum, bourbon, tequila, wine, Kalua and beer. Along the side of the table there were customized, extra-long colourful straws that could reach down to the bottom of a bottle of alcohol. Cult members crammed to look closely at the dazzling display.

Shantell scanned the members and noticed a guy with a handlebar moustache.

'That guy there is a cop, huh?' Azoma asked.

Shantell whispered, 'Shhish.'

Azoma nodded.

Beth positioned herself among the members, her eyes darting between the rows of vodka. 'Oh, it won't be long now," she muttered. 'The Zippy is the name of the game. You must use the straw to drink as much as you can. Whoever drinks the most in fifteen minutes wins.'

Shantell was about to pick up a straw.

'Wait until you hear the whistle,' Azoma told Shantell as she pressed her hand into hers.

Beth always wanted Brice where she could see him and she blew the whistle while Brice started the digital timer.

As soon as the timer started ticking, the crowd raced to the table. In a second the clanking sound of glasses against each other, and the gulping sounds as people drank, echoed within the chamber. Explosive pops like fire-crackers followed as the crowd surged to open sparkling wines and beer cans. Like parched African animals at a desert watering hole, the members guzzled the alcohol, burbling as they sucked it down.

After fifteen minutes the timer sounded. The members stopped immediately. Counting the empty bottles, Brice noticed that Bridgit had drunk the most bottles of gin and scotch.

It did not surprise the crowd as Bridgit was known to be the biggest pisshead in town. But the hospital staff had never suspected her coming to work intoxicated. She would drink alcohol whenever she could. As a Satan follower, all members came to replenish a spirit of simulated sobriety, which meant they could look sober when they were not.

Brice slurred, 'The winner is no other than Bridgit and she will receive a year's supply of alcohol sponsored by Bright Morning Star liquor, and a daily massage compliments of Lua Mata Massage Parlour.' He pointed to the Asian woman with jet black hair, cut in a sleek bob. 'Lua Mata came here to marry a New Zealander and they own many three-bedroom houses. Each house is rented out from twenty to forty migrants. They cram as many as they can into each house earning thousands a week.' In a standing ovation, the members cheered. 'What's better is they don't pay their taxes and they don't care,' the accountant commented.

While heavy metal rock blasted in the background, the group set out to drink and dance.

After half an hour the bell rang. Again, everybody fell line to go to the corner room. It was the toilet and changing room. In the changing room they removed their cloaks and their underwear and replaced these with a satin shiny dark purple shroud. The costume had an S, a snake logo, meaning Satan, in golden lettering on the left side. In single file, the Satan cult marched full of pride towards the second table.

Offering to roll the cover off the round table was a bald teacher. He belittled his students, by telling them they were hopeless and useless. The bald teacher had a fetish for women's panties and sneaked around people's backyard stealing girls' panties from clotheslines. He boasted proudly. 'I've been pinching panties for years. You should see my collections and you can join me in my sniffing session.'

Everybody gave him the thumbs-up and many yelled out, 'Good on you for not being caught for many years.'

Stuart Sullivan the lawyer, who wore woman panties, wondered whether the teacher had stolen his panties and smelt them. He smiled cagily. 'Enjoy your sniffing session, but that's not for me.' The lawyer rolled his eyes.

The teacher lifted the cover off the second table. On the table were cannabis bongs and pipes in an array of colours and shapes. The members' faces flushed in anticipation. The teacher bowed like a chef offering his great cuisine after revealing what was on the table. One by one the group surrounded the table. They sat in incredulous joy, helping themselves to the bongs and pipes. Soon the smell of cannabis dominated the air.

Azoma drooled at the sight of the colourful pipes and bongs. 'I declare this is my favorite table.'

Shantell grabbed one of the bongs. 'Me too.' She gave Azoma a high-five before pulling a chair over and sitting beside Azoma.

The secular Satan ritual began. Mechanically, the cult crossed their hands on their chests along with their raised index, and pinkie fingers. While the middle finger and the ring finger were folded touching the thumb, the group swung back and forth, from right to left. In unison they hummed and chanted their mantra: 'Kill, steal and destroy. Kill, steal and destroy'. Then they knocked their hands on the table three times, clapped three times, then drummed their feet on the floor three times in a rhythm, chanting 'Kill, steal, and destroy'. They continued humming, then everyone stood to declare, 'We beseech Papa Satan come.'

With a vibration of rolling thunder, Satan emerged as a James Dean look-alike. In tears the group applauded, hands to their cheeks, arms raised above their heads in awe of Satan, as they worshiped him.

To flaunt his evil supernatural power and to astound his followers, Satan sky-dived amid the tables. His red eyes glared with fierce scrutiny at the members. 'Yes, I stole James Dean's look-alike body this time but, more important, I gathered you here today to enlighten you. We have a staunch enemy. He is a menace to our mission. I demand you to zero in on him. He is Cameron Owen, recently arrived from America and he must be tortured. May the spirit of addiction, depression and suicide be with him.' Satan blessed the cult, hands waving and letting his spirit rest on everyone. He smoked a big pipe of cannabis.

Then everybody bellowed in a mantra. 'May the addiction, depression and suicide spell be with Cameron Owen.'

Shantell's eyebrows wrinkled and she whispered. 'Who's Cameron Owen and how does Satan know stuff like that about him?'

Satan heard what Shantell said. He looked through her mind. The spell darted into her forehead with a glow. A spell of deception pierced Shantell's thoughts. Within seconds Shantell's mind was tricked into accepting, without a challenge, all the lies that Satan said.

Shantell's thoughts possessed her, they told her to harm Cameron no matter who he was. She joined in the mantra. 'The addiction, depression and suicide spell be with Cameron Owen.' She inhaled one bong after another.

Suddenly all the candle lights were extinguished, the place thrown in blackness for a second, then replaced by a dim red light.

The group fell in line. Beth led them through large double red doors. A red light glowed all around the room. The floor was covered with beds with fresh white sheets neatly tucked under with hospital corners. Beside each mattress was a small low white table with boxes of condoms, lubricating gels, cannabis bongs and pipes. TV screens showed either erotic dancers rocking to heavy metal or porno clips. On the walls near the door were hooks for people to hang their garments.

Satan closed the door and in a few minutes, there was wailing, grunting and hooting. Shantell's initiation turned into an orgy

After an hour, the bell rang. One by one they came out of the room with their robes on, arrogance on every face. Their foreheads covered in a slimy white matter. Satan's oil for anointing his cult.

As the group staggered out of the room, 'How do you feel?' Azoma asked.

'Very alive and ready to do evil,' Shantell replied.

'Papa Satan has smeared us with his power. Now you can look people in their eyes, command any evil spell you want, then smash them with it.' Azoma looked slyly at Shantell from the corner of her eye. She smirked an evil grin. 'I'll try it on you.' Azoma fixed her eyes on Shantell's. A red laser shot like a missile from Azoma to Shantell. 'How do you feel?

'I'm very hungry. I could eat a horse.'

'That's the spirit of gluttony.'

Then Shantell fixed her eyes on Azoma.

'Oh, you pig, you just give me a spell of gluttony.' Azoma's mouth watered. 'I can fix that. I'll ask mom to give me a spell of anorexia then I won't eat for days.'

'Is that why you're so skinny?' Shantell asked, as her eyes widened.

After a few minutes, Satan stood at the third table. The group gathered around. Satan removed the cover, rolling it up and putting it aside. He stared at every member, giving them a spell of gluttony from head to foot. The table was fully laden with dish after dish of buffet food. All kinds of fizzy drinks sat between rows of food platters, which were stacked high with layers upon layers of fried chicken, bacon, hamburgers, nacho's dripping with creamed cheese, cakes packed with cream and smeared thick with icing and every brand of chocolate bar. Towers of pizzas, at least 100 inches tall like skyscrapers, looked down upon pyramids of fresh donuts in colourful glazes. Potato wedges with sour cream, hot dogs, jumbo style sandwiches, pretzels, sausage rolls, BBQ sauce, dips and everyone's favourite, red M & Ms, tempted the greedy group. Lastly there was a tall cake in the shape of the cross, but it stood upside down, mocking the symbol of God. No one could miss it as it stood proudly amongst the feast, with its sticky covering of blood-red almond icing and fine black liquorice outlining the edges. Drooling, the group looked over the feast. But the aroma of candles, cannabis, alcohol and food couldn't dull the stench of sex that filled the air.

The bell rang, and Beth announced, 'You know the game, whoever remains standing and eating is the winner.'

While the spirit of gluttony worked into their minds, the effects of cannabis gave the group a craving for food. Once the whistle blew, like scavenging vultures, they attacked the food. Using their bare hands, they shoved fistfuls of food into their mouths, like ravenous lions devouring their helpless prey. Eyes and cheeks bulged. Burps and farts followed. Some vomited on the tables, others rushed to the crowded toilets to spew; some didn't make it, vomiting on the floor.

After an hour most members lay on the floor, their stomachs distended like a full-term pregnant woman. Others sat on the floor leaning against the walls, exhausted from gorging. Only one was left standing: The lawyer. He stuffed the last piece of Satan's blood-red cross into his mouth and Satan announced him the winner.

The cop rubbed his abdomen while he laid on the floor, and commented, 'Good on him. I know some lawyers will screw you even when you're dead. They always win.' He had noticed throughout the feasting that the lawyer had paced himself, not gorging the food, taking his time so he could eat for longer.

Bridgit sat beside him and rested her hand on her stomach. 'What have you been up too lately?'

As he chewed on a toothpick the cop burped, then answered. 'As we all know our spell is more effective if the prey is under the influence of alcohol or drugs or when they're sick.' He sat up and moved closer to her, planting his elbows on his knees. 'But if there are Christians praying for them it's harder for the spell to penetrate their thoughts. About two weeks ago I took advantage of a young girl. I'm sure she had Christians praying for her. I succeeded in luring her into a toilet, groped her breast and her ass, but she managed to run away before I could finish with her. That's why I come to every wicked gathering - to recharge my evil power.'

At 3 am the group had changed back into their tuxedos and tiny black dresses. They gathered around the filthy tables covered in chunks of half-eaten food, vomit, empty glasses and discarded bongs and pipes.

With one of his lasers, the confident Satan pronounced the benediction. 'Go forth and multiply your evil deeds. May the power of darkness be with you.'

The group raised their hands with a cocky-as-hell grin on their faces as they accepted his benedictions and trusted that their evil powers had been amplified. Then Satan, as he glared at the group, slowly disappeared.

When all the members left, Shantell let out a nervous laugh and said, 'Who's going to clean up this mess?'

Brice grinned with amusement. 'You. Your initiation is not quite finished yet.'

Shantell's mouth dropped open. 'Okay. Where are the mops and the brooms?'

After the meeting Azoma, who had hooked up with the cop, they passed holding each other's hand as they made their way to the stairs that led out of the basement. She heard what Brice said. Turning her back to Shantell, she giggled. 'Oh you're so gullible. The professional cleaner will come tomorrow. See you guys later.'

Brice laughed hysterically and Shantell gave him the finger.

Before Brice could say something more to piss off Shantell, Beth approached him.

She put her hands on her hips. 'So, what's your plan for Cameron?' she asked as she lit a cigarette.

'I'll meet up with *my girlfriend* Tara at the flea market; the Owens will be there. I know you like surprises, mother, so I won't tell you what will happen next.'

'Okay, my darling Brice. Just remember a slow torture is more effective than a quick killing. If you kill him, he might go straight to heaven. And what good will that do? A slow torture makes someone look mangled and ugly. They suffer at your hands. Take time to kill him, slowly and brutally.' Beth flicked her hair behind her ear. 'Changing the subject, the documents forged by Shantell were perfect.' Beth gave Shantell a look of praise. 'Steven and Lora don't have a shit-show of claiming this house.'

The three of them climbed the stairs out of the basement.

'You can sleep anywhere you like, Shantell. Choose any of the guest rooms,' Beth said.

Brice offered his hand to guide Shantell. With anticipation she followed Brice up the polished wooden staircase. Looking down from the landing, they gazed at the vast lounge in the Victorian house. Posh theatre-type red velvet drapes hung in the windows. A white regency English sofa sat in front of an enormous fireplace topped with an ornate wooden mantel piece.

Shantell followed behind Brice. Watching Brice's muscled body as he gave her a tour of the top floor, her hormones surged, and she felt a tingling between her legs. While Brice was in the bathroom taking a shower, Shantell investigated his bedroom. She stared at Beth's portrait. She was wearing a red silk dress, her ample bust and cleavage spilling out the front. On his bedside table and on top of his dresser more photos of his mother were displayed. In one she wore a bikini, in another a wet t-shirt. She teased the photographer, her eyes full of lust. Something wasn't right. *Where were the teenage posters of beach blondes and heavy metal rock bands?* she thought.

After a quick shower, Brice laid down on the bed, naked under the sheet with two things on his mind: sex and sleep.

Shantell sat and rested against the plump pillows keeping a distance between them. Noticing the spotless room, she asked, 'Who cleans your room? She reached for her bag to search for a cigarette.

'What a ludicrous random question that Cameron could have a chance to hook up with his girlfriend, Tara. And it was unsettling him. He pulled open the bedside table drawer, and grabbed a bottle of sleeping pills, popping one into his mouth.

Shantell opened her hands. 'Give me one or two as I won't be able to sleep either.' After a few minutes they both dropped off to sleep.

Brice woke up with a hangover. He texted Tara.

Chapter 16

24 January, 11.30 pm

At Ruth and Terry's house, Steven explained Cameron's involvement with the gang. As Terry felt he owed Steven his life for taking a bullet for him in a scuffle outside a night club in Florida during the late 70s, he lent him his shotgun.

Cameron made a slingshot in Terry's Toolshed.

The next day Cameron's parents managed to buy a caravan and a station wagon to tow it. Then they took off to Kina Beach.

After having toast with peanut butter for breakfast, Cameron went for a walk in the sun. The wind blowing on the blooming red flowers of the Pohutakawa trees caught his attention and made him smile. Checking the slingshot he'd made, he tried to target a pine cone on a pine tree.

Explroring, his mind began to think of the event leading up to how he ended up in NZ. But his toughts were disrupted when he saw towering smoke rising in the distance as hee put more stones in his pocket. 'What the hell? Who would make a big bonfire in the middle of the day?' he muttered. As he drew closer, the smoke continued to rise but cleared for a moment. He saw an old man, beating up a guy who was already on the ground. Stunned to see that it was his dad being assaulted, his adrenalin raced. In a split second, Cameron picked a stone out of his pocket, his slingshot out of his pocket and launched the stone. He hit the man on the back of his head. Falling backwards, the man's head landed on a rock. Cameron sprinted to the scene. Steven was conscious but had cuts and bruises on his hands as he had used them to cover his face. The man Cameron struck with a stone appeared to be dead. He took his pulse, and it was beating. Yelling for help Cameron, started cardiac resuscitation quickly.

Steven remained on the ground. 'Give me your phone, Cameron.' He rang 111 and asked for an ambulance.

The dispatcher advised him to stay on the phone.

Within minutes, the ambulance came, along with a few spectators who had heard Camerons calls for help. In a green uniform, embroidered with 'St John' on their chest pockets, the ambulance staff took over. Once the man was stable they gave him oxygen. The ambulance staff found some ID on the man who they identified as a Mr Hartley, a famous and wealthy local man.

Relief spread over Cameron's face as Mr Hartley's color returned. *Jeez, I could've killed that man. I hope he's going to be fine*, Cameron thought. Once Mr Hartley was in the back of the ambulance, the ambulance staff attended to Steven dressing his cuts. They couldn't help but notice his intoxicated state.

'Thank you, young lad. You did well to save Mr Hartley's life,' The female ambulance officer said. They took a record of the event and his particulars and left.

Cameron's feelings were mixed. He hated his dad for being drunk but felt sorry for him for getting beaten up. And he was furious with Mr Hartley for beating his dad, but he hoped he would live as he couldn't bring himself to think what would've happened if he had killed him. He hoped Mr Hartley would be fine and the police wouldn't find out it.

But then the worse happened: a cop came.

It was Officer Daniel Fowler, who had a Maori designed tattto on his right arm. 'We have a report of an altercation here a few minutes ago. Can you tell me what happened?'

Cameron reported what happened while Steven sat on the sand.
'Thank you. You did well. You saved the man's life.

As soon as Officer Fowler finished talking to Cameron, he took Steven's statement, then drove away.

Steven quickly realized the consequences of his drinking and felt remorseful over sneaking out to buy alcohol. 'Cameron, please don't tell your mom. I'll get sober. I'll go for a swim. Lora wouldn't even noticed. Please. It won't happen again.'

Cameron fought to control his anger at the thought of his mom being tricked into coming to New Zealand and putting up with his dad's drinking. 'Whatever, Dad. Go and jump in the lake . I won't tell mom because it's her birthday today.' He then felt sorry for him and realized his dad had lied and not told Officer Fowler that he'd struck Mr Hartley with a rock from the slingshot.

As soon as Cameron left, even though he was intoxicated and had poor judgemen, he was determined to sober up and he became oblivious to his injuries and took off to find a swimming spot.

Hurriedly, Cameron returned back to the camp ground.

He opened the caravan door, noticing that Lora was sound asleep. He didn't wake her up. It would be better if she slept, which would give more time for his dad to sober up. He retrieved a fishing rod and lure box from a cupboard. He headed for the sea a short ways from the camp, srtiding through the native trees with their shiny leaves reflecting the sun, until he found a rock big enough to sit on. Throwing his first cast, he relaxed, but then he was hit with the smell of bug spray, suntan lotion, and strong coffee. Someone at the camp site was playing old eighties music.

The tide was rising fast when he spotted a boat off in the distance. The boat reminded him of their family cruiser, the Saga Sloop 43. Although Lora made it clear when she had purchased it that it was for the whole family, it still made James jealous because he thought Lora had bought it for Cameron because he loved fishing. Over the years Lora had bought him state-of-the-art fishing rods, and he had built up a handsome collection, but they had to sell the cruiser and the fishing gear to pay the mortgage.

His line wriggled. 'Wow. Man, this is a big bite,' Cameron yelled as he reeled a big snapper in. As he gutted the fish, James appeared.

'What a catch you made. That's for our dinner, aye?' James asked, holding up a miniature Noah's ark that he'd made from twigs.

Cameron eyes widened. 'Did you just make that? It looks so real, man. I hope one day you can make a real one so we can use it to escape this crazy world.' He gave James a hopeful look. 'There's another fishing rod by the steps to the caravan if you want to join me, but don't wake up mom.'

'Yip. Wait here. Where is Dad?' asked James, as he walked back to get the rod, then returned to join Cameron.

Cameron told James what happened. 'Mom will find out because it will be in the newspaper. But don't tell her dad is drunk.'

James swallowed hard. He lowered his head, and stuttered, 'L- let's h- hope mom won't find out.' He cast off his line.

They recast their fishing lines one after another and stood in silence on the shore, waiting for a bite. Cameron thought of the gang harming his family to get at him. Witnessing his intoxicated dad made it worse. What if the gang hit the town? How could Steven protect them? Could he use the shotgun safely? Cameron's thought turned to James and Lora; his mind debated whether they could protect themselves.

Then he noticed Steven walking towards them. A plastic bag full of stuff in both hands, Steven appeared sober. 'Where's mom? I've got fish and chips for tea tonight.'

Cameron's heart softened as he saw the sincerity in Steven's eyes and he was pleased to see fish and chips and fizzy drinks. 'Dad, thanks but we have to cook the snapper I've caught.'

'Oh, a good one,' he said, looking at the gutted snapper. 'Okay. I'll light the barbecue.' Looking down, he noticed the boat James had made. 'Wow, James. Did you make this today?' He picked up the boat and studied it.

James's fishing line started to jiggle. 'Yes, dad, but it took me all day. It's for mom. And I will cut out pictures of us and animals in pairs to put on the stairs of the ark,' James said as he reeled in the fishing line. He glared at his dad in silent disgust. *Cameron and I will beat you up if you carry on drinking,* James thought. 'Oh. I caught one. Yay!' James exclaimed, his eyes widening at the wiggling fish.

'That's a Trevally. Shame I already bought some fish, but we have four scoops of chips to go with it,' Steven said as he swallowed the lump in his throat.

At 8 pm, it was still daylight as Lora woke and looked at her watch. 'I had a good sleep hmm still day light,' she muttered as she noticed the time. Thinking of the boys she thought about what she could get for dinner from the supermarket. Then the aroma of fish cooking at the barbecue reached her and her mouth watered. She rushed out of the caravan and her eyes sparkled with delight to see the table with chips and fizzy drinks on it and Steven at the barbecue. In the distance she saw her sons fishing, chatting, and looking content. It pleased her to see Steven had organized something for tea. 'Wow. What a lovely surprise.'

'It's only fish and chips, love. We were just waiting for you to wake up so we can have dinner, and happy birthday,' Steven said, as he kissed her on the cheek then flipped the fish on the barbecue. Ten minutes later, the fish was cooked.

'Cameron, James. Dinner is ready,' Lora yelled.

'What happened to your hand?" Lora asked.

Steven told Lora what had happened, but he didn't mention being drunk. Cameron and James kept shooting each other looks as if to say, 'you're full of crap, Dad.'

After finishing the dinner, James gave the miniature Noah's ark to his mom. 'Happy birthday, Mom'.

Her eyes marvelled as she gazed at the miniature boat. 'It must have taken you hours just looking for the wood and then putting it together.' What made her even happier was the look in Cameron's eyes that held no hint of jealousy. Staring at the boat, Lora would never forget when Cameron made a boat that looked like a frying pan. That was over seven years ago. When Cameron showed it to her she had giggled as she thought the boat was cute.

Cameron thought it wasn't funny. 'I spent all day making that boat for you since you always loved James's boats. I thought you might like my one.' Squashing the boat with his hand he ran to his room crying. Seeing Cameron cry, had felt like needles were being stuck into her heart.

Cameron dug in his pocket and pulled out a velvet pouch that he purchased from the duty-free shop and gave it to Lora. 'Happy birthday, mom. I bought these at the duty-free shop.'

Lora's eyes widened as she opened the box and took out the golden hoop earrings. 'Thank so much, son. I love you. This is so nice.' She put the earrings on and kissed Cameron on the forehead. She wondered if Cameron knew they looked like the same earrings she had pawned back in San Diego and then been unable to buy them back.

Cameron was thankful that the day had not turned out to be a real disaster and catching the snapper had thrilled him. But the fear of the gang still lingered as well as the fact that he had almost killed someone. Cameron and James carried on fishing as they watched the sun sinking below the horizon. Orange and pink hues painted the clouds, and the pale blush of the moon started to rise.

Looking at James's boat, Lora touched the earrings and watched her sons. She sighed at the guilt that had been festering for ages. She took a folding chair and sat between them. 'I know I won't get a vote for the best mother from you guys but all I know is I will take a bullet for my sons. I messed up. I'm sorry, for the pain I've caused you,' she said, rubbing her leg.

James felt sad for her and cocked his head to the side. 'Don't worry, Mom. We made mistakes too.'

Cameron knew his mom was sincere. 'You're forgiven. Now can we carry on fishing,' Cameron asked.

Steven and the boys went off. Sitting in the camping chair, Lora felt as if a thorn had been pulled from her paw. She began to envision a bright future for her boys—with good friends, going to their school's prom, graduating high school, getting married and having a family, which would mean grandchildren for her. 'Oh God. Are my dreams too much to ask?'

Her thoughts were soon interrupted. When she heard the news on a radio nearby about a male tourist who was deported back to San Diego for possession of counterfeit money and a fake passport. She had no doubt it was a gang member. *Who else could it be?* she thought.

Steven returned and Lora told him what she'd heard on the news, which gave them reassurance that the gang could not reach them easily. Steven felt that New Zealand's security was tough after 9-11. 'I don't think he'll try to come again since I know New Zealand has high-tech gear to detect fake passports.'

'I suppose, but I believe that God's protecting us. And I'll tell Cameron once he's back from fishing,' she said.

'So, what is your plan for tomorrow, love?' Steven asked.

'We're so blessed. I've looked at the boxes the little old lady sold us with the caravan. You won't believe what I found. I can't believe she gave us jewellery, the vax cleaner, fishing rods that are almost new and other fishing gear. There should be enough money for groceries for a few months. I could sell it at the flea market tomorrow.'

'Well, we are indeed blessed with your bargaining skills. For the price we offered for everything, it was a steal,' he told her.

'What about you? What's your plan?' Lora asked.

'After the market I'll go to Hartley fisheries to see Murray. Do you remember him?'

'Yes. Murray the security guard at the gate, your old rugby mate. Could he get us jobs?'

'Murray will have some connections. You know Hartley is within walking distance from the campground, so it would be handy if we got jobs there.'

'We need to work ASAP. After being declared bankrupt, we don't have any credit cards, so if the money runs out, we're doomed.'

'Yes, but you need to sort the boys schooling out first,' Steven said.

'That won't take long. I sorted all the paperwork before we left for New Zealand. It's all good to go, I think. I've got an appointment at Honimoki High School next Monday. Hopefully the boys can start on Tuesday.'

Cameron and James fished until the sun went down at 9:30 pm, while Steven dozed on a blanket outside.

When Cameron and James returned, they set up the tent under the light of the full moon then, decided to light a bonfire, along the shore.

Lora sat outside the tent watching the stars as the bonfire crackled. 'I made up our beds in the tent.' She surprised them when she turned on the Christmas light, which highlighted the painting of a spiral loop of a fern, a koru, flags of different countries, and different kinds of fish on the side of the caravan.

'Oh, wow. Cool Mom, thanks,' Cameron and James said in unison.

'The tent rules are, if you want to fart, go outside,' James said.

'I bet you're the first one to break the rules, James,' Cameron replied.

James frowned. 'You've got a pimple on your nose; that's odd.'

Cameron touched his nose. 'I don't care.' But he did.

'Okay, guys. The fire is out so I'm going to bed now as we have to be up early to sell the stuff at the market so we can have some space in the caravan, and hopefully extra cash.' Lora said

'Mom, I still have US two thousand dollars. If you're short of cash, we can use it.' Cameron said.

'And I have almost same that amount if you need it,' James added.

'Thank you, but you can keep your money. Good night. Love you,' Lora said as she kissed them both on the forehead.' Cameron rubbed his nose and felt the pimple getting bigger.

Chapter 17

Sunday, 25 January, morning.

At Beth's place, Kyna, her Chinese housemaid who was familiar with Beth's rigid routine, ensured the place was spotless before she woke up. She polished the wooden furniture till it glistened in the sun's rays coming through the window. The intense scent of cleaning products floated in the air along with the smell of burnt bacon.

Beth appeared wearing a cream coloured, A -line frock with a deep neckline.

Kyna, who was cooking breakfast while cleaning the kitchen, apologized for burning the bacon. 'Sorry, ma'am. It won't happen again.'

'Don't worry about it, Kyna. I'll cook some more, but can you please go to Brice's bathroom to clean the fingerprints and smudges off the mirrors and the shower,' Beth said in a business-like tone.

Kyna frowned. *Hadn't she already cleaned it?*

'Okay, Mrs. Lomar. I no complain. Even me clean it already'

Beth read the Sunday newspaper while having breakfast with Brice and Azoma. 'We have a win-win situation here reading this paper. You see, I put a spell of the spirit of boiling rage on Mr Hartley after he backed out of the settlement and, of course, Azoma's spell on a spirit of addiction to alcohol on Steven the last time we saw him. So read the paper,' Beth said as she got up from her chair.

Brice forked bacon into his mouth. 'Well done, Mom. You're on to it. This will keep the town talking. Mr Hartley assaulting Steven on the beach. The rich and famous Mr Hartley. The hated guy in the community.' He got up to make a cup of coffee, then sat beside Azoma.

Breathing in the aroma of the expresso brewing in the coffee make, Azoma poured herself a mug of steaming black coffee. 'Hmm, coffee. This is all I'm having, but thanks for cooking all of this,' she said, as she smoothed her hand over her silky fuchsia body-hugging dress.

'Brice, when do we see the effect of your spell on Cameron? That jerk, peeing on my cool aid. How disgusting. I can't get over it,' Azoma said.

Brice simmered with jealousy when Cameron's name was mentioned. He struggled to appear cool. 'Don't worry. It will happen soon. That's why I'm going to the flea market today, to see the Owen's. From my source, they confirm they should be there. I'll be meeting Tara as well to show her off to our halfwit uncle and cousins so they can see I've got a hot girlfriend. And to check the spell one of our members cast on Cameron. While Cameron gave his statement to the ambulance staff, he put a spell, a zit, on his nose.' After a narcissistic grin, Brice continued. 'And that zit will grow like a cancer, which will eat up his nose. He will look like one of those characters in the movies who have leprosy, and then he'll die slowly from the infection.'

Beth's satanic faith heightened. 'Let's pat ourselves in the back. Papa Satan will be pleased at Steven being drunk. That will separate him from that silly cow of a wife. Breaking the family up is one of Satan's treasured goals. So we are winning.

Brice read the newspaper silently while he ate his breakfast.

Excerpt from the Nelson Evening mail:

A 60-year- old man was charged with assault with a walking stick. Mr Owen received multiple bruises and cuts after being repeatedly beaten by the man. Name suppression was granted to the assailant due to his personal circumstances. The assailant fell and hit his head on a rock and is lucky to be alive. Nelson Hospital reported the assailant suffered from a heart attack.

'What bloody good news. We'll have more of this soon. As all the members are on a roll after replenishing their evil spirit during the gathering.'

'Okay, my darling son. We've got to go. We're going at Silvanus Cafe at the marina. It's such a lovely day,' Beth said as she stared at the sun blazing into the kitchen and the glistening sea off in the distance.

Azoma thought of her boyfriend, huffed and crossed her arms. 'Would Kirk be there?'

'Yes, he will be there. That's why I asked you. And you know what to do. How to show off to Kirk so he becomes crazy about you. I need that as I have a business proposal for his parents.

'Yes, Mother, I know. I'll makes it hard for him to refuse your proposal.'

'Will see you then, darling. Ta, ta,' Beth said, rubbing Brice's arm. Within minutes Beth and Azoma were in Beth's Rolls Royce headed to the café, while Brice was in his BMW on way to the markets.

25 January, Sunday, 7 am.

Cameron felt someone covering him with a blanket as he woke up.

'Oh, sorry, son. I didn't mean to wake you up, love. It's cold this morning. It's 10 degrees Do you want to watch the sunrise? It's gorgeous,' Lora said, putting on a black cardigan over her flowery printed short sleeve top. She unzipped the tent flap revealing a pink sky in horizontal patterns like waves with the bright golden sun peeking over the horizon.

Cameron looked at his cell phone. 'It's only 7 am. No, Mom. I want to sleep more. Leave me alone.'

'Okay, if you want to go back to sleep then you can sleep in the caravan. We'll have to pack up the tent since we won't be staying here. We'll look for a more permanent caravan site later. We need to be at the market by 8 am. How can you sleep? The birds are so noisy,' Lora said, picking up the bundle of keys hanging on a hook on the top corner of the awning.

'Ok, Mom. I love the tweeting of the birds, it puts me to sleep,' Cameron said as he stood up with a blanket over his shoulder and a pillow in his hands, making his way into the caravan.

Concern covered Lora's face. 'Oh, your nose is so red. Is it sore?'

'It was a bit itchy last night. I must have rubbed it hard,' Cameron replied. He looked at himself in the mirror hanging on a nearby wall. 'Jeez. It looks bad,' he muttered.

'Where are James and dad?' Cameron asked.

'Out there watching the sunrise.'

After packing up the umbrellas, folding chairs and blankets they all headed to the flea market.

Cameron snuggled under the blankets on the bed, trying to forget a sinking feeling and the fear of the gang.

***

The noise of buskers singing with guitars, people talking, and kids' laughter woke Cameron. 'He peeped through the caravan window noticing they were now parked at the flea market.

At 10 am the temperature was already 20 degrees. It was sunny with clear skies. On Sundays, the large public carpark was used for the Motueka flea market. There were rows of stalls selling fruit and vegetables, honey, jam, handmade soap, jewellery, and scented oils. Down further, were booths of second-hand goods, knitted dolls and teddy bears. At the end of the row was a variety of food stalls: German bread and sausages, hamburgers, and Chinese takeaway, along with crowds of teenagers wearing signature sunglasses and clothing.

Familiar with the flea markets, Steven set up a folding table full of second-hand books, clothing, winter coats, jewellery, antique dinner sets, and ornaments.

115

Lora talked to the shoppers, and in between serving customers she talked to Steven about their worries, namely the boys and especially Cameron's nose where the zit had gotten infected and turned red and become inflamed. Lora had already made an appointment to see the emergency doctor at 1 pm.

Most of the time their stall was surrounded by costumers who wore colourful summer clothes and hats. Their stall attracted a lot of interest, making the other stall owners jealous. At around 11 am, Lora was pleased that they had sold almost everything.

A few metres away, a woman in her early forties waved to Steven. As she came closer, she said, 'Hello, stranger. What has brought you back to reality? I mean back home.'

Steven perched his sunglasses on top of his head. He felt a lightness in his chest at seeing his old friend, and he grinned.

'Karen, long time no see. We're here for good. This is my wife, Lora,' Steven said.

Lora felt sweaty and unkempt as she compared herself to Karen with her shiny, long, wavy brown hair, flawless light brown skin and deep-set brown eyes with perfectly mascaraed eyelashes. Feeling out of place, Lora smoothed down her crumpled top, and offered her hand. 'Please to meet you, Karen. So how did you guys meet?'

'We both went to Honi High,' Steven said, then added, 'afterward Karen went to US after high school. I heard you married a man in the US Air Force.'

'Yeah. His name is Paul, but he left the air force six years ago. He was last stationed in Las Vegas. It's a long story,' Karen said.

Lora and Karen chatted while Steven served a customer, while eavesdropping at the same time.

'What state are you from?' Karen asked as she looked through some books.

'From Nebraska, but I lived in San Diego for twenty-five years,' Lora replied.

After knowing Karen's husband came from the US and that he was in the air force, she could relate to her and her interest deepened. But before she could ask her more questions, Lora noticed a young girl. *Gosh, she looks like teenage version of Brook Shields,* she thought.

The girl approached Karen. 'Mom, can I go to the movies later?'

'As long as you're home before nine. You need to help me at the café early tomorrow morning,' Karen replied.

'Oh, this is Tara, my daughter,' Karen said, patting Tara's curly long blond hair.

Tara wore a white Nike T-shirt that showed her abdomen, and pink denim pants.

'I heard you have two boys. Are they in high school?'

'James is eighteen and Cameron is seventeen. Which reminds me, I need to wake Cameron up, and James is somewhere around here,' Steven replied.

'Stay here, Steven. I'll wake Cameron up.' Lora turned around and stepped into the caravan.

Cameron was sitting on the bunk, wearing a dirty, crumpled brown Quicksilver hoody and black low-waisted jeans, unshaven with strangled messy hair.

After a knock on the door, Cameron got out of bed. 'What's up, Mom?' Cameron asked. Outside he could see a girl who took his breath away: she looked like a cover girl from a teenage fashion magazine

As soon as Cameron opened the door, Lora noticed Cameron's nose had become beet-red and the pimple had grown larger. She tried not to look at it to save Cameron from embarrassment.

Tara had picked up a box full of old fashion jewellery from the table, and, despite Cameron's red nose, when her grey blue eyes met Cameron's, her heart raced.

Karen's jaw dropped as she looked at Cameron's nose.

'Karen, this is Cameron,' Lora said.

Instinctively Karen rubbed her nose as if it was Cameron's nose she was rubbing. 'Pleased to meet you, Cameron,' she said, struggling not to laugh.

'Likewise,' Cameron extended his hand.

'And this is my daughter, Tara.'

'Hi, Cameron. Nice to meet you.'

'Hi, I'm Pinocchio. I mean Cameron,' he said, pointing at his nose.

Tara giggled. 'Don't say that. I don't think you want me to call you Pinocchio.' She wondered why her heart felt so light and fought not to stare at Cameron eyes. 'How much is this?' she asked, holding up an old turquoise Celtic-looking set of earrings.

Cameron struggled not to stare at Tara as he pretended to tidy up the table. He remembered that he had felt like this when he first met Hollie. Cameron tried to talk himself out of how he felt. *No, you can't have these feelings.*

'Fifty bucks,' Cameron blurted out, stroking his mangled hair.

Lora and Steven gave Cameron a 'don't be ridiculous' look as this was an inflated price for the earrings. As they continued their conversation with Karen, Lora and Steven shot each other a look as to why had they been so worried about his nose.

So, it was a joke to have a huge pimple in his nose, Cameron thought.

Still exploring the jewellery on the table, Tara picked up an orange teardrop-shaped pair of earrings from the box. 'What about these?' Tara asked, her eyes fixed on Cameron. She could feel the heat rising in her cheeks and she let out a slow breath.

'Forty dollars for those, please,' Cameron said, avoiding eye contact.

'I only have ten dollars.' Tara frowned.

Trying to hide his true feelings, he said, 'Too bad, not my problem,' as he smiled inwardly enjoying the irate look on Tara's face.

Suddenly Brice appeared and Tara showed Brice the orange tear drop earrings to Brice. 'I like these, but 40 bucks is too much for them. Without a beat Brice dug into the pocket of his black jeans and pulled out a hundred dollar note and gave it to Tara. He looked at Cameron's nose and smirked, thrilled that the spell on Cameron's nose and worked.

Tara's square jaw clenched. 'No, Brice that's too much.' She paused. 'I don't want them now.' She put the earrings back into the box and handed the note back to him.

Brice flexed his arm muscles. 'Let's go, Tara.' He gave her a passionate kiss.

Tara was caught by surprise and looked out of the corner of her eye at Cameron.

'We'll be late for the movie,' Brice said, tugging her shoulder bag.

'See you, Mom.' Tara's face flushed in embarrassment.

Karen frowned in disgust. 'Gosh,' she said, then paused. 'What's wrong with that prick?' He's Steven's nephew, am I correct? How come he didn't even say hi to you guys? How strange? How could someone with an attitude like that think he is cool and have so many friends? No wonder Tara broke up with him two months ago.'

'What happened, if you don't mind me asking?' Lora asked, as she started to pack up the table.

Cameron and Steven helped as they eavesdropped on Karen and Lora's conversation.

'He slept with another girl,' Karen said, her chin dipping down as she paused. 'Tara took him back since all her friends are Brice's friends. Now, she's lost her friends because of him. You know how teenagers are. That's too much info, anyway. Nice to meet you again. Here is my phone number. Text me if you need to know anything for the boys when they start school,' Karen said with her slight American accent.

'Thank you very much for the offer. I'm looking for a job, any kind,' Lora said.

'There's not much around but you could do caregiving or waitressing? I'll be in touch. I've got to run. I need to pick up my son, Liam, from his violin lessons. Hey, Steven have you caught up with Terry?'

'Yes, we stayed the night. What about us all getting together one day?'

'What a good idea. It's been a long time since we got together. It was in Florida? Right? You can meet Paul and Liam soon I hope,' Karen said, as she waved goodbye.

Chapter 18

'Cameron, I've rung the doctor about your nose,' Lora said as she started to pack up the goods that were left, which included a baseball bat, a heavy iron frying pan, portable safe, vacuum cleaner, sewing machine, tennis ball machine and some ornaments.

'What about James? He could help. Where is he hiding?' Cameron asked. Across from their stall was a food cart selling baked potatoes.

Cameron couldn't resist the smell. 'Mom, Can I just get a baked potato before we go? I'm starving.'

'Okay. Hurry up. We've got to see the doctor in twenty minutes.'

Cameron walked up to the cart.

'What would you like? Kumara or potato baked with cream cheese or sour cream?' said the seller with an unbuttoned shirt and sagging belly.

'I'll have the kumara with cream cheese please. I'll have a ginger beer as well.'

'Don't worry. Take your time to eat. The GP surgery is just a five-minute walk from here,' the seller said, putting the vegetable salad and toppings on top of the kumara.

Amused at the nosey seller's eavesdropping, Cameron's eyebrows furrowed as he grabbed the food and drink.

'Thank you very much. Mmm. This looks delicious,' Cameron said, dipping his plastic fork into the kumara.

'Cameron, you can eat that on the way, it's time to go,' Lora said, taking the money pouch and giving it to Steven.

After visiting the doctor, Cameron was prescribed antibiotics and was advised to come back if the antibiotics had no effect.

When Cameron and Lora had finished at the doctor's, they went back to help pack what was left into the caravan, then headed to Humble Kiwi Holiday Park, located behind Hartley's food manufacturing.

The campground was only a few steps from the beach and nestled in between huge pine trees. It was a popular holiday park because it overlooked the ocean and had a playground plus a swimming pool. There was a public fishing area, which was also popular with the locals. Clouds covered the sun as they parked their caravan.

After paying the space rental fee, they sat outside watching the sunset.

'I have an announcement to make' Steven said.

***

As soon as Tara and Brice left the flea market, they went to The Warehouse, had lunch at McDonald's, then headed to the theatre to catch the 3 pm movie.

The people who were coming out of the last showing put their sunglasses on to shield their eyes from the sun that glared into the theatre's foyer. On the walls were posters showing the next movie releases. At the concession counter the staff were busy selling popcorn, ice cream, candy and soda. Throughout the lobby the smell of popcorn lingered in the air.

Brice watched a group of young men in line turn their heads to admire Tara's beauty and her flawless luminous complexion. He held her hand tightly and glared at the men.

Tara was aware that Brice was proud to be with her, even if it was in an arrogant way. What annoyed her the most though was that he hadn't even held her hand while they were watching *Mamma Mia* now, suddenly he was all over her trying to show her off.

'Why did you even bother coming to the movie when you slept the whole time?' Tara asked, trying to let go of Brice's hand.

Brice let her hand slip from his. 'Stop moaning I bought your ice cream, popcorn, drinks, and paid for your ticket. What more do you want? Stop your moaning,' Brice said as he handed the car key to her. 'I'm going to the loo so get in the car and wait for me.'

The way Brice talked to Tara today was normal. Usually Tara let it go, but not today. Brice's comments made her feel sick. Bored to tears, Tara waited for Brice imagining that he was admiring himself in the mirror in the loo. But her thoughts soon turned to Cameron, and she couldn't stop herself from comparing Brice to Cameron. It was not long ago that Brice had cancelled one of their dates because she had a little pimple on her chin. While Cameron looked rough today with his large pimple, it did not seem to bother him. He appeared not to be conceited in any way. Despite the pimple, Tara thought Cameron was handsome with his humble and caring eyes compared to Brice's eyes that showed... nothing.

In the car, Brice said, 'It's only five pm. We're going to Kirk's. He's having a party.' Rearranging the rear vision mirror to admire himself.

'Why didn't you tell me that before. I want to go home now,' Tara said, frowning.

'You're coming, otherwise you'll have to walk home, sweetheart,' Brice said.

'Seriously? She sighed. 'Okay.' Tara agreed grudgingly as the movie theatre was a long walk from her home, and her ankle still throbbed after she had injured it during soccer practice. Driving along the line of pine trees on the windy road, Tara couldn't wait to get home and ask her mom about the Owens. Since Brice was Cameron's cousin, she tried to dig for information.

Tara crossed her arms. 'You didn't tell me you've got cousins in US. And, why didn't you say hello to your uncle and cousin?'

'They're not worth mentioning. Their dad is a paedophile and their mom is a con artist,' he said, drumming his fingers on the steering wheel.

'How do you know?'

'Mother told me. They're here because the US Navy kicked Steven out because he molested young girls. Lora is a world class scammer. She slept with her CEO to get away with millions of dollars and she stole from the company to feed her gambling habit.'

'What about your cousins?'

'James stutters and Cameron is a fruitcake. And they are both high school dropouts.'

'Cameron is nuts you mean to say.'

'Yip. He's got an imaginary friend, King David, which got worse after their holiday to Italy. Steven sent him to a psychiatrist when he was about seven as he was obsessed with King David and a slingshot.'

'But they are still your blood relatives. You shouldn't bad mouth them like that,' Tara said in a weary voice. Although she had bit of a New Zealand accent, which she picked up after coming to New Zealand when she was ten-years-old, she hadn't lost her New York accent.

Brice fixed his eyes on the road. 'They are no bloody relations of mine. My grandparents adopted my mother from Romania when she was sev-en- years-old. So, I'm not really blood-related to those losers,' Brice said raising his voice.

'It sounds as if you hate them,' Tara said as she cocked her head to the side.

'Yes, I do, absolutely.' He paused. 'When we were young, our grandparents loved Cameron and James more than us. It was so obvious. They took them to Disneyland and Europe for a holiday while Azoma and I went nowhere with them. As far as my grandparents were concerned, when Cameron and James were here on holiday, me and Azoma didn't exist.'

'Oh, sorry to hear that,' Tara said, crossing her legs. The more Brice told her things about the Owens, the more she was keen to get to know Cameron. Tara thought it was only normal for their grandparents to make a big fuss over Cameron and James as they didn't get to see them much.

As they continued to cruise, Tara realized she had forgotten to ring her mom. She reached for her phone, but the battery was dead.

***

The car skidded to a holt. They had reached a cul-de-sac that led to the front of a multimillion-dollar house. Parked along the driveway were the latest ritzy sports cars.

Even though it was only 5:30 pm, the party was already in full swing. Brice knocked on the door.

With a boyish grin Kirk opened it. He wore a Nirvana black smiley T-shirt which accentuated his chest muscles.

'Come in,' Kirk said, as Tara looked up at six-foot-two Kirk. 'Who won the football game last Saturday? What was the score?' He asked as he shut the door behind them.

'We smashed the Mighty Panthers 54 -20,' Brice said. giving Kirk a knuckle to knuckle bump.

Tara covered her ears against the ear-splitting music. The air was full of cannabis smoke. She couldn't help but feel a high coming on after only a few breaths.

125

To make Tara jealous, Shantell moved towards them, her big russet-brown eyes were stuck on Brice the minute he entered the room. 'Hi, guys. It's so nice to see you. You know what? We all can stay the night as Kirk's mom and dad won't be home until Tuesday,' she said, throwing a teasing smile at Brice.

Two teenaged girls and Azoma, all in low-plunging necklines and skimpy denim short-shorts, sat at the bar. The girls kept checking their phones as they drank wine.

Shantell wondered why Tara wasn't responding to her attempts to make her jealous.

Tara sat beside Brice and turned away from him as Shantell strolled behind the bar. She reached into one of the cubic holes that held the alcohol and wine bottles and took out a bottle. The counter was littered with bowls of nuts and chips.

'Hi Tara. What have you two lovebirds been up too lately?' she asked, passing a cannabis pipe to the girl next to them who barely looked sixteen.

Already starting to feel high from inhaling the weed smoke, Tara still remembered to charge her cell phone when she spotted a power point nearby. 'Not much. No romantic getaways, that's for sure,' Tara said, plugging in her phone.

'Oh, how tragic. My heart bleeds,' Shantell responded, twirling her straight, long auburn hair around a finger.

'How was the movie, big bro?' Azoma asked, breathing in cannabis smoke from the pipe.

'It was so fantastic, I fall asleep,' Brice said, laughing loudly.

Shantell and the girls laughed with him.

'I enjoyed it. I loved the songs,' Tara said, her frustration showing.

Under the influence of alcohol and cannabis, Shantell couldn't help but flirt with Brice again, this time not to make Tara jealous but for her own lustful desire. She leaned forward to show off her cleavage. 'So, what do you want to drink cowboy?' she slurred. Ensuring that Tara wasn't looking, she gave Brice a wink.

'I'll have a Jack Daniels and coke, please. Make it two. Would you like to join me?' Brice asked her.

Seated on the red leather couch in the middle of the lounge, were two athletic-looking young men who were rugby players on Brice's team. They swayed in time to the music as they drank beer and passed the bong to each other. Azoma joined Kirk on the couch and snuggled up to him.

The girls at the bar talked about the latest party gossip and rumours about who had got with who.

Tara refused to drink and ignored the cannabis.

Brice gestured her to go to Kirk's room so they could have sex.

'I don't think so,' Tara said, shaking her head.

Brice bellowed, 'What's wrong with you? What the hell is going on?' He had put a spell of lust on Tara but it obviously hadn't worked.

By this time the boys and the girls were petting heavily, including Kirk and Azoma. She stared deeply into Kirk's eyes setting a spell of lust. Azoma and Kirk left and went upstairs.

Giggling and canoodling the boys and girls followed, falling into the bedrooms.

Shantell was on the counter dancing, stoned, with not a care in the world.

Tara felt miserable. *I should've walked home.* She picked up her phone to ring her mom.

Since the spell hadn't worked, Brice tried to pressure Tara. He stood up and planted his hands on his hip. 'As usual Tara, we'll go to Kirk's room, have sex, eat, then go home.' He wondered why the spell hadn't worked. He realized that if someone was praying for Tara, then his spell wouldn't have set in. *Well, I could find another vulnerable host as Satan's protocol,* Brice thought. He glared at Tara and said, 'Go away, Tara.'

Tara stormed out the door.

As soon as Tara left, Shantell jumped on Brice and they stumbled upstairs to Kirk's room where they had sex like lusty teenagers.

It was 8:30 pm. On the shiny granite stairs Tara sat reading her text messages. The golden sun was sinking against the pink sky. As the sun went down, tears flowed over Tara's cheeks, and she felt angry and sorry for herself.

Within fifteen minutes, Karen arrived in a white Ford truck. When she saw Tara with red eyes that she tried to hide, her heartbeat fast with apprehension. She raced to Tara, smelling the weed. 'What's wrong, babe?'

Overcome with self-pity Tara couldn't utter a word. Karen opened her arms and gave her a hug. Hugging her mom back, Tara cried like a little puppy.

In the truck, before turning the ignition on, Karen said. 'I love you and I'm concerned about you. Is there something that we need to talk about? A bath and a good dinner will do you a world of good, I think.'

'The whole room was covered in cannabis smoke that's why you can smell it on me. So please don't lecture me about drugs. I didn't smoke any.'

A guilty look came over Karen's face. 'Tara, I'm guilty for selling and using dope but I've learned my lesson. Tell me I'm a hypocrite but keep in mind dope is not good if you want to be in control of your life.' By now they were driving down the road. 'I love you and Liam. You know that, and I hate to see you get used.'

'I'm sorry. You're right about Brice. Love you too, Mom,' Tara said, blocking and deleting Brice's number from her phone.

'There, Mom. I've just blocked Brice from being able to contact me.'

Karen smiled through tears. 'It's for your own good. It's good to find out now, not later down the track.' She paused. 'You have a great future ahead of you'.

'Yes, I know,' Tara said, slumping in her seat.

'I've made your favourite – bacon, and macaroni with cheese. And there's cold iced tea with lemon in the fridge,' she said, stroking Tara on the back of her head. Her cell phone buzzed. 'Can you answer that for me, please? It must be your dad.'

Tara searched through her mom's bag for her cell phone, then read the text aloud. 'It's from Lora: We are at HKW holiday park.'

After reading the text, Tara's eyes popped open as she tried to hide her excitement.

'I'll visit her one day but not now as we're so busy with opening the café.'

A week had passed as Tara wondered why she hadn't seen Cameron at school.

Chapter 19

At the San Diego Red Serpent Headquarters, there was a debriefing about Tanner Sheldon, the guy who had been deported from New Zealand with a fake passport, then shot dead after leaving the airport.

Before Anton could talk about the next mission, there was a knock on the door. As he opened the door, the cigarette smoke escaped but the odour remained.

A guy in his late thirties, six-foot with a medium athletic build, entered the room.

Logan introduced him. 'This is Duane Dennet from Orlando. He will replace Tanner,' Anton said.

Everybody welcomed him with a hug and a knuckle bump. The gang didn't ask questions since they already knew what Duane's mission was: To eliminate Cameron Owen. The gang was aware Duane was given fifty thousand dollars in advance and would earn another fifty thousand on completion. After discussing the gang's problems and their accomplishments, Anton handed a manila envelope of cash to each of the members.

When Anton discovered Cameron had bugged the headquarters, he had double-checked every inch of the room to make sure that there were no other monitors, apart from his. Anton felt he had been ripped-off and hated Cameron even more after outwitting him. He felt smart that he had photocopied the notebook before it was stolen, but If the drug cartel found out that the original notebook was with somebody else, Anton knew he would be tortured to death. After assassinating Tanner, the only people who knew about the notebook were Mitch and Cameron. Anton had already planned Mitch's execution as soon as he got hold of the notebook. Anton felt no guilt for killing Tanner as he knew he was falsely acquitted for the charge of rape and murder.

Anton was delighted with himself that he had shot from a seventeen-floor building to murder Tanner Sheldon. And it satisfied him after hearing the news that there had been no witnesses after a thorough police investigation of the shooting. *Well, it looks like I got away with it,* he thought.

At Anton's apartment to find out more about Duane, he logged on to his computer and did a background check. He concluded that what made him trust Duane was when he put his life in danger to save the president of the Orlando Charter. He had made a secret phone call to Duane. 'You know who I am. Can we meet?

Reluctantly, Duane had agreed.

At the small bar on the outskirts of the city, they sat at a dark corner table.

Logan explained how the notebook had ended up in Cameron's hand. 'I'll give you ten thousand dollars for the return of the notebook and to keep this quiet,' Anton said.

Duane paused and figured out that Anton had killed Tanner and now that he knew about the notebook, he would be next. There was no way out of it. His chest tightened and he wanted to leave the bar quickly. 'I can't wack Cameron or any of his family until I got hold of the notebook. This needs a lot of planning. It will take time.'

'Do what you've got to do, then I'll take care of the rest,' Anton said as he looked around, then offered him the paper bag with the money in it.

Duane peeked into the bag. 'Okay, it's a done deal.'

Chapter 20

Before leaving the flea market, Steven and Lora counted the money.

Back at the campground, after Steven hooked the caravan to the power point, he gathered his family around the picnic table. 'So, guys, this is what I have to announce. First, we made one thousand five hundred dollars today. Second, I've had a phone call from my lawyer. They have concrete proof that Beth falsified the will.'

'It's no surprise the silly cow would do that,' James said, trying to help Cameron to set up the awning to the caravan.

'I don't get it, Dad. Why can't you see that Beth has been using you for as long as I can remember? The whole family is just out there for themselves. The only time she rings you is when she needs something,' Cameron said

After having a good day, Lora was determined that no one would steal her joy so she changed the subject. 'We'll give you one hundred dollars each for your help today.'

'No, Mom. Keep it for groceries or for whatever. I've still got some,' James said.

'Yes, we're okay with cash. We can keep it the portable safe,' Cameron said, getting his folding bed ready.

'Me too, Mom. I still have two thousand US dollars,' James said, handing the cash to Lora.

'Same here. I've still got over two thousand dollars plus, and you can use it if you need to,' Cameron added.

'Sorry, guys. I'm broke, but I'm hoping we'll be set for life once I get my inheritance,' Steven said.

After Steven helped his sons set up the caravan, he helped Lora with dinner. They made a salad, and Steven peeled the potatoes and cooked them on the stove. The cooked roast chicken he had bought was in the warmer tray of the oven. When all the preparation was done, they sat at the folding table to eat dinner while they watched the sun set.

'I like it here, better than that huge house,' Cameron said.

Lora gazed at Cameron admiring his cute smile. It was the first time she had seen him smile since they'd left San Diego. 'Me too. We have a million-dollar view here. Look at the sunset and the sky with my favourite colour orange. It's so gorgeous.' She sliced the roast chicken, and its aroma made her mouth water.

After dinner they went to bed. Lora and Steven slept in the caravan and the boys under the awning.

When James got up in the middle of the night to go to the bathroom, he noticed Cameron wasn't in his bed.

'Mom, Dad. Where's Cameron?' James screamed.

Chapter 21

25 February, 7.30 am

It had been three weeks since the Owens had arrived in New Zealand and they were slowly adjusting to their caravan lifestyle.

James had got used to the idea that if Cameron wasn't in his bed that he could've gone to the bathroom. It had alarmed the family, aware of the dangers, when Cameron was little and had started to sleepwalk. Now, it brought back bad memories for James.

They went looking for him and found Cameron in the toilets.

James had started school 2 weeks ahead of Cameron. Lora reminded the Cameron he would start school tomorrow since the doctor gave him clearance to go to school since his nose hadn't healed.

In the morning, the sun peeked through the gap of the awning, shining in Cameron's eyes. He turned over and covered his eyes with the blanket. The sound of the birds mesmerized him and he started to drift back to sleep. Then he smelled the sweetness of pancakes cooking.

'Cameron. Wake up, love. It's school today. Remember, the doctor said you can go to school now,' Lora yelled.

'Mom, look at my nose. It's still swollen,' Cameron said, looking at his face in the mirror that he kept under his bed. 'But if you want me to go I will.

'You don't have to,' Lora replied with a worried glare in her eyes. The swelling on Cameron's nose hadn't improved.

Stepping out of the caravan, and swallowing a mouthful of pancake, Steven said, 'It's still so big. Maybe you need to see the quack again.'

'The doctor took a swab,' James replied, rubbing his eyes and sitting up in bed.

'Okay, guys, see you later. I won't be home until 11:30 tonight,' Steven said, holding his lunch box. 'Love ya,' he added, kissing the boys on the forehead, then Lora.

'Love you too, Dad,' His sons said in unison.

'Have a nice day at work.' Lora said.

'Yip. Off to do my boring, monotonous, stinking job,' Steven muttered as he left the caravan.

'If you're going to school Cameron, you'd better hurry. The showers will be busy soon.' James shirked, with the towel and his uniform in hand, he headed to the communal shower.

After a quick shower James was ready and returned to the caravan. 'I wouldn't go to school with a nose like that,' he told Cameron, anxiously. Bitterly James thought of the bullying he encountered on his first day, but he had never told his family, he'd just got used to it. He sat at the table and ate his pancakes.

'I don't feel like going to school, Mom. I'll have pancakes though,' Cameron said, as he buried himself further under the blanket. His nose really hurt but he ignored the pain. He didn't want anyone to make a fuss. He did want to go to school. There, maybe he would see Tara again. He couldn't get her out of his mind and, she had seen his nose. He jumped out of bed. 'I've changed my mind. I'm going to school. Who cares about my nose?'

'You'll need to hurry,' Lora said, throwing him a towel.

Cameron returned to the caravan after his shower. 'Mom, this is so tight for me,' he said, trying to button his grey knee-length pants.

'They will have to do for now. I've ordered a bigger size for you, but they won't be here till next week. I've put your brown hoody and phone in your backpack, along with the gold pen you didn't want sold at the flea market, along with the notebooks,' Lora said.

With the big zit on his nose and tight uniform, he was suddenly indecisive again about going to school. He shrugged. 'These pants are so tight. I hope I don't fart, or else I'll rip them,' he said, then laughing.

***

At 8:30 am, they drove along the estuary heading to Hinamoki High School. The waves were coming in and stirring up the mud flats. Not being used to a left-hand drive, Lora looked ahead concentrating and driving cautiously.

James, who was sitting in front seat, turned around to Cameron. 'Tara has been asking about you. I didn't tell her you'd be at school today. I thought you wouldn't go by the look of your nose.' He took off his baseball cap with the Hinamoki logo on it and ran a comb through his hair.

'Karen, Tara's mom, bought that place. They call it The Possum Hall. She's looking for a waiter, so I gave her your name. It might be good pocket money,' Lora told him.

'Cool, Mom, I'll be into that,' Cameron replied.

Lora pulled into the carpark in front and parked in a visitor spot.

'See you later, Mom,' James said, hopping out of the car.

'You don't have to come with me, Mom. You told me the room number. I'll be okay,' Cameron said.

'Well, we have to see the principal. He asked me to see him before you go to class.'

'Why?'

'We'll find out. I think he just wants to welcome you, like James, and explain the rules.'

Cameron and Lora headed to the principal's office. Making a mental comparison to the school he had attended in San Diego, Cameron looked down the hallway. The lockers had no dents, were newly painted and the floor was shiny and clean with no chewing gum on it, unlike in San Diego. Cameron breathed in the fumes of newly painted walls, which irritated his nose. The giggling and shouting of the students brought back memories. Cameron shut his eyes tight and shook his head to get rid of the depressing thought. As the bell rang, students looked at Cameron as they rushed to their classrooms.

Noticing Cameron looking at the school's sports trophy case, Lora said, 'You can look at those later.'

'Oh, sorry. I was just interested in the rugby and netball trophies. It's interesting to know which teams are popular. 'I noticed Brice got the best in math award,' Cameron said as they passed a display board.

'I find that hard to believe when he still couldn't count on his fingers at ten. That's very strange,' Lora said, frowning.

Cameron continued. 'And Azoma won an art award with her painting called The Withered Tree. Can you remember, Mom, when I got a spanking from Dad? Because I said Azoma's painting looked like whirled up dog's poo when she tried to paint a picture of a snake. I was just being honest. How could that painting win an award when it looks like pubes scattered all over the place?'

'Don't be rude. I don't want to talk about them. I'm having a nice day.' Lora planted her hand on her hip.

'Sorry.'

'We're here,' Lora said as she knocked on the principal's door.

Mr George Bentley, the principal, opened the door. 'Hi, Mrs Owen. I won't be long, please take a seat,' Mr Bentley said, loosening his striped red and black tie.

'Thank you, Mr Bentley,' Lora said as she sat in a chair in the hallway.

'I hope you've noticed the difference, all clean and tidy, huh, but it won't be like that by the end of the year. I spoke to a cleaner and apparently they will do a major repair and a major facelift to the building during school vacation,' Mr Bentley told her.

'Why were you talking to the cleaner?' Cameron asked, after the principal went into his office.

'I'm looking for a job.'

'As a cleaner? Why? Don't you like your caregiving job?' Cameron asked, his eyebrows furrowing.

'I'm not interested anymore, after what one of the cleaners told me. They gave her a written warning when she left a bucket full of filthy water with red paint in the art room. And yes, I like my care giving job.'

'Jeez, they are tough here, huh, just for leaving a bucket,' Cameron said, clasping his hands behind his head.

'Apparently, a girl used it to throw the dirty water on a girl she was bullying. The bullied girl went home with her clothes saturated with red paint. The school board blamed the cleaner. They said if she hadn't left the bucket outside, this girl would not have thought of using it.

'How pathetic,' Cameron said, looking down.

Mr Bentley emerged from his office. 'Come in. Please take a seat.' He waved his hand towards the black velvet-covered chairs. His sky-blue eyes stared at Cameron's nose in sympathy. 'I've got a photocopy of your passport and prior grades so your enrolment is good to go.' He swivelled in his office chair and out of an overflowing filing tray, he pulled out a brochure. 'In this pamphlet is a map of the school, plus the rules and regulations. You probably have the same from your previous school.'

Across the table, Cameron stared at Mr Bentley's computer. He saw the agenda for the Board meeting, which was about bullying. It reminded him of the last time he was in the principal's office in San Diego. After a fight with Luke, the principal had suspended him. Cameron couldn't forget the terror on Lora's face after she had seen Cameron's bloodied nose. Cameron had knocked Luke unconscious, and he'd ended up in hospital. Cameron had retaliated as Luke had been bad-mouthing Lora in front of the other students. 'Your mom is a swindler. She robbed a lot of people out of their investments, including my grandpa's retirement fund. She's such a tart and got away with it because she'd been screwing the CEO.'

Cameron had punched Luke who had dropped to the ground, but Luke had gotten up and thumped Cameron on the nose. Cameron counter-attacked hitting Luke on the forehead, which knocked him unconscious. Luke was fine after hospitalization, but that incident had scared Cameron and he had to transfer from that school. Since then, Cameron had been in trouble at two more schools he had attended. He then dropped out of high school and left home. Cameron fidgeted and bit the inside of his lip.

Mr. Bentley noticed Cameron's agitation. 'I can see why you didn't let Cameron go to school last week. As much as I want you to start school as soon as possible, with your nose like that, the students will have a field day teasing you. To be honest, Mrs Owen, the bullying concerns me. That's why we'll have a meeting with the board about bullying.' Mr. Bentley leaned forward. 'But it's up to Cameron, whether or not he wants to attend class today.'

Cameron's leg jiggled. 'I'll be all right. If they're just going to tease me because of the zit on my nose, then what the hell. I can handle that,' Cameron said.

'Well that's good. I know honesty is the best policy, but if they found out you're one year behind and older...' Mr Bentley paused.

'I know, Mr Bentley. Say no more. I won't be telling anyone how old I am.'

'You're welcome. My pleasure, Cameron.'

Mr. Bentley thought his reverse psychology worked as it normally did. 'Okay then. Please let me lead the way,' he said, as they walked down the corridor to Room 32.

'Tara's brother is in your class as well. I met him the other day. At least there will be two people who you know already,' Mr Bentley reassured Lora.

'It's world history today, and your teacher is Mrs. Rundle,' Mr Bentley said, striding along.

***

Inside Room 32, Mr. Bentley introduced Cameron. 'Mrs. Rundle, this is Cameron Owen from San Diego, California.' With a quick phoney smile, still unsure as to how Cameron's first day would turn out, he shrugged then strode back to his office.

After a year away from school and today being Cameron's first day, made Lora nervous. *Please God. Protect Cameron today*. 'Have a nice day. I'll pick you up after three. Love you.' She said, then waved goodbye.

A trace of fear crossed over Cameron's face, but he managed to hide it with a false grin. 'Okay, mom. I love you too. See ya. I'll be fine, don't worry.'

As Cameron looked for a seat, Brice's eyes zoomed to Cameron's. The giggling and talking stopped at once when Mrs Rundle raised her eyebrow. 'This is Cameron Owen, and it's his first day. Please take a seat, Cameron,' Mrs Rundle said, waving her hand to an empty chair. 'Cameron comes from San Diego, California. I hope you'll give him a genuine Honimoki welcome.' Mrs Rundle pushed up her large oval spectacles. She wore a checked skirt with a mustard-coloured bow on her blouse. Being a good teacher and nice person, she was well liked, especially by the Christian parents and students. A few giggles came from the rear as students noticed Cameron's nose and his tight shorts, but they were quickly silenced by Mrs Rundle's stern eyes.

Cameron sat down. Right behind him were Azoma and Shantell, who were trying to look innocent, in their perfectly ironed uniforms with their hair tied back in banana hair clips. Shantell gave Cameron a once over and cast a spell of illusion. In the third row were Brice and Jerry Hunter and across the aisle Tara, Liam and Kirk Preston

140

Cameron blinked when he saw "Hell" in bold letters written on the whiteboard. He blinked again, and the word disappeared. His heart pounded. *Is this a joke, or is it time for me to visit a shrink?* Cameron thought. He scanned the room. Along the wall was artwork, which included Azoma's painting of a dragon and a goat with a huge horn, that stood out from the rest. The goat and the dragon flew out of the painting, breathed fire from their nostrils and tried to burn him. With these graphic visions, he fought hard to stay composed but broke out in a sweat.

Ensuring no one was looking, Shantell scurried around. She took a cardboard knife from her backpack. As Cameron would still be under the spell, she cut Cameron's pants. Unaware, Cameron shook his head in fear of the visions. He shut his eyes and the visions disappeared.

Mrs Rundle wrote something on the whiteboard, then turned around. 'Today's topic is the Philippines. This was your assignment. Can anyone tell me what they know about this country?'

No one answered.

Cameron raised his hand. 'Ferdinand Magellan discovered the Philippines. In 1951 and 1991, the Pinatubo volcano erupted and soon after they closed Clark US Airforce Base,' Cameron said.

Jerry, who was half New Zealander and half Filipino said, 'How do you know stuff like that? Cool.' He pushed his dark brown wavy hair from his face, but it fell right back over his tawny brown eyes.

'What about you Jerry? What can you add?' Mrs Rundle asked.

'Apparently it is one of the most corrupt countries in the world,' Jerry replied, stroking his arm.

'Oh, I think you could say more since your mom is from the Philippines,' Mrs Rundle said, shaking her head. She then turned her back to write on the whiteboard again.

Unseen, Azoma rummaged through Cameron's backpack stealing his wallet, pen, and phone.' She threw the phone on the floor in front of Cameron.

Cameron leaned down and picked it, up exposing his bare buttocks.

The students roared with laughter. 'Oh my God. He's got no undies on,' whispered one of the students.

Oblivious Cameron sat back on his chair and wondered why everybody was laughing.

Mrs. Rundle asked, 'What's so funny? What is everyone laughing about?'

No one answered and she turned around again to scribble on the whiteboard.

Azoma threw Cameron's golden pen. Cameron, noticing it, grabbed for it and exposed his bare buttocks again.

Another roar of laughter erupted, louder this time.

'Now, now, that will do. What on earth is going on?' Mrs Rundle bellowed, her eyes widening.

Jerry exploded out of his seat and rushed to Shantell. 'Don't you dare,' Jerry whispered, holding on to Shantell's elbow. He grabbed Cameron's wallet from her hand.

'Is this your wallet, mate? Don't get up; your pants are ripped,' Jerry whispered as he handed him his wallet, then returned to his desk.

Ashley was sitting beside Cameron. 'Hi, I'm Ashley Wiritana. Your pants are ripped, that's why they're laughing at you. Jerry stopped Shantell straight away once he saw she was about to throw your wallet. What a cow I see you have a jersey in your backpack. Do you want to wrap it around your hips?' Ashley said, reaching down to grab his backpack.

Ashamed and speechless, Cameron's face flushed.

Tara approached Mrs Rundle. Whispering, she explained what the laughter was about. Mrs Rundle's mouth dropped open.

'Can I take Cameron to the gym so he can find something to wear in the lost and found bin?' Tara asked.

Mrs Rundle released an angry breath. 'Please do.'

Chapter 22

Cameron left with Tara, embarrassed. With a braided hair style with some ringlets hanging on her shoulder, Tara looked stunning.

Currently there were no students in the gym. All Cameron wanted was to get something that fit and be done with it. He rushed to the clothing bin on the right side of the stage along the seating. Although the clothes stank of sweat, he dug around.

Thrilled to be with Cameron, Tara stood watching him as he searched. 'Why aren't you wearing any underwear?' she asked. At once Tara realized her question was too forward.

Embarrassed and battling to hide his feelings, Cameron considered that Tara's question was rude. He thought quickly of an impolite answer. He cleared his throat then stopped raking through the garments. 'Do I have to tell you?'

Irate with herself that she asked such a ridiculous question she replied, 'Oh sorry. That was a silly question.'

'Look at me. Do I look like I care? Cameron asked, pointing a finger at his face. 'Thanks for taking me here. I'll find my way around.'

She pressed her lips tightly before she replied slowly, 'Oh, okay.' She strode away feeling disappointed that her first time alone with him didn't turn out how she wanted it to be. Her step echoed eerily around the gym.

Since no one was around, Cameron changed into knee-length Nike loose shorts, then sat on the seats clawing his fingers through his hair. At this moment Cameron did not want to go back. Again, the word Hell kept going on and on through his mind like a blinking cursor on the computer screen that wouldn't go away, which drove him crazy. His eyes filled with tears. He pulled his shirt over his face to wipe his face. Staring across the seats and at the basketball hoops, he had a memory flash. It reminded Cameron of Hollie and Mitch cheering him on in one of the basketball games in the church basketball league. His embarrassment turned into an overpowering feeling of longing for Hollie and Mitch, and homesickness, which is where he wanted his heart to be. The word Hell continued to flash at him and the spell spirit of suicide was worming its way into his head. Cameron thought of killing himself to have a rest of from the flashing word.

Tara peered through the gap in the door. When she saw Cameron sobbing, her heart sank. But she thought that Cameron would be ashamed if she saw him crying. She walked slowly back to class.

Cameron also returned to class. Ashley remained sitting in front where Cameron had been sitting. The word Hell stopped flashing much to Cameron's relief, but nothing registered in his brain as Mrs Rundle carried on with the lessons.

'Okay, class, your assignment is on World War II and it will be on Chapter 23 of your history book. And prepare for the test tomorrow about the Philippines,' Mrs Rundle said. Then she pointed her finger to Azoma, and Shantell. 'I'd like to see you two in the principal's office after your morning tea.' Then the bell rang.

***

At morning tea, as soon as Cameron left the classroom, he looked for James in the canteen. Along the queues were students chatting and sniggering as they waited to be served. Sickened with the morning's events, the scrumptious aroma of the mince pies, and fish and chips didn't stir Cameron's taste buds.

Ashley spotted Cameron. 'Come and join me for morning tea, here, aye. We can sit outside on the benches in the sun, but on your baseball cap. I've got sunblock here. It's pretty hot out there,' she said as she stepped into the queue.

Suddenly Kirk jumped in front of Ashley in the line when it was her turn to be served.

Ashley's hazel eyes flick upward. ' Scumbag, whatever ?'

Kirk snarled a grin. 'And what are you going to do about it? Besides you're too tall to be in the front line, Miss Giraffe,' Kirk replied as he dug for some money in his trouser pocket.

Infuriated, Ashley stepped out of the queue. 'I hope you choke to death, dickhead.'

Kirk ignored Ashley's remark. He paid for his food, then left with a smirk on his face.

A student with purple hair blurted, 'Oh, Ashley, are you going to have lunch with Pinocchio later, huh?'

The other students giggled.

One of the boys with the blue-stud earrings who was in the same class as Cameron said, 'Yeah, Pinocchio, the mooner.'

Screw you, Cameron thought, and flashed a sardonic grin. 'Did you get a thrill looking at my ass? You, homo.'

The students rolled their eyes. The girl with the purple hair, gave him the finger and shot him a look as if to say, take that.

Ashely glared at the girl with hatred. 'Let's go, Cameron. I'll get some food at lunchtime,' she said, as she flung her backpack over her shoulder.

The school grounds at the back of the common room had a huge lawn with a concrete path surrounding it and a canopy. There were picnic tables and chairs in each corner and seats on the ground. It was the designated area for morning teas and lunches. During the period breaks or their morning teas, the students were divided into groups. The groups were mainly Asians students with one or two white students in the right corner. Jerry and Tara were in this group. In the corner adjacent to them were Kirk, Azoma, Brice, Shantell, students who were on the rugby team, and young pretty girls who liked to hang out with the rugby players. Along the seats there were students in pairs, and in other groups were a mix of Europeans, Indians, and Maoris.

After texting James, Cameron and James met at a picnic table with Ashley.

'Hi, I'm Ashley Wiritana. You're Cameron's brother I gather?' she said as she gathered her long thick dark brown hair onto one side of her shoulder.

'James, I'm older.'

'Yeah, by only fourteen months,' Cameron said.

'How's your first day going, bud?' James asked.

Cameron winked at Ashley, indicating don't say anything about this morning.

'It was alright. Do you want some of my sandwiches? Mom, always packs lots of peanut butter and jam sandwiches?'

Ashley took a mouthful of the sandwich and tried to be polite. 'Umm. Thanks. Yum, taste like peanut butter and jam. You know what? Tara was only in Jerry's crowd today to make Brice jealous, by flirting with Jerry, but what I hate about that is Jerry seems to like it when Tara flirts with him.' She rummaged through her backpack to find some sunblock.

'Tara. She's hot, huh. If she flirts with me, I'll enjoy that too,' James said.

'But she won't be the prettiest. There's a girl who's just as pretty as Tara, aye. She's in your class, James,' Ashley said. She smoothed sunscreen over her flawless complexion.

'Yes, Melissa Jennon is from Auckland. I've met her. She's out of my league as you can see. She's in with Azoma's troop. They call them "The beauties of Honi High," TBH for short,' James said, taking a bite of his sandwich.

'I think Tara's got the hots for you, Cameron,' Ashley said, stroking her long dark thick brown hair.

Cameron licked his scarred lower lip, 'But she's still with Brice, huh?

'The gossip is that she just broke up with Brice yesterday,' Ashley replied, biting her fingernail then spat out the little nail she had bitten.

Cameron shrugged, but his heart fluttered at the rumour.

'Where are you from, Ashley'? James asked, rubbing his shorts.

'From Kaeo. It's a dump up north. But I live with my nana on Queen Victoria Street. Nana Moana adopted me because my dad was in prison. I'm not proud of what he's done, but he's my dad and I love him.' Ashley paused and crossed her arms. 'Too much info, huh. No one knows about it. I think they gave him name suppression to protect me. Please don't tell anyone, aye. I wanted to let you guys know that Azoma has spread a lot of rumours that she is supposed to be your cousin, what a cow.'

Cameron and James realized now why they sat with only Ashley. Sadness crossed over their faces. Cameron and James eyes met with pity for each other thinking that they thought they'd moved on from the shame of their parents and now it had returned as if it had never left them.

'Thanks for the heads up, Ashley. So it's okay for you to join us despite of the rumours. The gossip about my dad wasn't true, you know,' Cameron said, frowning.

'True or not, I don't mind hanging out with you guys. It must be hard coming from the other side of the world to find no one wants to be friends with you. At least with me I've got so many cousins in this school they accept me for who I am.'

Concerned for Cameron, James changed the subject. 'Tara is hot, huh? She can get any guy she wants,' he said, putting on sun block.

'Look who's coming,' Ashley said as she cocked her head to the side.

Jerry approached them with a paper bag on his hand. 'How is it going, mate?' he asked, handing the brown paper bag to Ashley.

'This is my brother James, Jerry'

'And I'm Jerry Hunter.' They gave each other a knuckle bump. Jerry stood five-feet ten-inches and with an athletic build.

'Hey, guys do you want to be in the rugby team?' Jerry asked.

Cameron and James felt the warmth of Jerry's presence.

'Yes, we do,' James said

Ashley opened the bag. 'Wow, thanks. Moro and Crunchie bars, peanut slabs and Jaffas. Thanks, Jerry.'

'That's not all for you. Actually, I bought some of them for this guy knowing that they come from the US,' Jerry said as he cocked his head on the side.

'Of course, I'll share it; I'm not greedy,' Ashley said as she spread the chocolate bars on the table. She took the Jaffas since it was her favorite.

James knew that Crunchie bars were Cameron's favorite. 'I'll have the peanut slabs thanks, Ashley,' James said, grabbing the peanut slab chocolate bars.

Cameron picked up the Crunchie bars.

Jerry crumpled the empty paper bag and threw it into the basketball hoop. 'Well, I'll tell you, all you have to do is register at school.' He put his hands in his pocket and stood with his feet wide apart and rolled his shoulders back once. 'Hey, would you guys like to play Xbox after school? I'll text you after taekwondo practice'

Ashley swallowed the last bit of the chocolate and put the wrapper in her pocket. 'Jerry, forget the taekwondo practice you're a black belt so no need to practice, what about your cool aquarium and the fish that you just bought?'

'She'll be right, Ashley.'

'Cameron will be into that. He's world class when it comes to aquari-ums. He was an aquarium wonder back in the day,' James said, rubbing his jaw.

Cameron blushed with the memory of his old aquarium. 'Stop talking crap, James. You know I haven't bothered with that for years,' Cameron blurt-ed.

The bell rung for the next period. James rose to his feet and waved goodbye, eating more chocolate bars on the way.

'Hey, thanks for the choccies,' Cameron said.

'No worries, mate,' Jerry replied. They walked together side by side with Ashley following behind to their next class.

Cameron noticed out of the corner of his eye that Tara had her eyes on him the minute he entered the room.

***

At the principal's office, Mrs Rundle, Azoma and Shantell sat across from Mr. Bentley.

Azoma pinned her eyes on Mr. Bentley placing a spell of deception on him.

After hearing Mrs Rundle's report, Mr. Bentley frowned. 'Is it true that you planned the seating so you could cut Cameron's pants?'

A grin of self-gratification and triumph at the spell, covered Shantell's face. In a low respectable tone, she replied, 'No, we noticed Cameron's shorts were way too small for him and they were second-hand, that's why they ripped so easy.'

'It's not our fault that he hadn't worn any undies,' Azoma said.

'And who threw his phone and pen, so he had to bend down and pick them up?' Mr Bentley asked.

Like innocent children trying to tell the truth, Azoma and Shantell looked down at their feet. 'Not me,' Shantell and Azoma said in unison.

'What can you say about that Mrs. Rundle?' Mr. Bentley asked, rubbing his chin.

As Mrs. Rundle was an elder of All for Jesus Church, when Shantell gave her a spell of deception at this moment it didn't affect her. The historical unresolved case of bullying was getting to her. A flush of anger washed over her face. 'We all know that's an utter lie,' Mrs. Rundle said, planting her hands on her hips.

'You can go back to your class now and please shut the door behind you,' Mr Bentley said, waving his hand towards the door.'

As soon as the door shut, Mr. Bentley folded his arms.

'Well, if you can't prove it, Mrs. Rundle, I have no reason to detain those students after school.'

'Oh, bollocks. You know Shantell and Azoma. If I tell them who told me about their plan for Cameron this morning, they will torture my source. Remember what happened last time?' The girl left this school... and killed herself,' Mrs. Rundle answered, flaring her nostrils.

'What do you want me to do? I have to follow the protocol as per school detention policy and the girl who committed suicide had schizophrenia. And...'

'Grow some balls. You are too soft and gullible with these girls. And, again, you have no idea how serious this is. I'll get to the bottom of this. It will be my mission to prove what Shantell and Azoma did to Cameron. Watch me,' Mrs. Rundle said, getting up and slamming the door behind her.

Chapter 23

Lora arrived twenty minutes early to pick her sons up from school. Turning the ignition off, Lora pulled out her Bible from the glove box.

Suddenly Karen knocked on the passenger side window.

Lora beckoned her to get in the car. 'Hi Karen. I really appreciate your taking me to the prayer meeting today, and for the info about the caregiving job. Oh, and thanks for your prayers for my sons.'

'No worries,' Karen said. 'Thank you too, for praying for Tara. Amazingly God answered your prayers immediately.' She shifted her back from side to side to make herself comfortable. Her phone buzzed. 'Liam's just texted me. Tara has broken up with Brice.' She paused, then continued. 'I'm really relieved that when we pray for our children with the blood of Jesus, man, that's powerful. Let's read Eph. 6:10-12.'

They read it together. 'Finally, be strong in the Lord and in his mighty power. 11 Put on the full armour of God, so that you can take your stand against the devil's schemes. 12 For our struggle is not against flesh and blood, but against the rulers, against the authorities, against the powers of this dark world and against the spiritual forces of evil in the heavenly realms.'

Lora blinked in dismay. 'As I said at the prayer meeting, I think Cameron is quite depressed.'

'Just trust that God will answer our group prayers. Sometime that's all we can do is trust God, that our children are in the palm of His hand,' Karen said.

Then Lora confided everything to Karen, apart from Cameron's involvement with the gang. And Likewise, Karen confided to Lora.

'I know we have to trust God, but you can also try the school counsellor, but I think you have to ask your GP for referrals and that will take long. Please don't think I'm trying to scare you but what Jenny said at the prayer meeting makes sense,' Karen said.

Lora grimaced in fear. 'I agree with what she said that there is a Satan cult operating in this town. Just look at the statistics for the number of crimes per population in this little town. Honi has the highest incident of crime, teen suicides, drug related deaths, arson, and unexplained accidental death; you name it and we've been in the news lately.' She buried her palms in her cheeks. 'That's why counselling won't work. The best thing we can do is to pray for this Satan attack.'

Karen's eyes widened in apprehension. 'Yes, I'm afraid that this girl committed suicide. She'd had counselling and was on high doses of Prozac but still...' Karen sighed.

'Say no more,' Lora said as she stroked her forehead. She couldn't bear it if Cameron committed suicide.

'I can only understand his depression. We can pray for him right now,' Karen said.

With their heads bowed and eyes closed, they held each other's hands and prayed.

Karen started speaking in tongues, 'Shisaka, ribba, Kanika, Shika, rraabba, kanga.'

Then Lora begun to pray. 'Oh, Heavenly Father, I know you love my sons, Cameron and James. I ask that you to protect them, cover them with the blood of Jesus, and surround them with your angels. Lord, you know what is going through Cameron's mind. I surrender it all to you in Jesus's name.'

Karen continued to pray. 'Praise you, Lord Jesus. We trust in you, Lord, that you will protect our children, especially Cameron, who you know is de-pressed. Put him in the palms of your hands. Save him from the Satan spell. In

Jesus's name. Amen.' After a few more minutes of praying for the community and world peace, they opened their eyes.

Karen unlocked the door letting herself out of the car. 'Text me. See you at the next prayer meeting love. Drag you sons to church on Sunday, aye. It's at the High Street All for Jesus Church. Oh, look there's James and Cameron. It looks like they've found a friend,' Karen said as she walked back to her car.

To meet James and Cameron, Lora stepped out of the car and headed toward the pathway that led to the main building of the school.

***

Walking along with her sons as they headed back to the car park, Lora gazed endearingly at her sons and beamed at the girl. 'How did the first day go?'

'It was alright.' Cameron shot Ashley a *don't tell mom*-look.

'Mom, this is Ashley,' Cameron said.

'Hi Cameron's mom,' Ashley responded.

'Hi, call me Lora. Pleased to meet you Ashley.'

'Likewise,' Ashley said.

'Bye for now, my bike is just over there,' Ashley said heading to the left where the bike stand was.

At 3:30 pm the sun was the still glaring. The stink of the crude oil was in the air. By the time they got in the car they were hot and sweaty. James sat in the back and Cameron sat in the front seat looking into the distance. Lora drove off.

'How was your first day, Cameron?'

'Mom, you've asked me already. I told you it was alright.'

'What happened to your old uniform? Why are you wearing those shorts, love.'

'Mom, leave me alone.' Cameron clasped his fingers at the back of his neck and shut his eyes, trying to control the tears.

Lora stopped the car. 'I'm sorry,' she patted Cameron's shoulder, 'but something must be upsetting you.'

Cameron cocked his head to the side and his eyes met Lora's, then he told her of his humiliating moment at school.

James felt for Cameron and was infuriated that he couldn't do anything about it other than to support him so that he didn't feel alone. 'This is not the first time. I heard this girl at school who has a fetish for cutting bags, dresses, and all sorts of clothes, but the school has not caught her. I wonder if she is the same girl who ripped your pants.'

Cameron unclasped his fingers, then rubbed his arm. 'I wish I hadn't taken off my undies. But it felt comfortable without them, so I went to school not wearing any,' Cameron said, fiddling with his watch.

Lora imagined how embarrassed Cameron must've felt. She stroked his hands wishing that she could say something that would take it all away. 'I think this girl who ripped your pants is under Satan's spell.'

'Mom, you know there is a simple psychological reason as to why she would do that,' James said as he scratched the back of his neck. 'Don't blame Satan or bring witchcraft into it.'

'Yes, Dr Phil. Get a life, James. You watch too many talk shows. Now you think you're a shrink,' Cameron said, raising his eyebrows.

James thought of the bullying he'd had but he didn't want to tell anybody. He grimaced. 'It's not all about you, Cameron,' James said, his nostrils flaring.

Cameron didn't answer. He immediately realized he had said the wrong thing. *I shouldn't say that, he's just trying to help. Thinking of Satan putting a spell on this girl. Did someone put a spell on me today?* Cameron thought. 'I'm sorry James. I didn't mean to say that.'

Lora felt awful that she was neglecting James. She turned her head. 'Oh, I'm sorry, James. How was your day?' she asked.

'I'm okay, Mom,' James said.

Then Cameron noticed the blue Ford Maverick that had seemed to be following them since they'd left, had stopped.

They heard banging at the back of the car.

'Oh, that is Ashley,' Lora said, looking in the rear vision mirror.

Ashley hopped off her bike. She walked slowly to the passenger side of the car. 'Hi, guys. Do you want to come to Jerry's house? He could do with some tips as I'm not sure about the fish he's put in the aquarium. I'll show you.'

James's mood changed and he grinned in agreement. 'Go, Cameron. You're the aquarium wizard. I'll help mom get the groceries.'

Ashley's invitation pleased Lora after the humiliation Cameron had been subjected to. 'Yes, it will do you a world of good,' Lora said.

If I walk with Ashley to Jerry's house this will prove if the Ford is following me, Cameron thought. 'Ok, Mom. I'll text you for when you can pick me up,' Cameron said as he stepped out of the car.

Chapter 24

Walking with Ashley, Cameron was still thinking about the Ford and struggling to control his growing fear.

'Oh, there's, Jerry,' Ashley said, waving to Jerry in the distance.

They met up with Jerry and headed to his house. The sun was beating down on them. The gardens were blooming with Canterbury bells, fuchsia, and gladiolas as they passed an apple orchard.

'Don't pick that apple, 'Jerry said

'Why not?' Cameron asked

'It could be sprayed. You'll get sick,' Ashley and Jerry said in unison.

'Hmm. It looks so yummy and smells so sweet,' Camerón said, biting into the apple.

'What did you get up to? I thought you've gone home.' Ashley asked

'After taekwondo I played rugby with Kirk and Brice and forgot the time.'

Jerry strode beside Ashley and Cameron. 'What do you think of rugby, Cameron.

'My dad taught us how to play and he played with us a lot when we were young. But as dad got older...' Cameron paused rubbing his head, '...he didn't play with us as much. He said it was a silly game, a bunch of stupid people chasing a ball on the field.'

'So true, like a lot of sports though,' Ashley said.

'Hey, where did you learn about volcanoes in the Philippines?' Jerry asked.

'He googled it, duh,' Ashleigh said sarcastically.

The Ford passed them on the opposite side of the road. They turned their heads. Cameron swallowed his fear. 'Well, Dad was supposed to have a tour of duty in the Philippines around that time. Of course, Pinatubo erupted before his tour of duty started so Dad was assigned somewhere else.'

'So, your dad was in the US Navy, right?' Ashley asked.

'Yes, but not now,' Cameron replied as he looked behind him to see where the Ford was. It was parked next to the curb.

'Thanks for what you did for me at school,' Cameron said to Jerry.

'No worries, mate,' Jerry responded.

Cameron needed to get away from the Ford. 'Can we hurry up? I want to go to the toilet,' he said.

'No need to hurry, mate. We're here,' Ashley said as she opened the brown gate next to her.

***

The path was lined with camellia trees, and behind them, a meticulously trimmed hedge. There was a white swan ornament in the middle of the lawn. As they walked up the path, Ashley picked some grapes from the climbing grapevine that covered the veranda and ate them.

As soon as Jerry opened the brown aluminum sliding door, their eyes widened in astonishment at the big eel wriggling of the floor, along with broken glass and other fish.

'Oh my word, Jerry. You're in deep shit,' Ashley said.

'Holy camoly! Get two buckets of water. We can save the other fish. They're still breathing,' Cameron said.

Ashley sprinted past the kitchen into the laundry, Jerry following close behind. They carefully picked up the goldfish, some of them goggle-eyed, and put them in one bucket.

They put the big eel in the second bucket, then swept up the broken glasses, wrapped it in newspaper and threw it in the rubbish.

Cameron looked at the eel. 'Well, I think your aquarium is far too small for eels. I think it tried to get out but tipped the tank over and broke it,' Cameron commented.

Jerry shook his head. 'It looks like I'll need to buy a new aquarium. I'd better get it now, otherwise Mum will skin me alive.'

'But we need to clean water and other mess up before your mum arrives, otherwise you will be grounded for weeks,' Ashley said.

'Or disowned,' Jerry said.

'Doubt it,' Ashley replied.

'Let's get on with it. Crikey, Mum will be home in three hours. She told me not to put that bloody eel in the aquarium.'

'I'll get some towels,' Ashley said.

'No, Ashley, it won't work. We have a wet vax cleaner. I'll ring Mom and get her to drop it off,' Cameron said.

He rang Lora and explained what had happened and Lora arrived within half an hour with the vax cleaner.

'Okay, Cameron. I'll text you when dinner is ready. See you later,' Lora said.

Cameron vacuumed the water off the carpet. Ashley and Jerry threw the dirty water outside onto the lawn.

After an hour the carpet was almost dry.

'Now, Ashley, you can use the towel to damp it dry,' Cameron suggested.

'Where did you learn how to clean like a pro, man?' Jerry exclaimed, clasping his hands behind his head.

Trying to avoid painful memories of when he used to work at the gym, he didn't reply.

After drying the carpet, they put the couch back in place and the mahogany coffee table as well as the wall cabinet full of old 33 records.

'Wow, man, we did well, all done and dusted within an hour,' Ashley said.

Ashley and Jerry gave Cameron a knuckle bump and Cameron beamed.

'Thank you very much, mate. I've got to get cracking to get a new aquarium,' Jerry said, waving goodbye.

Cameron and Ashley continued to dry the carpet, finishing just as Jerry returned.

'That was quick,' Ashley said.

'Can you give me a hand to get the aquarium out of the car please?'

As soon as the aquarium was in place, they put the moss and water in the tank then the fish they had managed to save.

Ashley had her eyes on the eel. 'Well, if you don't want the eel I'll take it. My nana will cook it. Can Lora drop me home?'

'Of course. I'll ask mom,' Cameron said.

Jasmin Hunter, Jerry's mom, arrived home. Her brown eyes stared at the carpet and the aquarium. 'Why is the carpet so clean? What happened here, Jerry? What happened to the eel?' A Filipino of Chinese and Spanish descent, she stood 5 feet tall, and had olive skin and dark brown hair.

'I'm taking the eel home coz Jerry doesn't want it anymore,' Ashley answered.

'Thank goodness for that,' Jasmin said with a sigh of relief.

Jerry reluctantly told his mom what happened.

'Don't worry, son. I don't want you to keep worrying about it. I won't tell your dad.'

'Mum, this is Cameron Owen. I told you about the new student from school, James. This is his brother Cameron.'

'Pleased to meet you, mam,' Cameron said, offering his hand.

'Just call me Jasmin,' she said. Her long brown ponytail swung against her shoulders. She offered her hand to Cameron. Her eyes turned to Jerry tenderly. 'I'm so proud of you, Jerry.

Jerry's eyebrows raised as if to say, "what have-I done". 'Why, Mum?'

'Because you always welcome new students at school,' she said, moving toward the kitchen. 'Okay. Let's get something to eat. Are you guys hungry? Jerry get the pansit (a famous noodle dish in the Philippines) and heat it up and get some pandesal (a sour bread made the Filipino way) from the freezer and put it in the microwave please.'

'Ok, Mum, and the pandesal too?' Jerry asked as he strode into the kitchen.

'Yes, love.'

There was a knock on the door. 'Hi. I'm Lora, Cameron's mom. This is his brother, James. You must be Jerry's mom.'

'Yes, Jasmin,' she said as she put her hand out.

'I heard about you. We work at the same place. I start at four and you leave at three. That's why I haven't met you.'

'Me too. So you're the nice American lady they were talking about. Were you at church last Sunday?' Jasmin asked as she gestured for her to come into the kitchen.

'You know Karen?' Lora asked.

'Yes, she's my friend. We go to the same church,' Jasmine replied.

After a brief introduction Lora accepted Jasmine's persistent invitation to share a Filipino meal. The smell of the big platter of pansit and the fresh heated pandesal was inviting.

Ashley showed James and Cameron around and Jerry followed behind them. The back yard had a well-kept vegetable garden. A huge old plum tree with big hanging branches stood in the rear of the garden. There was a tool shed and a room for Jerry that had a pool table, and dart board on the wall.

'When we were young, we always raided the plum tree. Jerry and I used to sell the plums for pocket money. Jasmin dug a hole around it and filled it with sand so if we fell we wouldn't hurt ourselves. Since then the next-door neighbours' kids' use it as a sand pit,' Ashley said.

'How old were you and Jerry then?' James asked.

'Ten-years-old I think, and that's how I met Jerry. I used to live six hous-es away from here. I asked him if I could have some plums as it was loaded, and they were falling on the ground. I suggested to Jerry that we sell them so we'd be mega rich. But Jerry sold more plums door- to-door than me, and they sold like hot cakes, because he's so cute. He was only 5 foot and I was five feet eight I think, so I guess no one wants to buy plums from a giant girl like me, I thought. Since then Jerry has been the seller and I've been the plum picker.'

'Did you become mega rich selling plums?' Cameron asked

'Nah,' Ashley replied.

'It looks like that plum tree has done her dash. There aren't many leaves, and it's so dry. Is it dying?' James commented, rubbing his ears.

'I hope not. It was my hiding place when I was in trouble with mom when I was young,' Jerry said, looking down.

'Okay, Jerry. You carry on. I'll play pool while you give them a tour,' Ash-ley said.

Next to the room was a tool shed and a bench. When they entered the tool shed, Jerry noticed Cameron's eye had widened when a slingshot, lying on the table among the hammer and other tools, caught his eye.

Jerry picked up the modern looking slingshot, which was made of metal and had red rubber weaving. 'My dad bought this for me when he was in the UK.' Jerry led them out and picked out some cans out of the rubbish bin. He lined the cans up on the bench. He aimed and hit the first can, then three more out of six.

'Do you want to have a go, Cameron?'

'No, thanks.'

James knew that Cameron didn't like being watched and he'd be embarrassed by the attention.

'I'll have a go,' James said. He was about to launch the first stone when Ashley poked her head out of the shed.

'Hey, come over and play me a game of darts,' she yelled.

Thrilled to have a game of darts, James dropped the slingshot and went in the shed. Jerry followed.

Cameron picked up the slingshot to aim, but his attention was diverted by a familiar squeaky wail. His heart raced as he noticed a black hairy, big fat rat on top of the shed's roof, about to jump at him. Threatened and reminding him of the rat attack at Beth's house, Cameron aimed precisely at the rat hitting it smack on the forehead with a big thump. The rat fell in front of him. After hearing the crash and the rat's high pitch whine, James, Jerry, and Ashley ran out of the shed. They stared at the rat, repulsed by the stone between his eyes.

Ashley rubbed the goose bumps on her arm. 'Oh, holy crap. That was the rat Jerry tried to kill. It has been prowling around here for days.' She paused clasping her hand to her chest 'Jerry has been trying to kill it with a stun gun and the slingshot, but he kept missing.'

James's face flushed. 'Get rid of that revolting creature, Cameron, as mom will faint if she sees it.' He pointed with disgust to the rat on the ground.

'Why can't you? I've already killed the dammed thing,' Cameron replied with the slingshot still in his hand.

Jerry stood motionless at the sight of the dead rat. 'Don't look at me. I'm not touching it.'

'Okay, wimps, I'll bloody do it as Lora will go hysterical at the sight of it.' Ashley took a shovel from the shed, scooped up the rat and threw it in the rubbish.

'Cameron, you're the man! You killed the bastard,' Jerry said as he gave Cameron a knuckle bump.

'Jack of all trades, professional cleaner, and a rat killer. That's awesome, mate,' Ashley said, giving Cameron a high five.

'That's my little brother. Fantastic job, bud. I'm so proud of you. Back home they call him Slingshot Guy,' James said, giving Cameron a thumbs-up.

Chapter 25

Lora and Jasmin remained at the table conversing while the young ones were having fun, content at hearing their voices and laughter. Now and then they could hear Cameron's deep booming voice and Jerry's loud ridiculous laugh.

Lora felt quite comfortable and welcome at Jasmine's house.

'Excuse me, I'll just get the electric heater to dry the carpet faster,' Jasmin said.

With the short encounter with Jasmin, Lora felt quite at home and welcomed at her house.

Jasmin came out from the corridor with an electric heater in her hand. Then the phone rang.

'Do you want to answer the phone? Can I plug the heater in for you?' Lora asked

It didn't take long for Lora to plug in the heater and close the door.

After the phone call, Jasmin said, 'It's my husband. He works overseas. I told him briefly about what happened today. Jerry is busy with his friends so he will ring later to talk to his son.'

'What does he do if you don't mind me asking?' Lora picked up the dishes from the table.

'He works as a petroleum engineer. Jerry and I miss him a lot. He works three months on then one month off.

Lora looked at her watch surprised that the time had gone so fast. 'I'd love to stay longer but Steven, my husband, may think we've got kidnapped. Just joking. School tomorrow. It's a battle to get them ready. Sorry we've got to go.'

'No problems. Let's see what they're up too,' Jasmin said, waving her hand towards the back door.

Ashley was playing darts with Cameron while James played pool with Jerry.

As soon as Lora and Jasmin entered the room, Jerry, put his pool stick down and said, 'At last that big rat is dead. Cameron hit it with the sling shot.'

Imagining the big fat rat made Jasmin shiver. Her body jolted for a second, then with a deep sigh she said, 'Thank goodness for that.'

Suddenly a fire alarm went off. Everyone realized that the fire alarm sound was coming from the kitchen, so they rushed into the house. They could see the lounge shrouded in smoke behind the closed glass panel door.

They shot each other a look of disbelief. 'Seriously, is this really happening?' Ashley said.

'Leave that door closed,' Jasmin said calmly as she dialled 111 on her phone.

'Come on, guys, get out,' Lora said, covering her nose to avoid inhaling the smoke.

They gathered in front on the lawn in anticipation as they waited for the fire brigade to arrive. Within ten minutes the fire engines arrived and the firemen extinguished the fire. Neighbours lined the footpath.

'No excitement here now since they caught it in time,' one of the male spectators with a ponytail said.

In a yellow oversized uniform, the firefighter approached Jasmin. 'Are you Mrs. Hunter?'

'Yes, I am ,sir.'

'Lucky the only damage was a large burnt patch where the heater was placed upside down, which burnt the carpet.'

Immediately Lora realized what she had done with the heater. 'Oh, I am sorry, Jasmin. That was me. I thought that's how the heater is supposed to stand facing flat on the floor.'

Feeling sorry for their mom, Cameron and James looked embarrassed.

'Oh, don't worry, Lora. It's an accident, and I've got insurance.'

We've contained the smoke but to be safe I suggest for you guys not sleep in the house tonight. And leave all the windows open.'

Blaming herself, Lora thought she needed to make it up to Jasmin and Jerry. 'We have a tent and sleeping bags. Can we stay the night to keep you company?' Lora asked as she put her arm around Jasmin.

'We have camping gear too. We can camp on the front lawn or out the back,' Jerry said.

Lora took Ashely home, who was thrilled to take the eel home for dinner. Then she phoned Steven, told him what had happened, that the boys were going to stay the night and to bring over the kids' school uniforms. With fun and enthusiasm, they finished putting up the tent before dark. Camping on the front lawn were Jerry, Cameron and James and in another tent out back was Lora and Jasmin.

Cameron could not sleep as the thought of the Blue Ford came back. Images of his family being tortured by the gang played like a movie in his head. He then realized how much his family loved him regardless of his faults and he felt the same too no matter what. Thinking of both the good and bad times they'd been through Cameron thought the world of them, and he did not want to lose them. After losing Hollie it had become clear to Cameron that you cannot see that person physically anymore but the memory stays in your heart. All he could do was to hug his backpack with the notebook and the slingshot in it, to feel protected, even though Jerry and James's snores were deafening. Drained, Cameron finally dropped off to sleep lying between them. But the sound of a car engine woke him up. Convinced it was the gang, he sat up, put the backpack on and crept out of the tent.

'Where are you going?' James whispered.

'I'm just going to pee. Close your eyes, go back to sleep.'

As soon as he was out of the tent, Cameron heard the car drive away. Then Cameron went back in and fell asleep again.

When he woke at 8 am he wondered where everybody was. He went inside the house to find Jerry and James in the kitchen having breakfast in their uniforms.

'We didn't wake you up as your mom said to let you sleep in since you left the tent last night,' Jerry said.

'You were sleep walking,' James said.

'And I heard you talking in your sleep, 'Jerry added.

'What did I say.'

'Something like, why, why do I need to?' James replied.

Cameron's sleep walking worried Lora, and anxiety covered her face. 'Hurry up, Cameron. Take a shower. You have forty-five minutes.'

Within half an hour Cameron was ready. While having breakfast his mind filled with questions. Did the car belong to gang? What are they waiting for? There had been many chances to take him, but why hadn't they. Who was in the blue ford car? Or was it all a dream when he was sleep walking?

Chapter 26

After a week, Lora got the right size uniform for Cameron.

Shantell and Azoma got a written warning after Mrs Rundle's investigation. She encouraged Cameron to see her if he experienced any more bullying. Kirk and Brice took all the opportunities they could to bully Cameron when Jerry and Ashley were not around; kicking, shoving him, throwing his lunch away and more.

Friday after school Cameron came home pissed off with himself. Throwing his backpack on the floor he huffed out an angry breath. He sat on his bed and cuddled the pillow, his body curled around it, thinking, *Why didn't I stick up for myself?* I should've kicked Brice when he tripped me, but I was too slow. With an effort, he pushed the thought of Tara's heartsick expression to the back of his mind, guessing that she had witnessed the bullying. *Why am I so scared of them? How long will they keep doing it? Am I under Satan's spell of fear? Why had Lora's prayers not stopped Satan's spell? Did God let it happen?*

With the sun glaring in his eyes and the wind blowing on his face, Cameron went for a walk. To vent his fury, he began hitting the water with stones shot from his slingshot. His eyes widened when he hit a fish. He didn't take his shoes off to get the big snapper that floated on the water. Ecstatic he put the fish beside him and carried on shooting at the water. When he saw people coming from a distance he stopped. But when he looked to his side the fish was gone. Disheartened at losing the fish, he sat on his bed wondering why his shoes were not wet. *How did I get into the water without getting wet?* He covered his face with his hand. *Am I having hallucinations again? King David, my friend, is that you?* At this point Cameron's confusion escalated and he felt like he was going mad. Hating to recall when he was young and being questioned over and over by a psychologist; sitting in a room, bored, trying to convince him that what he was seeing was only a hallucination. Since no one was home he felt that it would give him a good chance to read the notebook properly as he hadn't had much privacy to read it alone. Turning the over the notebook's pages, he noted a list of names. Some had been crossed out. *Are these the names of the people they've killed*? This thought sent shiver to his skin. Before drifting into the thought of Hollie's brutal death, Steven arrived.

With a big fish in his hands, he said, 'It's been a hell of a day, but this man gave me this big snapper, which has made my day. Look.' He lifted his hands holding the fish.

'What did the man look like, Dad?

'Who cares? He looked like a king. Just kidding. I can't remember what he looked like. I'm so tired. Can you gut this? I just have to take a shower.'

'Okay, Dad,' Cameron said softly

'Anyway, I don't think he's a bad guy if you are thinking of the gang. I couldn't really see his face since he was wearing a white hoodie.'

As Cameron gutted the fish, he wished King David would visit him as he yearned for his old friend. He had no doubt it was King David who gave Steven the fish.

***

It was Sunday morning, and a half-asleep Cameron struggled to move. But on his way to the shower, he stared at the beautiful feather-like clouds in a horizontal layer, which covered the pale blue sky. The bright rays of the sun motivated Cameron. Although it was summer, the sea breeze was cold. While the smell of the sea filled the air penetrating the shower cubicle, Cameron pondered his dream the last time he was in the tent at Jasmin's. His dream came back to him in bits and pieces.

King David had visited him and told him to go to church before he could help him, and he recalled answering back, *Do I have too? Why me? Is this the thought that is the guiding energy for me to go to church this Sunday?* Thinking back to what he'd been through, Cameron decided not to tell anyone about his dreams or his hallucinations. Not like when he was seven-years-old. He despised the advice of the psychologist to his parents; King David was just a make believe figure.

Because they were desperate to find a solution to Cameron's sleepwalking when he wandered off in the middle of the night, they sought the advice of a psychic. Although he didn't want to tell King David to leave following the advice of the psychic who said, 'It was this ghost who was luring him to get lost when he sleepwalked and if Cameron tells him to leave, he may.' Cameron was advised to tell King David to go away 'If you don't tell your friend King David to go away something really bad is going to happen to him. Believing what the psychic said was true, young Cameron did not want anything bad to happen to King David. As he remembered, he could still feel the pain of losing a friend, actually a best friend. Cameron could not forget when he was desperate to talk to him.

King David had visited him when they were at Queen's Garden in Nelson on a sunny afternoon at the bridge while he was feeding the ducks that were swimming in the pond. King David, wearing a white hoodie, joined Cameron to feed the ducks. While throwing the bread, Cameron said, 'Sorry, you have to leave me alone. I can't see you anymore as you are just a figment of my imagination. With his young tender emotions, Cameron struggled to convince himself that King David was make believe and not really his friend. Since then the dreams and hallucinations had faded and Cameron believed King David to be a ghost.

Because Cameron didn't show any enthusiasm for going to church, Lora ironed his favorite Fila T- shirt and his stonewashed blue jeans and told him that Tara would be there. She felt Cameron had a huge crush on her and the mere sight of Tara would make Cameron happy. *Mom is right in one thing. Tara would be there, but I'm also going to church because of my friend King David as he might visit me again If I do.* In a few minutes they were in the car headed to church.

Cameron's heart raced as soon as he entered the church since he hadn't seen many people since Hollie's funeral. Below a large screen was a tall wooden cross. As the music played, the parishioners sung along to the lyrics that appeared on the huge screen. White decorated pots with an array of colourful flowers were set on each side of the stage. Strumming guitars were Jerry and Liam. A girl wearing a flowery-print frock played the keyboard. On drums, was an obese middle-aged man. In the centre, leading the song with a microphone in her hand was Tara singing "With all I am" by Hillsong.

To calm himself, Cameron took a deep breath in slowly.

Lora and Cameron had come in late, sitting in the last row of the pews. Listening to the softness of Tara's voice and the lyrics, touched Cameron. When the group stopped playing, Tara prayed.

'Thank you, for your unfailing love. We love you, Lord. Thank you, for you are always there to pick us up every time we stumble. Thank you, that you are in the midst of us. Lord, let your holy spirit guide us to listen in your word today. In Jesus's name, we pray. Amen.' Putting the microphone down, Tara sat in the second row between Liam, who wore a light brown polo shirt and black trousers, and Jerry who wore a black V-neck body stretch T shirt, which showed the contours of his muscly body.

Seeing Jerry and Tara's closeness as they whispered and giggled and listened to the weekly sermon, Cameron resisted feeling insecure while he watched them.

Nick Creighton, the pastor, wearing a white polo shirt with a black bow tie, spoke from the pulpit. 'Today we are going to talk about forgiveness. Open your bible.' Pastor Nick stroked his handlebar moustache and read Luke

7:47-48. 'Therefore, I tell you, her sins, which are many, are forgiven—for she loved much. But he who is forgiven little, loves little. And he said to her, 'Your sins are forgiven. Ephesians 4:31-32 Let all bitterness and wrath and anger and clamour and slander be put away from you, along with all malice. Be kind to one another, tender-hearted, forgiving one another, as God in Christ forgave you.' Closing the Bible, Pastor Nick continued. 'Brothers and sister, sons and daughters if there is unforgiveness in your heart, hatred and fear because someone hurt you so bad, God will understand why you could not forgive. But God will not forgive you if you cannot forgive. Because God love us so much, he did not want us to suffer from the hatred and the torture of unforgiveness in our heart.

'Because God is love. He wants to fill our hearts with love but if our heart is full of hatred, and unforgiveness, love will have no place in it,' Pastor Nick said as he extended his arms across the pulpit. He carried on preaching for half an hour, and at the end of the message he said, 'If the message today touches, your heart, come. I'll pray for you. Would you like to give your heart to Jesus, to be your saviour, your guide, your friend? Do you want to have a relationship with Him? He is waiting for you right now to make that decision. God gave you a choice. If it's not in your heart God knows when you are ready. He is always waiting for you.'

No one came forward. The music team was requested to play while people began walking to the front. There was a long introduction of the music then Tara sung "Turn Your Eyes Upon Jesus" by Helen Lemmel. This time Tara's voice was husky and bold touching the very core of Cameron's heart.

The message and the lyrics of the song moved Cameron's spirit. He felt that the pastor was singling him out as the messages of hatred, fear, and for-giveness sounded right for him. Unforgiving Hollie's killer was like a toxin pes-tering his whole body. Suddenly the word "surrenders" kept flashing on the screen like a digital alarm clock. *Oh, not in church as well. God, you mean forgive?* Cameron thought. Then he felt a light pressure on his chest going around and around as if it was an electrical massager. Cameron felt as if this massager was softening his heart. *Why am I feeling this? Is this the holy spirit?* With his eyes shut, Cameron muttered, 'Oh God. Forgive me for not forgiving Hollie's killer. And I forgive Andrew now.' Bit by bit Cameron felt like a big arrow full of venomous blood was being released out of his chest. Cameron sobbed.

An old lady with a blue hat gave him a tissue, and Lora put her arms around him. He kept crying as the lyrics to the music together with Tara's beautiful voice tenderly stirred his soul. At this moment, Cameron felt as if his heart was like a wound full of blood being cleansed in running water. As he opened his eyes, he could not believe what he was seeing as Hollie appeared on the screen. She was wearing a white robe. Hollie was on a white, endless staircase, surrounded by white fluffy clouds and rays of sunshine. She waved her hands as if she were telling Cameron to come. *Yes, Hollie, I want to be with you.* Cameron listened to his inner voice, which was saying Hollie was happy where she was, and that he must let her go.

Hollie shook her head. Cameron nodded to her indicating that he had understood. Yes, Hollie, I know this is what you've always wanted; for me to accept Jesus into my heart. Yes. Yes. I accept Jesus into my heart. But please don't go. In a flash, Hollie's image disappeared. Snivelling loudly, the congregation turned their heads toward Cameron with sad smiles.

The old lady felt sorry for Cameron and offered him a tissue. 'God is asking you to come forward, my dear. Go, don't hesitate.' She gestured with her hand to Cameron to go forward.

Timidly, Cameron stepped out from the pew. Lora followed him.

In front of the congregation, Pastor Nick approached. He was tall and towered over Cameron. He kneeled to be at the same height. 'What is your name?' Pastor Nick asked rubbing his wrinkled hand.

'Cameron Owen, sir.'

'Cameron, do you accept the Lord Jesus as your personal saviour?' Pastor Nick asked, putting his arms on Cameron's shoulder.

Still sniffling, and with red eyes, Cameron replied, 'Yes, I do.'

'Let's pray together. Repeat after me, Cameron. Lord, I know I'm a sinner. I repent my sins. I choose to follow you from this day forward. I give you my heart. I'll put you first in my life.'

After repeating this prayer, Cameron felt his heart cool down like cold water had been thrown onto a flaming frying pan that was full of unforgiveness, fear, and hatred. As Cameron stood up, he felt like a block that was weighing down his chest was taken away. Suddenly, Cameron felt weightless as if there was a spring in his shoes. He could not help it, he started laughing.

The congregation didn't react to Cameron's laughter as if they understand that it was the Holy Spirit working on Cameron. Lora remained standing and speechless. Her arms rested on his shoulders. 'God, thank for you saving me,' Cameron muttered. Looking down, he looked up at the screen and again, there was Hollie smiling. Cameron took a long deep breath. *Goodbye, my love, I'll see you in heaven one day*, Hollie said spiritually to Cameron, then her image slowly disappeared as she waved goodbye.

Pastor Nick noticed Cameron's nose. 'Do you want us to pray for your nose?'

Before Cameron could answer Lora answered, 'Yes, Pastor.' Lora clasped her fingers together on her chest.

Pastor Nick waved to the elders in front of the church as if to say - pray for Cameron. Two elders of the church came up, a bald guy and a woman with a multi-coloured bandana on her head.

The bald guy laid his hand lightly on Cameron's nose 'Oh, Heavenly Father, you shaped this nose. You can turn this nose into normal shape. I speak healing in this nose.'

The woman spoke in tongues at the same time. 'Shitake shisnande, ricnassed, bricandes,' she said as she laid her hands on Cameron's shoulder.

Pastor Nick left to talk to some people who were waiting for his attention.

After talking and praying to the congregation, Pastor Nick announced, 'We'd like to invite everybody to our usual morning tea.'

Jerry approached Cameron after the elders finished praying for him.

'Hi. What are you up to today?' Jerry asked.

'Going home to sleep as I was up all night,' Cameron answered, combing his fingers through his hair.

'Fair enough, but I'd like you to have this though,' Jerry said, offering the red-covered Bible to Cameron. 'There is a leaflet there on how to start and how to read it, but for me I start on the Book of John first.'

'Cool. Thanks,' Cameron said as he grabbed the Bible from Jerry.

'See you at school tomorrow then. We have a youth group meeting every Wednesday. Come, you might like it,' Jerry said as he waved goodbye.

'I'm just going to catch up with Karen. Are you okay here?' Lora asked, waving her hand to Karen in the distance.

Tara and Liam walked over to Cameron.

'What are you doing after church? Do you want to come with us to watch some videos or play guitar? I heard from the music class that you can play guitar,' Liam said, as he shot Tara a look as if to say: I did what you want me to do. I've asked him.

'As I told Jerry, I'm going home to sleep. Maybe next time,' Cameron said, covering his nose.

'Okay, next time then,' Tara replied, as a hint of disappointment crossed her face, then she approached Jerry.

'Jerry, are you coming with us?' she asked.

'No, Tara. I'm going to see Ashley soon,' Jerry replied.

'Okay. See you guys later,' Liam and Tara said in unison.

Cameron turned his eyes on Tara the moment she turned her back, and he watched her as she walked away. As she came out of the church, he saw them with Karen in the big black Holden truck. Cameron felt miserable to see Tara upset for him not accepting her invitation, but he felt that he had made a commitment today to put God first. 'I'm sorry, Tara. One day you'll understand,' Cameron whispered to himself.

After catching up and having a cup of tea, Lora found Cameron sitting in the pew by himself after everyone had left. She sat beside him and patted his knee. 'Okay. What do you want to do? As I promised I'll take you to the movie or the bowling alley in Richmond.'

'I just want to go home and catch up on my sleep.'

'Okay, home it is. I thought you wanted to hang out with Jerry and Tara.'

'Can we go home now please?'

'So, what are you going to do at home? Don't you want to even go to the flea market?'

'No, I want to read this today,' Cameron said, raising the Bible in the air.

'Oh, okay, great.' Lora shook her head in disbelief.

James had texted Lora: *I will not be home for tea as Melissa has invited me to go to McDonald's.*

Driving along, Lora felt Cameron wanted some space after being in the large crowd in church. Lora said, 'I don't think you'd want to come with us to the supermarket, so I'll drop you home first. Do you need anything? What do you want for dinner?' There was no answer. 'Hello? Okay, since you're not answering I'll make spaghetti Bolognese for tea.'

'Oh, sorry, mom. Just get me some toothpaste and a deodorant,' Cameron said as he stepped out of the car and headed to the caravan.

***

'Okay, see you. I'll be back soon,' Lora said, waving her hand as she drove off.

Once Lora left, Cameron tidied up his folding bed. He looked at his phone and was pleased to see it was only 12.30 pm. He opened the awning of the caravan and sat on the folding bed with pillows behind him leaning on the back with the Bible in his hand. He faced the calm ocean with the sun glaring off the water. There was a cool breeze occasionally that almost compensated for the scorching heat of the sun. The sound of kids laughing and playing echoed from the distance. Oblivious to the smell of meat on a nearby barbecue, Cameron began reading the Bible.

When Lora arrived back, she hurriedly cooked the spaghetti and left for her 3-11 pm shift at the Golden Age Rest home, which was a ten-minute drive from the caravan site.

Steven poked his head through the awning. 'Oh, you're home. Do you want to go fishing later?'

Engrossed in reading the Bible, Cameron didn't answer and continue reading loudly from 14:11-16 King James Version (KJV).

Believe me that I am in the Father, and the Father in me: or else believe me for the very works' sake. Verily, verily, I say unto you, He that believeth on me, the works that I do shall he do also; and greater works than these shall he do, because I go unto my Father. And whatsoever ye shall ask in my name, that will I do, that the Father may be glorified in the Son. If ye shall ask any thing in my name, I will do it. If ye love me, keep my commandments. And I will pray the Father, and he shall give you another Comforter, that he may abide with you forever—

'Dad, you see as it is written. If you ask in my name it will be given to you. You've been battling with your addiction to alcohol for ages. God could help if you asked,' Cameron said, as he closed the Bible.

Guilt flashed over Steven's face, and he swallowed hard. 'Yes, Cameron. Been there and done that.' He paused. 'If you don't want to go fishing with me later, I think I'd rather work as I need it to pay for the lawyer.' Steven took a towel from the drawer and left the caravan to take a shower, then headed for work.

Cameron wondered each time he opened the Bible about the page on Samuel. So, he read about King David and became captivated. He finished reading the Book of Samuel. His perception of King David after reading Samuel took on a new meaning compared to when he used to attend Sunday School at church. Later he wondered why the pages kept turning around the verses of dream and vision; Joel 2:28: And it shall come to pass afterward, that I will pour out my Spirit on all flesh; your sons and your daughters shall prophesy, your old men shall dream dreams, and your young men shall see visions. Numbers 12:6: And he said, 'Hear my words: If there is a prophet among you, I the LORD make myself known to him in a vision; I speak with him in a dream.' Cameron meditated with these words; his growing beginner faith led him to question whether his hallucination was a message from God.

Stinking of cannabis and with red tired eyes, James came home at 9:30 pm.

As he spoke, James's voice was slow and sing song. 'I've got you a Big Mac and your favorite, apple pie. I've bought one for you and me, and can't wait to eat with you, just like old times, when we were in San Diego.'

Cameron's heart sunk. His former perception of James being a normal loving brother, son, and just a typical student changed. This time Cameron looked in James's eyes and, as if he could read the message there: I'm lost, help me. 'Can I pray for you, James?'

James giggled in a combination of surprise and disappointment. 'Whoa. Don't tell me you just went to church today and now you're a preacher? Seriously, you're too young for that career. Leave it to someone who can't get a real day job, mate.'

'I'm not hungry,' Cameron said his eyes on the Bible as he continued to read.

'Okay, I won't hold it against you. I won't feel offended … No in fact, I'm pissed. I looked forward for you and I looking at the sunset. I hope this is only one of your fetishes like the aquarium, fishing, guitar, Tae Kwando, and the sling shot. I know you'll grow out of it. Jeez, you are high maintenance. Just as well mom was loaded back then. But who cares, I get to eat all of this then, thank you very much,' James said, as he opened the paper bag and pulled out the Big Mac. He made himself comfortable with a pillow behind his back as he sat facing the ocean; marvelling at the sun sinking on the horizon in an orange-painted sky. Thinking back on what he said to Cameron, it pleased him that he hadn't mentioned Hollie as one obsession as well. If he did, Cameron would probably have never spoken to him again.

James continued to waffle on. 'Wow, this is heaven. I had an awesome time with Melissa. He stared captivated by the view of the sunset while eating the two hamburgers. 'I'm going to ask Melissa to the school formal. I think she's into me,' James said as he swallowed the last bite of hamburger.

Absorbed in reading the Bible, Cameron didn't answer. He continued to read until dark. As James fell asleep talking, he slid down on to lying position. Cameron turned the lights on and zipped the awning closed. At 10.30 pm, he rested his eyes but didn't sleep because he wanted to continue reading. His eyes felt heavy and he dozed off.

At 11:15 pm, Lora arrived home. She felt contented to see that her sons were sound asleep, safe in bed. On the floor, she picked up the McDonalds wrappers. Even thought it was hot, she put a blanket over her sons, watching them. Seeing Cameron clutching the Bible pleased her and looking up, she thanked God. But on the other hand, it worried her that James smelt of cannabis. With a huge sigh, she prayed as she placed a hand on James's forehead. At midnight, she went to bed reading a text from Steven: Won't be home until midday.

At 3 am, Cameron got up. He turned the light on waking Lora. 'Mom, we have to pray for dad and James'.

Half asleep Lora responded, 'Okay, sweetheart, let's pray.' She poked her head out the door. She was stunned to see Cameron's red eyes, but she was so tired she went back to bed.

'Get down here, mom,' Cameron said as he laid his hand on James's forehead. 'Oh, heavenly father, I pray for my brother as you say in your word if there is one…' Cameron wasn't able to finish his prayer.

James pushed Cameron's hands away. 'What… what's going on? You're a dick. This is weird. You went to church this morning and it seems you've been instantly brainwashed. It takes many years for a cult to brainwash people. Jeez, there must be something else. It could be something you've eaten. Mom, help, Cameron is going crazy,' James yelled, raising his hands in protest.

'James, you've got to believe me. You need to be saved otherwise you won't go to heaven,' Cameron said.

'Get off my back. I've got school tomorrow. Get away from me. Let me go back to sleep, you dickhead,' James said, covering his face with the blanket.

Exhausted, Lora blinked many times in confusion. 'It's three am, Cameron, and you both need some more sleep for school. God will understand if you don't pray for James now, love.'

'But I'm so hungry, mom. I've not eaten since breakfast,' Cameron said, rubbing his stomach.

'Oh my goodness. Not since breakfast. No wonder you're acting like that. Ok, no one touched the spaghetti so you can have it all, Lora said, stepping into the caravan.

Cameron ate all of the spaghetti letting out a big burp afterwards.

The next minute there was someone trying to unzip the awning.

'Who is that?' Lora asked.

Whoever was trying to open the awning wouldn't answer and continued to zip it open, then stopped.

Cameron took his slingshot from his backpack. Anxiously he stood by the awning aiming, ready to hit if anyone who entered the caravan. Thinking it could be the gang, Cameron's heart raced like an athlete on the track field, racing to the finish line.

Holding a baseball bat, James hid under the bed and wondered if someone had been observing them and knew about the money in the safe.

'Mom, dial 111,' Cameron said softly.

Lora put the knife down on the folding bed. She was about to dial but the zipper of caravan opened, and Steven emerged.

'What the hell? A baseball bat and the bloody slingshot. What for?'

'Well, why didn't you answer when I asked who you were?' Lora asked, raising her hands.

'Oh, my mouth was full of mussels, and I thought you would know it was me. Here, try some. They're real nice,' Steven said, handing her the plastic container of mussels.

'You scared the living day light of us, 'James said, grabbing the container of mussels from Lora and putting one mussel after another in his mouth. 'Mmm.'

'Why you didn't you text me that you would be home early? I thought you were doing over time? Lora asked as she stepped back into the caravan.

'My phone went flat, and they ran out of fish, so we got sent home early,' Steven said, holding out his palms.

'I'm tired. We have school tomorrow. Good night,' Cameron said, burying his head in the pillow, dropping off to sleep in a second.

James and Steven shot each other a look as if to say was Cameron alright?

Lora whispered, 'We'll talk about it tomorrow. Good night.'

Chapter 27

February 28, 8:00 am.

It was cloudy, but the temperature was 15 degrees with a gentle wind.

Rushing to make peanut butter on toast for breakfast, Lora yelled 'Wakey, wakey, love. You've got half an hour to get ready.' The smell of toast was in the air and made it feel homey.

At 8:30 am, Cameron and James got ready for school. Their eyes were puffy, and their uncombed hair was still wet after showering.

On their way they ate their breakfast which included a chocolate milk shake in a tetra pack. Wearing a red old Levi's T-shirt and blue jeans, she said, 'Comb your hair. The hairbrush is in the glove box.'

James sat in the passenger side while Cameron sat in the back. 'Cameron is fast asleep, Mom. What happened to him?' James asked as he combed his tangled hair.

'Good for him. Don't wake him up they say a power nap is better that a long nights' sleep. There is a deodorant I bought for Cameron in the glove box if you want to use it,' Lora said, drumming her fingers on the steering wheel.

'Don't change the subject, Mom. Why did Cameron wake us up at three am as if he was going crazy? Is he goanna be alright?' James asked, putting the comb back, then grabbing the deodorant.

'Cameron isn't going crazy. That is the work of the holy spirit and Cameron will be more than fine now as he has accepted the Lord as his saviour,' Lora said, driving into the roundabout.

'I hope the Holy Spirit does not work on him at three in the morning,' James said, opening and closing the glove compartment.

'Actually, I'm not worried about Cameron. I'm more worried about you. Last night I smelled weed on you. I'm disappointed son,' Lora said as she stopped the car in the school car park. She was aware that her sons knew that she used to smoke weed. She felt like a hypocrite, but she had to tell James that it wasn't okay to smoke weed.

James didn't answer as embarrassment spread over his face. He knew that Lora had not smoked cannabis since she had become a Christian.

'Cameron, wake up, love. We're at school. Can you pass the deodorant to Cameron?' Lora asked.

Cameron woke. 'That's my deodorant I smell.'

'It's ours now. Mom said I could use it,' James said, passing what was left of the toast, the milkshake, and the deodorant to Cameron.

As they stepped out of the car, they hung their backpacks over their shoulders. Cameron applied the deodorant under his armpits. Then he handed it back to Lora.

'I didn't have time to make your lunches. Do you have some money to buy lunch?'

'No, I left all my money in the caravan, Mom,' James said.

'Me too,' Cameron added.

'I hope you put it in the safe,' Lora said.

'Yes, we did,' Cameron and James said at the same time

'Okay, get yourself some lunch,' Lora said, handing them ten dollars each.

'Thanks, mom, love you,' James and Cameron said as they waved good-bye.

In the distance, Cameron saw Brice and Kirk laughing and passing a rugby ball.

***

At 10.30, after morning tea break, the temperature had risen to a roasting 26 degrees, but there was a cool breeze just enough to be refreshing.

In English literature class Cameron sat beside Liam. Sitting behind Cameron was Brice and Kirk. In front of Cameron, Tara sat in the second row with Shantel, Azoma, Ashley and Jerry.

After roll call and everybody was accounted for, Mrs Rundle looked at the students. 'Good morning, class. I've marked all your homework from the book I'd assigned you to read.' She gave the papers back to each of the students.

The minute Mrs Rundle turned her back, Brice signalled Kirk as if to say to do it now. Out of the blue, Kirk took his wet middle finger, full of saliva, and spun it hard into Cameron's ear.

Although Cameron felt disgusted and humiliated, he did not respond. Words from the Bible that he had read last night reminded him to turn the other cheek.

Liam appeared disgusted at what he saw.

Kirk punched Liam on his shoulder almost tipping him out of his chair. Some students watched but didn't react, used to his typical fooling around.

Jerry and Ashley, who usually stopped Kirk and Brice's bullying, were not aware of what happened. And the students who did see it, wouldn't say anything for fear of Kirk's and Brice's intimidation.

Cameron prayed quietly. 'Oh God, gave me patience right bloody now.' The words "pray for your enemy" and "blessed them from the Bible" kept flashing through his mind. Secretly he prayed for Kirk. *Oh God, please forgive Kirk for he does not know what he is doing*. Cameron felt conflicted that his prayers weren't doing anything, and he felt sick. Normally, Cameron would have given Kirk a thump on his head. But after reading the Bible, and when he remembered back to San Diego, where he'd knocked Cullum unconscious and was kicked out of school, Cameron backed off. For the whole period his mind mentally battled and he commanded himself not to retaliate, but a part of him wanted to beat Kirk to death. He imagined Kirk dead, his head cut off and bleeding in front of the class.

Mrs Rundle finished handing out the graded homework assignments. 'Where is your homework, Cameron?' she asked.

'I beg your pardon, Mrs Rundle,' Cameron said, shaking his head.

'Have you completed your homework, Cameron?' she asked again,

'Oh, I'm sorry, Mrs Rundle. I was up all night reading the Bible. I'd forgotten all about the homework.' He wiped a bead of sweat from his forehead and rubbed it on his shorts.

Once the class heard what Cameron said, laughter thundered around the room.

Mrs Rundle clapped her hands twice forcefully. 'Quiet, everybody. Okay, Cameron. I'll give you another two days to finish your homework considering you started late this school term.'

Hair glistening with gel, Brice stood and glared in irritation. 'Because you know Mrs Rundle is churchy, you are using the Bible as an excuse. Oh, what a lot of codswallop,' he said, folding his arms defiantly.

'Brice, sit down and mind your own business,' Mrs Rundle said, placing her hands on her hips.

From English class and up to fourth period, Cameron's mind was blank. Nothing sunk in from the lectures. When the lunch time bell rung, he didn't notice it as the episodes of bullying dominated his thoughts.

In the blistering sun, students played rugby and football, their shouts and laugher echoing in the air.

As usual Ashley and Jerry sat across from James.

'We bought extra fish and chips to share,' Jerry said, opening the cream-colored wrapping paper

'Yeah, we noticed you didn't have anything for lunch,' Ashley said, digging into the fish and chips.

'Thank you so much. It's smells great,' James said as he grabbed the biggest bit of fish.

'The formal is in November,' Ashley said. 'Are you guys going? I bumped into Melissa; we got talking. She's into sewing like me. So, we are going to get together one day to look for some material for our dresses. I can hardly wait,' Ashley said as she cocked her head to the side.

Jerry opened the tomato sauce sachet and dipped a chip in it. 'That's cool. Brice will be taking her to the formal, so I heard. Their parents know each other, and both are in real estate. He's a mega property developer and both are loaded. Melissa's dad was on the news. He bought a huge block of land worth millions of dollars. That was sold by a real estate agent, your aunty Beth, Brice and Azoma's mom. I don't think she'll hang out with us cos we're budget,' Jerry said, scratching the back of his head.

'Budget? What does that mean?' James asked, frowning.

Ashley giggled girlishly putting her fingers over her lips. 'Budget means you're hard up.' She paused. 'You retard,' she added jokingly.

James's heart plunged after hearing what Jerry said. He felt cheated and humiliated. His eyes blinked, trying to control the tears as he was about to announce that the hottest girl in school had asked him to be her date.

Cameron sat quietly, to upset to talk, knowing James was so thrilled about last night when he told him that Melissa had asked him to be her date. This upset him even more hearing what Jerry said as he felt pity for his brother.

James and Cameron sat listening to Jerry and Ashley, laughing at each other's jokes and putting on a big act as if they were okay. The bell rang and they raced to demolish the fish and chips, then ran to their next class. Cameron tried to catch up to James who was walking along the corridor.

'Are you okay?' Cameron asked anxiously.

'I'm okay. I'll catch up with you later. Mom is picking me up at 2:30 as I have a job interview at the supermarket, so you'll be walking home on your own,' James said, waving goodbye, heartache written all over his face.

After Math, in the passageway to the music room, Cameron saw Ashley.

'You look dazed. Are you okay? Would you like to hang out at Jerry's?' Ashley asked as she stopped next to the lockers.

'Oh cool. I'll text you later to let you know. I've got to go to music class now.' Heading to the music room, and out of the corner of his eye, Cameron noticed Tara had entered the music room. He hesitated.

***

In the music room, there were rows of keyboards, and a grand piano at each end of the room. In the corner were stands with guitars and banjos and on the shelves were music books. There were three people in the room: a girl with a green Koru necklace, a boy with a mole on his eyebrow and a chubby girl with green-streaked hair. They were playing the keyboards and flutes. Trying to strum the guitar with a music book in front of her was Tara.

'Hi, how's it going?' Cameron asked.

Tara begun to strum. 'This is my second practice,' she replied.

Cameron focused on tuning his guitar.

Feeling ignored at trying to get Cameron's attention, she strummed the guitar harder. Abruptly the number six string snapped. To replace the string Tara went to the shelf. She was confused which replacement string she need-ed.

Noticing Tara was having difficulty, Cameron walked up to Tara, 'Can I help you?' A scent of sweet spice sent heat through Cameron.

Tara turned around and retied her hair. 'Please, I don't know which one to pick. They look almost the same to me.' Facing Cameron, she could feel the heat between them. A burst of excitement aroused her, as she inhaled Cameron's manly scent.

Tara's beauty became more distinct. He stared at her sweet smile, her high cheekbones, and flawless pale skin. Her blue greyish eyes captivated Cameron. With ease, Cameron chose the right string. 'This is the number six string,' Cameron said as he opened the packet. 'Do you know how to change it?'

'No. Can you please show me?'

'Okay,' Cameron replied as he set the guitar onto Tara's lap.

'Pull that peg out,' Cameron said, pointing to the black peg where the guitar string was attached. It was too hard for Tara to pull. 'I'll help you,' he said, pulling the peg out.

Tara's heart flickered as she felt the warmth of Cameron's muscly hand.

'Hold on to the string and thread it through the tuning peg,' Cameron said as he passed the string to Tara's fingers.

'Yip, okay,' Tara said, trying to thread the guitar but her finger was shaking.

Cameron looked in Tara's eyes with passion, and he guided her finger to pass the string through the peg hole.

Their eyes locked. Instinctively they wanted to kiss one another.

Tara closed her eyes, but Cameron held back. *I can't have you. You don't deserve to be mixed up in my complicated world,* he thought. He pulled away.

Tara opened her eyes, hurt spread over her face. Blushing she said. 'Okay, now I know how to do it. Thanks.'

'Can I ask you a personal question?' Cameron asked.

'It depends... Okay, fire ahead.'

'You and Brice. Are you two still an item?'

'Nope, not anymore...' she was about to explain further but the teacher entered the room.

'Okay, guys, if you have any problems, let me know,' the teacher said as she sat on the chair facing the computer.

Cameron and Tara carried on with their lessons.

In half an hour, the home time bell rang.

Tara put her blue guitar in the case, then approached Cameron. 'Thanks for helping me change the string.'

Cameron couldn't hide his feelings anymore seeing Tara's glum eyes. 'That's alright, but would you go out with me this weekend for lunch at Silvanus café at the marina and a movie after?'

Tara's eyes glistened with surprise. 'Yes, see ya, bye,' Tara said her heart full of anticipation. Along the corridor she headed towards the car park. Although it was only a brief encounter with Cameron, Tara began to savour the thought of being close to him. She reminisced in his scent, his strong hands and her body with just a short distance between them. She stopped at her locker and closed her eyes, taking a long deep breath imagining the date this weekend. While her eyes were closed, suddenly someone kissed her. She wished it was Cameron, but when she opened her eyes, she was appalled to see it was Brice. Out of the corner of her eye, she saw Cameron in the distance, and he seemed to be shaking his head. Tara assumed that Cameron saw Brice kiss her. She felt disheartened with herself for not telling Cameron that she hadn't finished the relationship with Brice. And now how could she gain Cameron's trust and be close to him after what he had witnessed?

Brice tried to put his arms around her. 'What's wrong with you? Don't play hard to get. Melissa asked me if you want to come over to her place after school.'

'No, and for your information I don't want you in my life. Leave me alone,' Tara said pushing Brice's hand off her shoulder.

'Oh, my heart bleeds. Are you sure?' Brice said, fixing his eyes on Tara and giving her the spell of lust for him.

'Yes. Consider yourself dumped, Brice Lomar,' Tara said. She ran to the car park. Karen's truck pulled up, and Tara jumped into the passenger's seat.

'Hi, chickadee. How was school today?' Karen asked, kissing Tara on the forehead.

Brice had taken off scheming to put a spell on Tara next time hoping she would be weak and under the influence of drugs or alcohol. He was disappointed that the spell of lust didn't affect her thinking and that Cameron had something to do with it, and his hatred for Cameron deepened.

Chapter 28

Along the hallway, Cameron remembered his dad urinating in public. That cost him a $200 NZD fine, and he didn't want to do the same thing. In case, he felts the urge to urinate on his way home, as it was a half an hour walk, Cameron decided to go to the toilet. Moving towards the toilets, he heard footsteps. He felt someone was following him. As he turned his head, he noticed two students that were in his class. Tom Manning, who had a blue stud earring, and Scott Ellery had ginger hair. They were the same size and as tall as him. When Cameron entered the toilets, the two students grabbed and held his arms tightly pinning him on the wall beside the mirror.

Astounded Cameron prayed to God to give him patience not to fight back. Calmly Cameron said, 'If you want my lunch money, I have eight dollars in my pocket.'

Tom and Scott shot each other a look, chuckling as if to say "Really, how-dumb." They chuckled nailing him harder to the wall.

Kirk entered the toilets and carried a thick pen in his hand. He pushed Cameron's hair away from his forehead and wrote in capital letters SON OF THE PEDOPHILE in the middle of his forehead. Kirk was about to give Cameron an uppercut. Suddenly, Jerry appeared. They quickly let Cameron go and Tom ran off. Kirk tried to punch Jerry in the head, but Jerry ducked.

With adrenalin rushing Jerry's hand curled into a fist and he ploughed a punch into Kirk's left eye. Staggering, Kirk took off. Scott tried to kick Jerry. Cameron kicked him in the groin. Stumbling on the floor for a second, Scott left holding his groin in agony.

As Jerry read the words written on Cameron's forehead, his heart sank with pity. He pulled out his handkerchief and rubbed the words off Cameron's forehead using some soap from the dispenser. 'Just as well I heard them talking about you on my way out. I came to check when I saw them go into the toilets.'

'Thanks, mate. That was God's will,' Cameron said, as he tried to grab some paper from the holder to help Jerry.

Jerry pushed Cameron away from the mirror to stop him from seeing what had been written on his forehead. Jerry scrubbed it away quickly before he could read it.

'Can you sit on the sink so I can scrub it good, you're much taller than me.' Jerry said, holding on to the wet handkerchief.

'Okay, shorty… just kidding,' Cameron said, holding his hair back from his forehead.

Jerry smiled as he knew it was a term of endearment, and he felt sorry for Cameron knowing what is written on his forehead.

As Jerry continued to rub, Cameron's forehead started bleeding.

'I think that will do. Ouch!' Cameron blurted out, patting his head with a paper towel.

'Oh, I made it bleed,' Jerry said as he looked at his watch. 'It's 3;15. Got to go, mate. I have a dentist appointment. If I miss the appointment this time, Mom will have a heart attack.'

'Hey, buddy, thanks,' Cameron said an expression of gratitude on his face.

Since the words on Cameron's forehead were still readable, Jerry felt that he must tell Cameron. 'I hate to say this but the words on your forehead say, "son of the paedophile."' Jerry paused lowering his eyebrows. 'Come around. I'll text you when I'm done,' Jerry said, waving goodbye.

Once Jerry left Cameron, he looked in the mirror at his forehead. 'Oh, God. Why didn't you stop them from doing this? Are you for real?' He struggled to stop thinking of getting even with Kirk. This time he pictured that he was strangling Kirk; Kirk's face was blue, and his tongue and eyes were hanging out, he was dead. Leaving the toilets, Cameron headed for the long walk home. He decided to take a short cut at Redwood Lane along the kiwifruit orchard. The smell of the grass and the perfume of the flowers in bloom were in the air. Cameron's mind was like an agitating washing machine, recalling what had happened. After seeing Tara and Brice kissing, he swallowed hard and clenched his teeth with this thought. *I cannot see the sense of this. I thought accepting Jesus was the answer, but this is like hell for me. Why God?* As he turned around, he saw the Ford slowly cruise by him. 'Oh, thank God,' Cameron muttered. With relief, he realized that it was only in his mind that this car had been following him for the last week.

Feeling hungry, Cameron walked briskly. Then suddenly he saw Brice, Kirk, Tom and Scott who had ambushed him in the toilets. They were smoking cannabis, passing a joint to one another. Cameron's adrenalin spiked. He was tempted to use the slingshot, but God told him not to. They came charging towards him. He thought he could go to a nearby house and people would help him. Running for his life, Cameron took off, but Tom and Scott caught up to him. They tackled him and pinned him against one of the posts of the kiwifruit vines. He tried to free himself, but they were stronger and he gave up the struggle. Brice and Kirk stood in front of him lighting a big fat joint. *What is the point of this is if they just want to beat me up?* he thought.

Brice glared with such hatred and jealousy that Cameron felt it was like a sword slashing into his body.

'I think you need this before we kill you,' Brice said, smoking the joint. Pushing up Cameron's hair and reading what was written on it, Brice smirked. 'Well done, Kirk, mate.' Holding the joint and blowing smoke into Cameron's face, he continued. 'Hmm, I think you'll like this, Cameron. I know you've been hanging out for this since you arrived. I bet, so here it is cousie, bro.' Then he blew more smoke in Cameron's face.

Cameron thought he would go with the flow as he couldn't see the point of struggling. But he wondered why they had to subdue him. High on cannabis, he couldn't have cared less if he lived or died.

Brice grinned in wicked enjoyment at seeing Cameron's vulnerability. Brice thought if he was high on weed, he'd lose this fight for sure. 'Okay, I'll give you a fair fight, one on one. Kirk, are you ready for this? Show us your black belt moves. Let go of him, guys,' Brice commanded, rubbing his knuckles. Promptly Scott and Tom released Cameron.

Brice stood between Cameron and Kirk. He was self–assured knowing Cameron had never been a cheat for as long as he had known him. 'All right then, Cameron. Kirk, are you ready? With a knuckle bump, Kirk and Cameron nodded.

Despite being high on cannabis Cameron's wit remained. For a moment he thought Brice had always cheated at Monopoly, card games, and short-changed him. And accusing his mom of stealing Nana Mollie's jewellery when he had been the one who stole it. He suspected that this would not be a fair fight. His faith told him to forget about turning the other cheek; an eye for an eye was a stronger message.

To initiate the fight Brice said, 'On count of three. One...'

Cameron wasted no time and abruptly gave Kirk a flying kick, damaging his right eye and adding to the black eye from Jerry's previous punch. He staggered in hellish pain, and he couldn't strike back. Elated at seeing Kirk struggling, *Oh, God I'm sorry. I know I will get beaten up regardless, so I hit first. Please forgive me*. Cameron prayed inwardly.

Brice raised his hand shaking it in disbelief. 'Oops, I didn't see that coming. No more Mr. Nice Guy.' He gestured to Scott and Tom to grab Cameron again and hold his arms. Without a beat, Kirk gave Cameron a huge upper cut, his fist colliding with his jaw and nose.

Cameron fell to the ground unconscious, his nose bleeding profusely.

'Stomp him to death,' Brice said, pointing to Cameron.

Kirk grimaced. 'No, it's not meant to be like this.'

Brice blinked. 'What's the matter with you?

The two of them stood watching Cameron, unsure of what to do.

'If you won't, I will.' Brice was about to stomp on Cameron, but out of nowhere the blaring sound of a car screeching interrupted Brice. They noticed a Ford truck coming toward them and instinctively they fled, leaving Cameron lying on the ground.

Chapter 29

Cameron woke. He looked at his cell phone, 4:30 pm. He rose to his feet and made his way home along the line of box hedges and houses with beautiful gardens. Clotted blood covered the front of his shirt and his face. His mind was packed with questions: Did they leave me thinking I was dead? If I played dead, why did I not get up as soon as they left? It had been over an hour since they'd left. Had I fallen asleep? Did I fall unconscious? Feeling elated Cameron wondered whether he was still high. *I guess I am and that's why I couldn't feel any pain from the blow to my nose and jaw.*

In the distance, although the sun was glaring in his eyes, he spotted a dairy. Feeling hungry, he entered the store. 'Can I have two scoops of hokey pokey ice cream please and a ginger beer?' Cameron requested, wiping the beads of sweat from his forehead.

'That's eight dollars, please,' the man with a full beard said as he handed the drink and ice cream to him.

'Thanks. That's great. How did you know I only had eight dollars, and where is that accent from? I can't place it,' Cameron said.

The seller didn't answer his question, but said, 'We have a free bin of second-hand books, ornaments and clothes if you want to change your T-shirt.' The man stared at Cameron's T-shirt, which was covered with blood. He gave Cameron a wet wipe and gestured to wipe the blood off his nose and cheek.

'Thank you very much. God bless you, sir,' Cameron said as he grabbed it wiping his nose and cheeks quickly.

Cameron glanced at the display counter, which had an array of chocolate, candy and nuts.

The seller noticed Cameron had his eyes on the Milky Way chocolate bar. Instantly the man gave it to Cameron. 'Actually, you can have it has it expires today. April 2008.'

Cameron frowned. 'It's only March. It hasn't expired yet.'

'You can have it anyway,' the man said.

'I've been craving for these. Thanks a lot, sir,' Cameron said, biting a big chunk out of the Milky Way.

On the other side of the counter was a grocery shelf and behind it was a mirror. Between a gap in the cans, Cameron caught a glimpse of himself in the mirror. It surprised him to see his nose was back to normal. Cameron set the ginger beer and the ice cream on top of the counter. He took a yellow Wilson t-shirt, which was hanging out of the bin. Then he took off his old T-shirt and put the Wilson T-shirt on. There were all sorts of things in the bin: a flower vase, elephants, birds, teddy bears.

An ancient looking Bible caught his attention and he wondered why it was in the free bin. He picked it up and as he was putting it in his backpack, a shepherd slingshot and leather cuff dropped onto his shoes. He assumed these had been in the Bible. He picked them up and put the slingshot in the backpack and slipped the leather cuff on his wrist. 'Hmm, this looks cool,' Cameron said, admiring the lion logo in the middle of the cuff, which had an interlacing design curbed along the edges of it. 'Thank you, sir, again,' Cameron said, grabbing the ice cream, soda and then his backpack off the floor.

As he continued to walk home, feeling humiliated at the words "Son of the Paedophile" written on his forehead, he felt he was losing his faith. It was as if the sky had fallen in remembering Jesus and the thorny crown that had been wrapped around his forehead. *My saviour suffered humiliation too. Why can't I?* This reminded him to keep the faith. Some of his memory started to return. Cameron recalled Kirk tried to stop Brice from stomping on his face. Kirk had given his nose a good punch, which had exploded the abscess on it. This must be a God thing, Cameron reckoned, believing when he prayed for Kirk to forgive him. As a result, he hadn't followed Brice's evil plot to kill him.

However, Cameron felt disheartened, recalling how Brice had kissed Tara while her eyes were closed after she had told him that she had broken up with Brice. Watching Tara sing in church and praying so pure and honest, he had put her on a pedestal, but it was all a lie. This made him think more of Hollie. Although she had been a prostitute, she had been upfront with it. Cameron realized since he had become a Christian why Hollie hadn't wanted him to sleep with her until they got married. More than ever Cameron missed Hollie as he compared her to Tara. He felt like shouting Hollie's name, but he didn't as there were people coming.

Chapter 30

3 March 2008, 9 pm

After drinking and smoking weed with another group of friends, Brice left for the monthly meeting of the Scorpion Venom Gang (SVG). As soon as Brice entered the lounge the scent of alcohol and weed on him filtered through the living room. The chandelier chimed like music from the wind blowing. Azoma sat on the white regent couch with the computer on her lap. Spread around on top of the couch beside her was a US passport, credit cards, driver's license and some papers, which looked like receipts.

'Where is everybody my lovely, gorgeous little sis?' Brice asked

'The meeting has been cancelled,' Azoma said, her eyes glued in the computer.

'Why has it been called off?'

'They're in the cellar as the security guy caught a prowler'

Azoma cocked her head to the side. 'I was there but I left cos I'm not in the mood to see a guy being tortured.'

Brice stared in amazement as he couldn't believe what Azoma said as she always enjoyed something, or someone being tortured. Brice always re-membered when Azoma tortured a kitten hitting it with the golf club until the kitten had died. And when she pushed a migrant kid, she knew who couldn't swim into the water and watched her almost drown till someone came, and she pretended she had been trying to save her.

Speculating what this guy could look like as Azoma had a weak spot for older handsome guys, Brice's mood changed quickly. With his typical erratic mood, he switched from wonderful to obnoxious, thinking of the several men, young and old, Azoma slept with. His face flushed in anger and disgust. 'I'm bloody tired. Just tell me, don't mess me around. Give me the stuff about this guy.'

'Okay. You're being psycho again, stop it now. Our informant said that he's got a fake passport. His real name is Duane Dennett and is about thirty-eight-years-old, a suspect on drug trafficking, aggravated robbery, fraud and three murders. He is a member of The Red Serpent gang from San Diego, and he's a hit man.' Azoma's eyes gleamed in anticipation of what she could do to him later, thinking of Duane's physical attributes.

'So, what do you think he's here for?' Brice asked.

'They're down in the cellar so you can find out yourself and take this computer.' Azoma inserted Duane's stuff in the computer bag before closing it. 'Let them know what I've found.' She handed him the laptop.

Brice quickly told Azoma what had happened to Cameron, like it was just another day in the office.

Azoma rose to her feet. She smiled but the smile quickly faded when she thought that Brice would be edgy for not killing Cameron. 'Well done. Shame you didn't kill him, but we have members in the hospital that would finish him off.' Then she headed upstairs to contact the hacker so she could sleep with him to gather more information about Duane.

Brice stormed down to the basement. The cellar had the air conditioning on as Beth didn't want to sweat. Although the gang disagreed as the heat would torture Duane even more. Inside the basement the only sound was the faint noise of the traffic in the distance.

Sitting on the folding chair across from Duane was Beth in a black skirt, coat and white blouse. Guarding the interrogation was a gang member wearing a bandana and holding a baseball bat. Duane's hands and feet were tied with yellow nylon rope to the back of the chair.

Brice arrived with the laptop. Irritated with the musty odour of stale wine in the cellar, he rubbed his nose. Then he opened the laptop. 'Here read this,' Brice said, offering the laptop to Cedrick Granger.

After reading the screen, the forty-five-year-old, six-foot two-inch, medium built head of the SVG said, 'Now we know who you are.' He pointed a knife at Duane's face. 'Who sent you?'

Duane trembled and hesitated for a minute. There was no way out of this. For a moment he assumed his face was his asset for getting the most of what he wanted in life. Like when facing the jury, he believed his good looks helped. As Duane had learnt from the statistics that showed that the jury favoured the plaintiffs more if they were good-looking. So, fearing that his face would be slashed, Duane said, 'I was sent here by the Red Serpent Gang to kill Cameron Owen.' He drew a quick breath. 'And... this is his address.'

'And why do you want to kill him?' Cedrick asked, digging the knife deeper.

A droplet of blood rolled down Duane's chiselled nose 'They cannot afford to keep Cameron alive as he knows too much about the gang's activity,' Duane said, trembling.

Beth and Cedrick shot each other a look. Turning her head Beth gestured to the bandana guy. Soon they were next to the bar with racks of wine and wine glasses behind them and far enough away for Duane not to hear.

Beth stood by the granite bench, rubbing her neck. 'Well, I think we can use this guy. He's not a threat to us, but he is our ally.'

'And looking at the security camera he has not seen the lab. So, he isn't a danger to us. We have his passports so he can't leave the country,' Judd Morton, wearing a printed bandana said sitting across from Beth.

Cedric's eyes narrowed. 'Oh, you think you're so smart, dickhead. If you were watching the screen cautiously instead of watching Azoma,' he put his hand on his head, 'you would've caught this guy before he climbed over the fence.'

The bandana guy reddened, and looked at Beth, who shrugged.

'So, I hope you had some fun. Let's get on with the business. Okay, you can go back to your post.' Brice helped himself to a bottle of wine and sat beside Beth.

Beth updated him on the Will and assured him that using Duane to kill the Owens was a brilliant idea as she poured wine into Brice's glass.

Cedrick put his arms on Brice. 'Cameron is unconscious, but it was a good job for not using any of my boys to beat him up.' Cedrick gave Brice a firm handshake.

'It's only a warmup. Next time if he lives, he'll be in the box,' Brice said drinking the wine. Once Brice finished the wine, he left.

Beth, who was sitting on a bar stool, said to Cedric, 'Can we have a catch up since the gang meeting has been put on hold until the next week? We need to get rid of the Owens pronto.'

'I thought you only wanted to torture them as death is far too easy. I've got someone who can trash their caravan and steal their money to piss them off. And they won't have any money to pay for their lawyer. I decided that Duane should do it instead of my men, so it won't have a connection to us if he screws up,' Cedrick said.

'Yes, you can do that as well, but listen, the Owens' lawyer said he cannot release my parents' estate over to me as the document Shantell forged was not authentic.

'Which one?'

'The certificate of mental incapacity. He found out dad's GP did not generate this document at all,' Beth said as she poured another bottle of wine. In bitterness she consumed one mouthful after another.

Cedrick's eyebrows furrowed. 'How did he find out? The signature Shantell forged looked exactly like the GPs. I thought we'd sussed this out.'

'It was the date.' She slumped down on her stool. 'Shantell just put in any date, and I didn't double check as I was so amazed with the similarity of the forged signature.' Sighing in revulsion Beth continued, 'His lawyer said that his GP could not have signed the mental incapacity document at that time and date as the Health Centre was closed and had been set on fire the day before. It was on the local news that it was closed and apart from that-his GP was on holiday that week.' Beth huffed out an angry breath.

Cedric flushed in panic. 'So, if we can't prove that your dad wasn't of sound mind then the paper that you and Shantell falsely generate doesn't have a show of standing up in court,' he scratched his head, 'even if it was signed, sealed, and delivered by our legit lawyers.' He squinted. 'I'm afraid to say we're in dire straight'

'Yes, we're in deep,' Beth said, as her face hardened.

'It isn't fair that you've only got a box of old coins and Steven has the rest of their estate, after you looked after them,' Cedrick said.

Beth raised her hand in protest. 'Yes, tell me about it. What an asshole of a dad.' Her eyes narrowed. 'When I found out, instead of putting a pillow over his head to kill him I threatened that I would accuse him of molesting me when I was young.'

'That's real nasty, but it works even with celebrities nowadays. Look at Michael Jackson.' Cedrick stroked his finger against his cheek repeatedly. His eyebrows furrowed. 'Have you ever been molested by your dad?'

Beth licked her lip then bit the bottom lip. 'To be honest... no.' Her throat muscles tightened 'When I was young, I could not get the attention I wanted after Steven was born so I've accused dad, then later told the police it was a lie. Dad was cleared of this allegation, but his reputation was tarnished. He sold the accounting business and moved up here to Honi.'

'Quite frankly now I can see why you did not deserve an equal share of the estate, apart from the fact that you're only adopted. Your dad begrudged you for what you did.'

Beth clenched her hands into fists. She stood up and rolled up her sleeves. 'Whose side are you on?'

Cedrick put his arm around her. Cool down I'm on your side, darling.'

'You better bloody be. Remember it's all my idea to buy Rick's peanut butter jam factory to disguise your drug operation. We're doing well. It's almost six years and no one is suspicious.'

'I know, sweetheart. The wheeling, dealing and the connections and all your plans worked. And you're very clever, making your dad sign the will in your favour by threatening him.'

'But my dad was so shrewd changing the will a week before he overdosed on morphine, killing himself. But little did I know that Dad changed it again a week before he died giving all of the estate to Steven. Oh, I'm gonna puke. So, without the mental incapacity document to prove that Dad wasn't of sound mind when he made the second will, if the Owens win their case, we're in hot water. They have to be eliminated.'

'Let's get cracking as time is of the essence,' Cedrick responded.

Cedrick stroked his face. 'I thought that plan was so impeccable that the GP would believe that he signed the document, and the original was burnt.' His lips curled. 'We successfully made it look like the surgery fire was accident.'

'What a shame. It was almost a perfect crime. It's just because of the date. What an insult ' Beth shrugged.

'It is just a matter of time before they find out. So, if we rob the Owen's of their money, they can't pay the lawyer. It will give us more time to plan and make it look like an accident killed them.'

'Why don't you just buy them off?' Cedrick asked, looking down at Beth.

'With what? Our cash? As of now I'm having trouble trying to work out how I can put all the cash into a different business account. Knowing Steven and Lora, they're very street wise. I have no doubt they know the ins and out of money laundering. They will not buy into this.' She folded her arms in agitation. 'And this is personal, Cedrick… Steven is not getting this property. Period.'

'Yes, of course, darling. They can't have it after the renovation, with the value now 23 million. But keep in mind, you did that because of the money we get from the drug operations. You did very well paying the tradesmen and builder with cash,' Cedrick said.

Beth exploded with fury, screaming, 'Steven is not having any of this.' Her hand reached for a bottle, and she threw it against the cobblestoned wall, which made an ear-shattering noise. 'I hate him. The golden boy. creep!'

Quickly, Cedrick clutched her and held her hands, preventing her from throwing another bottle. 'Let's sit down.' Cedrick pointed to the bulky grey armless couch in the corner of the cellar. He poured her another glass of wine. 'Have another drink. There is no problem so bad that an expensive wine like this can't ease.'

After several glasses of wine, Beth had regained her composure.

'How do you feel now?' Cedrick asked his eyes penetrating her with desire. He kissed Beth, and one thing led to another, and they had quick sex. While putting their clothes back on, they heard footsteps.

'That must be Azoma. Good. We need to talk to her,' Cedrick said.

Cedrick couldn't take his eyes off Azoma. She had on a see-through thin lace top which showed her belly, and tight white jeans displaying the V-shape of her groin.

Cedrick explained to her that they would use Duane to trash the Owens place and make it look like a threat, and robbery with vandalism. 'If there are any witnesses, it won't be linked back to SVG.'

Beth rubbed her eyes and the back of her neck. 'Well, I'll leave it to you it then. I have to get some sleep. I've a big day tomorrow. See you guys,' she said, waving goodbye.

Beth headed to her bedroom, walking as though she hadn't noticed a light through a gap beneath the door of Brice bedroom from the bed side lamp. Brice was under the sheath naked, Beth cuddled into him.

Back in the cellar, Duane had overheard their conversation.

Azoma came in to see Duane. 'Untie him. I'll take care of the rest,' Azoma said.

Staring like an idiot, Judd said, 'Okay, lollipop, he's all yours,' as he untied Duane.

Chapter 31

March 4, 10 am.

Azoma had a sleepless night, frustrated as her seductive look and the spell of lust to Duane had not lured him into having sex with her. Although still feeling very tired, she woke up early to hunt for more information. She didn't trust Cedrick's men. She'd always thought they were thick, and assumed they'd not searched for Duane thoroughly. She sneaked into the guest room, while Duane snored with saliva dribbling from his mouth. Cautiously she tiptoed over to Duane's dirty clothes on the floor. She couldn't help but yearn to be in bed with him as she stared at Duane's roughly handsome square jaw, olive skin and solid muscly form. She shook all his clothes and found nothing. Then in the Fruit of the Loom jockey shorts, she could see something inside it. A revolting thought came to her. *Is it a blob of poo?* she wondered, cautiously lifting it up with two fingers. It was a cell phone. 'Bingo,' she muttered, watching Duane. She opened it slowly pressing "favorite." Duane groaned. She put the phone back carefully, then froze. Disappointed for not being able to copy the numbers, she memorised two of the names then tiptoed into the bathroom.

There was a knock on the door. Beth stood outside the bathroom. 'Azoma, get cracking. The guy from the pig farm will be at the gate in half an hour.'

Azoma stood up and grabbed a towel. 'Yes. I'll be there soon, mother.'

'Brice has gone to school. He's pissed off that you took his favorite T-shirt.'

'It was not his favorite, mother.'

'Well, it is now.'

'I've told the school you have an appointment with a counsellor in Nelson, remember, just in case they ask you why you're not at school. There's bacon and eggs in the warmer drawer for breakfast. I'm going. See you.'

After breakfast, Azoma outlined the plot of trashing the Owen's place with Duane. Azoma drove the Holden pickup, heading to the Thorp Pig Farm,

Duane stepped out of the passenger side. The smell of pig manure was horrendous, intensified by the heat of the sun. He cocked his head to the side, his ocean-blue eyes glared at Azoma with growing self-blame as to why she wouldn't stop hounding him. 'Why do you guys have to do this, huh? And to this extent? It doesn't make sense,' Duane grumbled as the wind hit his face with the pungent scent of urine.

Azoma remained sitting in the truck with her Oakley dark sunglasses on. 'Just hurry up. Be thankful. I've already organized it for you. Look,' Azoma said, pointing to a guy with a khaki hat, who was holding a wheelbarrow full of pig dung waiting at the gate. Azoma dug her hand into her pink Gucci handbag. 'Here, wear some gloves. You may need them and give that guy the two hundred bucks.' Duane grabbed it quickly and she closed her bag.

At 2:30 pm they arrived half an hour before Steven would be home from work. The heat of the sun increased. They pulled into the beach car park as planned. Noticing how calm Duane was, Azoma figured he was a professional and assumed he had done this before.

It took twenty minutes to trash the caravan and steal the money.

Half an hour later, Azoma's nerves were rattled. She stepped out of the truck and looked around cautiously. She peered back into the caravan, noticing Duane was looking in every pocket of the trousers.

'Hurry up. You've been in here for over ten minutes. Whatever you're looking for obviously is not here.' Quickly Azoma went inside and wrote something on the mirror using her red lipstick. Hearing a car engine coming, they took off hoping nobody had seen them leave the caravan.

***

Cameron sprinted towards the caravan, noticing Officer Daniel Fowlers was occupied taking notes while Steven gave information. Cameron felt ignored as if he was not even there as Steven and Lora continued to talk to Officer Fowlers. James sat outside the caravan on the folding chair, his face buried in his hands. Onlookers surrounded the caravan. Cameron wondered why no one had told him what had happened. As he ran inside the caravan, his heart pounded and he covered his nose to the unbearable smell of feces, which was smeared on the walls. Clothes and underwear hung out of opened drawers. He tiptoed sideways avoiding some globules of feces. On the floor was cutlery, a frying pan, plates, and the wide opened empty safe which looked like it had been dropped hard so it could be opened. Cameron felt his heart cut into pieces after seeing the broken fishing rods and guitars, parts thrown all over the caravan. Noticing the trousers on the floor, each pocket was inside out, and he became suspicious. *Were they after the notebook?* Then he checked the shot gun his uncle terry lent them--- it was not under the bed. As looked around. The word 'paedophile' was written in red lipstick on the mirror by the kitchen bench. Cameron took off feeling nauseous, then threw up in the bushes outside.

The thought of the gun being stolen, and that it might be used to kill his family terrified Cameron. 'Oh my God, help me,' he yelled.

Shocked, Cameron ran, not knowing what to do. He ran and kept running, finding himself on the beach far away from the caravan. Swaying with the strong wind along the shore were countless tall pine trees. The sun was setting in the orange and pink sky. Devastated, Cameron picked up a handful of stones and using his slingshot, shot the stones at the surface of the ocean, one after another. The stones skidded like little jet boats skimming across the water. He imagined that each stone was for Brice and the gang. He believed that the trashing of his house had been done to hurt his family. Cameron felt like a frightened little mouse that had been chased and tortured by a big fat black cat. He had nowhere to go. Exhausted and with no energy left to fire the last stone, Cameron dropped to his knees trembling. He cried out to God.

'God, where are you? If you are for real, help me. I'm sorry I put my family in danger. Brice, his mate, and the gang were after me. They want me dead. And they want to hurt my mom, Dad and James. I'm trying to be good. Help me God. I'll do anything for you to save my family. You said to ask for help and it would be given. Answer me please, please… now, God.'

Suddenly Cameron saw the tallest pine tree in the row begin dropping pinecones one by one. He saw the man in a white hoody put a stone into the pouch of a shepherd slingshot, swing it round and round, increasingly faster than release the stone and hit a pinecone accurately.

Awed, he stood staring. 'Oh God, that looks impressive, but I don't need entertainment right now.'

The man in the white hoody with the words "peace love and hope" on his T-shirt approached Cameron. 'Greetings, peace be unto thee Cameron Owen! God sent me. I'm King David. You've been reading about me. Well done,' he said, pulling the cowl of his hoody over his head. He appeared to be in his thirties, tall, muscular and with brown curly hair.

Cameron shook his head. *I must be dreaming this can't be real.* 'God sent you when I cried for help. Did God send you too when I kept getting lost? Are you my old friend?'

'Yes, but this time it's for a mission. You are chosen Cameron,' King David said.

Cameron's heart melted as King David's eyes were full of compassion. For the longest time, since he'd said goodbye to him, he hadn't felt a warm kindness. With his presence, Cameron's spirit lifted. He felt as if he'd been raised up from the dead. Looking up in the sky, he read: Save my people from harm and danger.

'With all due respect, does God really think I can do his mission? Surely, God has a good sense of humour.'

'Why me? I have nothing to offer but my problem. I'm the one who needs saving?' Cameron asked, putting up his palms.

'Because of your inherent extraordinary talent with the slingshot, and because God knows your heart, please accept God's mission in your heart,' King David said.

'B- but what about all my problems? God knows that for sure.'

'You've read about me, the conflicts of my life, and what I've been through. I empathized with you. I know what it's like being chased and having to go into hiding... but God still chose me to lead my people.'

'You've done great things; I've done nothing.'

'We would not understand how deep the mystery of God is. God does what pleases him,' King David said.

'So, it will please God if I accept what he asked me to do. But I don't think I can do this mission,' Cameron said. 'I couldn't save myself, let alone save the world. How could I?'

'With faith. God will give you supernatural powers. Do you accept the mission?'

Although, he trusted him, his mind was full of questions, hoping that it wasn't a dream. The thought of having supernatural powers to save his family and the people meant the world to him. Confused, his head said no, but his heart voted strongly to accept it. 'Yes sir, lord.' He knelt with eyes closed accepting the mission.

With a bottle of oil, King David anointed his hands, head, eyes and feet saying, 'I sanctify your eyes, head, hands and feet with the supernatural power. Repeat after me.'

Cameron followed. 'I am to use this power only for good and not for evil. Not for revenge, only to save. I will practice my power fervently with faith and prayers. And I will do everything I can to keep my supernatural power hidden. In God's name, Amen. But how will I go about it. When do I start?' Cameron asked.

'I will speak to you in visions, thoughts and dreams to help you discover how to practice your power, and the image of future danger. KEEP THE FAITH. Remember God's favour is in you,' King David said, giving him the sling-shot, putting the bracelet in his hand, then waving goodbye.

Chapter 32

Cameron couldn't open his eyes, but he could see a white shield over his face. 'Where am I?' He wanted to push the shield away, but his hand wouldn't move. There were many questions in his mind, but his mouth wouldn't open. *Am I in a coffin? Am I dead? What is going on here, God? I've accepted Jesus as my saviour. I should be in heaven with You. You promised. Why I am not with You?'*

Suddenly Cameron heard a booming voice. 'Because you're not dead, my son.'

Ecstatic, Cameron yelled, 'I'm alive, I'm alive.' Finding himself in bed, with a heart monitor connected to his finger, an IV line in his arm, nasal cannula, a curtain surrounding his bed. Once his eyes opened, he noticed James. 'James, slap me, so I can feel that I am alive.'

Overjoyed with excitement to see Cameron out of his coma, his face lit up. 'Okay,' James said with hesitation, giving him a little tap on his face.

'Harder, James. I can't feel that,' Cameron said, squinting.

'Okay, this time,' James said as he hit harder.

Suddenly Cameron went limp.

'Oh, no, no! I didn't mean to do that,' James said frantically.

Cameron opened his eyes again. 'Just kidding, James, I'm having you on.'

'Don't do that ever again, Cameron. It isn't funny,' James said, giving Cameron a big hug, adding an appreciative sigh of relief.

Lora rang the call bell at once, then held her hand to Cameron's cheek and cried with joy 'Thank, God.'

Steven held Cameron's other hand, speechless and also in tears.

Dr Gavin Finlay, who was in his thirties and wearing a light blue uniform with a stethoscope hanging around his neck, appeared. Holding a chart was a haggard, wrinkly nurse with a navy-blue uniform.

'Hi, I'm Gavin. You've been in a coma for the last three days. Someone found you on the beach under the pine trees. The witness said they left you at the kiwifruit patch. How did you end up on the beach? Can you remember what happened?' Dr Finlay asked with a Scottish accent.

Cameron hesitated. He wanted to tell him about the beating, but he didn't want to incriminate Kirk as he remembered him trying to stop Brice.

'I can't remember, sorry. Can I have something to eat?'

'Of course, you can. Please order some food from the kitchen,' Gavin requested of the nurse. 'While we wait for your food, can you tell me your name and address?'

Cameron's family stood proud and confident as they listened to Cameron answering all the questions correctly. After a sequence of routine questions to test for memory and confusion, Gavin gestured at Steven and Lora to meet them outside the curtain.

While James sat beside Cameron, he picked up the cannula to put it out of the way. He told him what had happened to the caravan. 'The worst thing is when Mom and Dad came home to pick up something while I looked after you, they found the caravan had been trashed and our money stolen.'

With a bitter smile Cameron said, 'Oh poor mom, how is Dad?'

'As you can see, relieved to see you conscious.'

'Do you know what time they found me?' Cameron asked as he rubbed his temple.

'After three days, a huge search party went looking for you. We were on the world news with headlines about *The slingshot guy from America, missing in New Zealand*. The investigation stopped after a confession from a witness. A guy on his way to go fishing found you. He's got a cool car - a blue Ford Maverick. Did you fall unconscious before you changed into your T shirt because it looks like you had a nosebleed?' James asked curiously.

Cameron figured out that he must have dreamt about the caravan and King David when he was unconscious. Feeling strange as James described how the caravan looked, it sounded just like it was in his dreams. And why had the Ford been following him, but no one had noticed. Had God sent the Ford to save him?

Brigit, a nurse with the orange hair, that Cameron and James had previously met, arrived with a tray of food and loitered as if she was eavesdropping.

Cameron waited till she was finally gone before continuing. 'What about Uncle Terry's shotgun?' Out of the corner of his eye he caught the heart monitor flashing the words "keep the faith". As he blinked, the words stopped flashing. He wondered whether he should mention this to the doctor.

'Dad returned it just a day before the burglary as he didn't think there were any more threats. That was lucky, huh.' He smiled in affection and delight. 'But we have some good news, you know Mr. Hartley? He saw you on the news and visited while you were unconscious. And guess what?' James eyes widened.

'What?' Cameron asked.

James's eyes sparkled with enthusiasm. 'He offered us one of his properties by the beach, not far from the caravan for free rent, and for the caravan to be professionally cleaned. Hmm... of course, we accepted.' Pulling out what looked like a card from his pocket, James rose to his feet. 'And he gave out vouchers for the music store, fishing, and hunting, for you and me. How cool is that?'

Cameron shrugged. 'That's nice of him.' He didn't feel enthusiastic as he didn't feel he deserved it.

'By the way, Jerry and Ashley came by many times, waiting for you to wake up. And Tara as well. Can you remember who beat you up? The police are investigating.'

'No, I'm still wondering what happened,' Cameron said, not wanting to reveal anything to James.

After twenty minutes, Lora and Steve came back, pleased to hear after a brief discussion with the doctor that all the tests were clear. Gavin advised that Cameron could be discharged within the next twenty-four hours, but he still had to be observed for hallucination, confusion and change of behaviour.

Lora's heart leapt with joy at Dr Finlay's information. 'Thank God, you're fine. I love you, son. We can take you home tomorrow. The doctor said you're okay.' She patted her teary eyes with a tissue.

'Love you too, Mom,' Cameron replied, ringing the bell.

'What do you want love?'

'I want to ask the nurse if they can take the drips off. I don't think I need them anymore,' Cameron said, taking the cannula out of his nose then pulling it over his head. With two hands, he grabbed the club sandwiches and started eating.

James stared at Cameron. 'You look so good. The rest from the coma must've done you the world of good.' He handed a glass of orange juice from the tray to Cameron. 'And not to mention your bloody Pinocchio nose now looks normal.'

'Now, now, James. That will do,' Lora said.

Steven moved closer to Cameron. 'We missed you… the last three days was like…' He paused, his eyes filling with tears. He gave Cameron a hug. 'I thought we'd lost you. We've got to go before we miss the last bus to Honi.

At this moment Cameron felt unconditional love for his dad and knew that no matter what, his dad loved him.

Waving goodbye James and Steven left.

'Aren't you going home with them, Mom?'

'No, I'm going to stay here.'

'I'll be fine, Mom. Go home and have a rest.'

'Mom, where is my backpack.'

'Why, sweetheart?'

'I want to read my Bible, please.'

Lora smiled. It pleased her that Cameron was seeking help from God. 'Okay, I'll get it.' Lora retrieved the Bible from the backpack in the closet and handed it to Cameron.

It was a relief for Cameron to see the notebook was still in the compartment of the backpack. As he took the Bible, it fell open at Psalm 114- 140; the message was to keep the faith. After reading the words, Cameron felt at peace. 'Thank you, Lord, for reminding me,' Cameron muttered.

Lora dug into her handbag to search for the digital camera Bianca gave her. 'God works in mysterious ways. Even though the caravan was trashed, God gave us a new home,' Lora said as she showed Cameron a photo of the house.

'I can't wait for you to see it. Oh, Jerry and Ashley just texted me. They want to visit you,' Lora said as she cocked her head to the side.

'Can I text them that it's okay to visit you now?' she asked.

'Yes, Mom,' Cameron answered.

Ten minutes later after ringing for the nurse, Bridgit, arrived. 'Well, the doctor said we have to give you your meds in your IV for an hour before I can take this off.'

Lora glared at Bridgit in total disbelief. 'Are you sure about that?'

Bridgit gave Lora and Cameron a spell of deception, but it didn't work. She reddened as she fought to hide her frustration. 'Oops, I'm very sorry. I am reading the wrong patient's chart. My mistake.'

'Thank you very much,' Cameron said fiddling with the cannula. *God must be watching,* he thought.

Bridgit struggled to be polite. 'You're welcome. Is there anything else I can help you with?'

'No, thank you,' Cameron replied.

Bridgit left, her footsteps thundering down the hallway.

After an hour Ashley and Jerry arrived with a box of chocolates. They both rushed to hug Cameron. Ashley wore a tube top, which showed her belly and Jerry wore a black The Doors T-shirt.

'Hi, Lora. You must be relieved,' Ashley said, squeezing Lora's arm.

'Oh, I'm kicking myself for not walking with you. I wish I hadn't gone to my dental appointment,' Jerry said, looking down.

'Can you remember who did this to you?' Ashley asked, handing him the chocolates.

'No. Apparently, I have temporary amnesia. That's why I can't remember much,' Cameron said, opening the box.

'So, can you go home? You look pretty good now and… man! No more Mr. Pinocchio for you. Just kidding,' Ashely teased.

'I want to go home now, but I can't until tomorrow. I wish the doctor would give me three weeks off school so I can go fishing,' Cameron said then offered everyone the chocolates before putting one in his mouth.

'Fishing? Choice. I'll show you all the good fishing spots around here, mate,' Jerry said.

'Can I get you something? What about a smoke?' Ashley asked as she sat close to Cameron.

'I'm hanging out for one. Don't tempt me, Ashley… I've quit. Thank you very much,' Cameron said.

After an hour of catching up about the gossip at school, it was time to for Ashley and Jerry to leave.

'Cameron, we've got to go. I'll see you at school whenever,' Ashley said as she gave Cameron a hug. 'You could do with a shower though, bro.'

Jerry gave Cameron a hug, and a knuckle bump.

'Is it that bad? Alright then I'll take a shower,' Cameron said, as he grabbed the towel on the bedside table.

'Oh, here are your clean clothes,' Lora said, handing the clothes to Cameron as he headed for the bathroom.

As they were about to leave, Tara, Liam and Karen arrived. As Karen knew what had happened between Tara and Brice, Karen and Liam left to give Tara and Cameron some privacy.

After Cameron had his shower and as he dried himself, he could hear Tara's whispers.

'Do you think Cameron will still like me, even after I told him that Brice and I were finished, and he saw Brice kissing me?' Tara asked.

'Why would Brice kiss you?' Ashley asked.

'I don't know, he just kissed me. I've broken up with him before, but he won't accept it. I've threatened him that if he does it again, I'll report him for sexual assault, and he backed off.'

'This is how you to handle the jandal, sis. Tell him that he's such an egg. Tell Cameron how you feel, Tara,' Ashley said.

'What if he says I don't really care?' Tara asked.

Ashley changed the subject as she didn't know what to say. 'That's a cool top; it really suits you'.

Tara suddenly became conscious pulling the plunging neckline up.

Jerry thought that he should give Tara and Cameron some space, so he said to Ashley, 'Hey, Ashley, let's get something to eat from the café.' He gestured at Ashley to follow him.

After hearing what Tara had said, Cameron's feelings for Tara came back. After drying his hair and putting on a clean white Dickies T–shirt and blue jeans, he looked like a teenage version of Robert Redford. He opened the bathroom door, and asked, 'Where's, Mom?'

Tara's eyes burned with passion as she stared at Cameron's clean and clear face. Wrestling to compose herself, she took a few tiny breaths. 'Liam took her for a cuppa. I mean my mom took her for a cuppa and Liam went with them. This is for you,' Tara said, handing him a balloon with "get well" written on it, and a box of Rocher chocolates.

'Cool, thank you very much,' Cameron said.

'It wasn't what you think when you saw me and Brice kissing,' Tara said, her eyes blinking briefly to fight back the tears.

Cameron's eyes met Tara. 'You don't need to explain. You aren't my girlfriend. It would be a different story if you were,' Cameron said, struggling to fight his emotions. Avoiding sitting close to her, he sat at the top end of the bed. Tara sat on the chair at the foot of the bed.

Although Tara felt that Cameron was avoiding her, her instincts told her differently. Gazing into his eyes, she felt sure that Cameron felt the same way.

Keeping his distance from Tara but still wanting to seem friendly, Cameron initiated a conversation. They spent twenty minutes chatting and laughing about their childhood; mostly comparing New Zealand to the US and the different places where Tara's dad had been stationed. They agreed on one thing, they didn't like to be called an army brat.

'So how are the guitar lessons?'

'I've learned to play with "All I am" by Hillsong so far.'

'Is it a gospel sound, like a rock love song?'

'Yes, it is.'

'Anyway, what is your favourite song?'

'Hero, by Mariah Carey.'

Unaware sorrow had spread across his face, he took a small breath to control his reaction.

Noticing Cameron's sudden bleakness, she said, 'I'm sorry. Did I say something wrong?'

'No, it's just that was also Hollie's favourite… my first girlfriend.'

Tara realized the significance. Karen mentioned what had happen to Hollie, but she hadn't known it was Hollie's favourite song as well. Without hesitation Tara rushed to Cameron and gave him a sympathy hug. Cameron didn't pull away, but they stopped hugging when they heard footsteps outside.

'Good afternoon. I'm Kelly. I'm a student nurse. Can I take your OBS please?'

Karen, Lora, and Liam arrived back as soon as Kelly left.

'You better have this before it melts,' Liam said as he handed a cone with two scoops of hokey pokey ice cream to Cameron.

'Thanks, Liam,' Cameron said as he took the ice cream. He was touched by Liam's kindness and felt guilty for not sticking up for him when Kirk had punched him.

After half an hour, Karen looked at her watch. 'We'd love to stay longer, but we have a big day tomorrow.'

Tara's eyes stole a last glance and spotted the grief on Cameron's face.

Cameron waved goodbye. As soon as they left, he buried his head in the pillow. *Why can't I have a normal life? I hate being a fugitive. I love Tara. But I can't. Oh, God, help me.*

Chapter 33

Lora's heart ached for Cameron when she saw him hiding his face in the pillow. She felt so helpless. She sat and scratched his back as she knew this would pacify Cameron. After half an hour, Cameron got up. 'Mom, I'm going for a walk around the hospital.'

'Can I come with you?'

'No, mom, I won't be long,' he said, as he swung his backpack over his shoulder.

'Ok,' Lora said, wondering why Cameron had to take his backpack. She didn't want him to feel that she is prying so, she didn't ask. Maybe this strange behaviour was part of his condition caused by the coma, she thought.

Along the corridor, Cameron saw an arrow saying: 'hospital church'. Looking around he followed it, went in and sat at a pew in front of the large cross. He dug his hand inside the backpack and felt the bracelet. He stopped rummaging when he heard a voice. It was nurse Bridgit, yelling at a patient for messing his pants. A few minutes later, Bridgit came out of the ward, dragging a portable blood pressure machine with her.

'Hmm, there you are,' Bridgit said, then gestured to Cameron, coiling her finger to hurry him up. He zipped his backpack closed at once, and realized it was time for his four-hour vital sign check.

With a cat like curiosity, Bridgit glared at Cameron. 'I've been looking for you. Sit down,' she ordered, pointing to one of the blue chairs against the wall of the corridor. 'You've wasted enough of my precious time looking for you, you little twit.'

'Oh sorry, the extra walk won't hurt your big fat ass,' Cameron fired back, then whispered. 'Oh, sorry Lord. Didn't mean to say that.'

Bridgit thought Cameron was underfed, angry, lonely, and tired and his condition would result in depression for anyone. She tried to give Cameron a spell of deception again 'Can I look at your eyes?' she asked, as she started examining him. Bridgit's eyes darted to Cameron's as she flashed a light into his eyes. 'Your OBS is not in normal range. You may need another night or more, so you don't drop into a coma again.'

Cameron's mind fought hard, not to say stick that OBS up your arse nurse Brigit. Instead, he rubbed his temple and said, 'Guess what nurse Brigit, I don't really care.' Cameron was feeling good that his faith in God had soared at that moment and her spell didn't work. A fuming Brigit rushed to the door, slipping then falling with a huge thud as she plummeted to the floor. The emergency bell sounded as a staff member rushed in and found her, her head bleeding.

Cameron said, 'Sweet as it might seem, I did not pray for that.'

Later, noticing Cameron was sound asleep, Lora left to go to Marama Trust Housing, a charitable organization that offered free accommodation for families of a patient who lived far from the hospital. But Cameron had pretended to be asleep, knowing that as soon as he dropped off to sleep, his mom would leave.

Waiting to be sure she had left the hospital, Cameron grabbed his backpack from the bedside table. Rummaging through it, he found the bracelet, a stone and the rope from his slingshot. In another compartment, he found the ancient Bible from his dream. Cameron's mind had wrestled all night, wondering if it was all a dream, was King David for real? It can't be a dream. I have all the visible evidence right here.

Suddenly he saw the vision of King David sitting across from him on the bed wearing white hoody printed with *I'm real*. He stared at Cameron. Am I dreaming?

'No, you're not, Greetings my friend I will read this to you, and it will give you peace and answers,' King David said taking the Bible

Seeing King David - Cameron felt the same old feelings - loved and secure, he recalled when he was lost in the crowd in Italy, King David took him back to the hotel safely and when he visited him many times at age six to read children's bible story books. 'Oh, thanks my friend.'

Reading the bible King David turned the pages open to Numbers 12:6 and he said, 'Hear my words: If there is a prophet among you, I the LORD make myself known to him in a vision; I speak with him in a dream. Acts 2:17 'And in the last days it shall be, God declares, that I will pour out my Spirit on all flesh, and your sons and your daughters shall prophesy, and your young men shall see visions, and your old men shall dream dreams; King David read more chapters in his book in psalms , the chapters 13, 15, 19 about peace and safety.' Then he prayed laying

his hands on Cameron forehead. 'Oh Lord. Keep Cameron as the apple of your eye, hide him in the shadows of your wings, lay him down to sleep in peace. Make my friend Cameron dwell in safety.' Finally, at peace with himself waving King David goodnight, Cameron dropped off to sleep at 2 am.

It was 10 am, Saturday. The intense heat of the sun pierced the window of the hospital. Dr Gavin Finlay's usual morning routine rounds began. The nurse with grey hair and an upside-down watch, pick up the chart from the trolley and handed it to Dr Finlay. 'The results of your blood test, and x-rays are all clear and your vitals are all within normal range. You can go home today, Cameron,' the doctor said, then handed a discharge note to Lora.

'I can't give you any medical explanation as to why you were unconscious for three days. Nor, why all your results are clear after three days of being unconsciousness,' Dr Finlay told him.

A smile spread over Lora's face. 'Thank you very much.'

Cameron was still in his Dickies T-shirt and raring to go, his backpack on his shoulder. 'Thank you, doc. very much,' Cameron said.

'All the best to you Cameron,' Dr. Finlay said, as he left the room.

After reading the discharge summary, Lora phoned everyone that was concerned about Cameron. She told them to understand and be considerate with him and advised them not to make comments or react when Cameron acted weird. This would likely be a part of his condition, she told them, especially if he wouldn't let go of his backpack. She also mentioned that Cameron might express whatever was on his mind. Lora basically advised them to ignore any strange behaviour.

Chapter 34

11 am

They arrived at Overbeek road and the Humble Kiwi caravan park. The bungalow style, two-story house was nestled in big pine trees and 200 meters away from the neighbours, with a wooden handrail along the four steps and surrounding the veranda that looked over the ocean. It pleased Cameron to see Lora happy as it had always been her dream to have a house by the sea. But his guilt regarding Mr. Hartley's sling shot stuck like chewing gum at the back of his head.

The front door opened.

Approaching Lora was Karen wearing a dark blue A-line sleeveless frock. 'Oh, it's so nice to see you guys,' Karen said giving Lora a hug.

'Thank you so much for organizing the housewarming and welcome home party for Cameron,' Lora said, raising her hands in appreciation.

His backpack hung over his shoulder, Cameron scanned his surroundings. 'Where's James and dad?' he asked.

'They're in the garden in the backyard cooking BBQ,' Karen replied.

'Go check our house out but your friends are waiting so do what you want love, this way,' Lora said, waving her hand towards the house. It was a joy for Cameron to see Tara in the corner of the back-yard gazebo, the climbing jasmine in bloom. She sat next to Ashley, Jerry and James inside the gazebo. They were all laughing, talking and munching on potato chips and Cheerio's. In the other corner of the backyard, across from the gazebo, was the BBQ. It was made up of terra-cotta bricks with a large triangular awning over top for shelter. Liam was sampling food as soon as it was cooked, unable to resist the smell of meat and sausages. He was in the company of several older friends, all still wearing summer clothes since it was still 26 degrees in the beginning of March.

Cameron rushed to see his friends and took a seat beside Tara.

'How are you?' Cameron asked.

'I'm fine thanks,' Tara answered.

Ashley squinted trying to focus on Cameron's nose, a smile on her face. 'They might not recognize you at school,' she said. I think you looked better with a long nose,' She kidded.

'Hey, it's nice to see you back. That's a beauty. Mr. Hartley gave you this house aye?' Jerry said, plunging a potato chip into the dip.

'Not only that, but he also gave us a cheque so we could buy a bike, fishing rod and whatever,' James added, showing the cheque he'd taken out on his pocket.

'Seriously, there are heaps of second-hand cars you can buy for that,' Ashley said.

'My little brother saved his extraordinary precious life,' James said, his eyes widened.

'Even though, it's not like him to do that,' Jerry said, then shrugged.

'He's known for being shrewd. He pays his employees minimum wage and I've never heard of anything he's donated,' Tara added.

'That's true and most people in this community would have left him for dead, so he's pretty lucky. If that happened and it was me, I'll probably walk slowly. I won't be in a hurry to save his life,' Jerry said, scratching his head.

James spoke up. 'Can you guys show us where a good hunting and fishing shop is around Honi?'

'Sure thing. As long as you take me fishing,' Jerry said.

'Maybe you can ask Mr. Hartley to take us fishing in his flashy boat,' Ashley blurted out.

'Yeah, come on Cameron, that boat is super posh. You can't miss it at the marina and people go for long drives just to have a look at it. I bet it cost a mega million,' Jerry said.

Cameron tried to pretend he was excited, even though he felt he didn't deserve all the attention. Trying to forget the event with Mr. Hartley, he changed the subject.

'When do we register for rugby?' Cameron asked.

Out of nowhere a voice in his head said practice, practice and, as he blinked, it appeared in front of him. Cameron swallowed hard, trying to convince himself this must be a hallucination, like the doctor had told him.

Laughing, joking and talking, the group continued to catch up with Cameron's events. He held onto his backpack as if his life depended on it. Jerry and Ashley shot each other a look, as if to say they understood why Cameron was acting weird.

In the distance Cameron saw Steven, drinking beer with a guy with an eagle tattoo on his right arm. Suddenly, a nauseous feeling came over Cameron as he thought of what Steven might do if he got drunk. He worried about what Tara would think of him if she found out he had an alcoholic father. Looking at the sudden change in Cameron's state, James' eyes widened. He watched as Cameron's mood changed, his skin turned pale, his breathing was heavy, and beads of sweat formed on his forehead.

They shot each other a look, James silently asking are you okay? As anxiety spread over his face. 'Do you want to have a rest, Cameron?' he finally asked.

'Sorry, I'm feeling a bit tired... if I can be excused, please,' Cameron asked, wiping the sweat from his forehead.

'Sorry Tara'

'It's ok Cameron, have a good rest.'

'M... mom, Cameron's not feeling well,' James yelled as Lora and Steven rushed over.

Ashley, Jerry, and Tara shot each other a look of worry, concern and compassion.

'Get Jasmin to check on Cameron,' Steven said.

Cameron saw the beer bottle in Steven's hand and his eyes lit up and his color came back.

'Oh thanks,' he whispered, taking the bottle and then a big swig, thinking it was a beer. He quickly realized it was ginger beer, in what look like a beer bottle.

Since everybody believed he was feeling sick. Cameron thought that he might as well take this opportunity to sneak off and find a secret place to hide the notebook.

James stared at him, concerned. 'You better have a lie in your bed. This way. I'll show you where your room is.'

Jasmin wearing grey leggings and a light green, loose top came up with Lora to check on him.

'Wait, a minute James. I want Jasmin to check on him,' Lora told them.

Jasmin watched him for a minute, studied his eyes, then checked his pulse.

'Have you eaten? Do you feel nauseous?' she asked.

'I had a little breakfast, no lunch, but I feel ok.'

'I think Cameron is exhausted and nervous with all the excitement,' Jasmine finally said, shaking her head. He seems fine but keep an eye on him. He needs a good rest,' Jasmin reassured Lora and Steven.

'I'm feeling ok now. I just want to take a nap. I'll go back to the party once I've had a rest.'

Looking doubtful, Lora finally said, 'Okay, Cameron.' Then gave him a hug.

Steven cocked his head to the side. 'Are you sure'

'Yip,' Cameron answered.

'Alright then, I'll let your big brother show you to your room.'

A trace of fear hidden in their smiles, Steven, and Lora went back to the party with Jasmin.

James took Cameron for a quick tour of the place. Waving his arms and obviously excited, he told Cameron, 'This house is better than our Chula Vista home, look we have a real fireplace,' he added, pointing his finger at the fire-place in one corner of the lounge.

'Yes, for sure. Look at all the beautiful surrounding stone,' Cameron re-plied.

Passing the lounge he noticed a maroon-colored corner couch, and across from it a wall unit displaying all kinds of family trinkets. They walked past a bay window with thick dark blue curtains. On both sides of the fireplace were built-in wooden bookshelves with a colourful array of books and orna-ments. On the right was a wooden stairway with guide rails. Along the top the second floor overlooked the lounge and the open-plan kitchen with double sliding doors to the outside, where a wooden deck led to the backyard.

Before climbing the stairs, Cameron said, 'James's wait. I'm thirsty. I just want to get a glass of water.'

'Fine I'll be back in a minute,' James said as he went back to the BBQ ar-ea to catch up with Liam.

With no one around, Cameron took a knife from the kitchen drawer and quickly put it in his backpack. Taking a sip of water, his mind drifted back to his mom being homeless and the day before leaving San Diego. Now here she was with the house by the ocean that she had always dreamed of. Overcome and feeling blessed, Cameron wondered if all this was too good to be true. Then he remembered the words in the Bible from Eph 3:20: Now to him who is able to do immeasurably more than all we ask or imagine, according to his power that is at work within us. 'So, we really deserve this.' he muttered looking up and praising God.

When he returned, James considered Cameron's vague look. Then, convinced it was just another symptom of his condition, he didn't ask why he look so dazed.

Cameron and James climbed the stairs, then at second floor deck, they stopped and briefly looked over the railing into the lounge. Finally, heading to the bedrooms, James entered first, Cameron following. 'So, what do you think of your room? It's big enough to fit a giant aquarium in it and still have plenty of room,' James told him.

'Oh cool, yeah.' Cameron said, as he threw himself onto bed. 'I want to go to sleep now I'm tired,' he continued.

James stared at him, his frown showing deep concern. 'Ok, see you later.'

Once James left, Cameron pushed the chest of drawers against the door since there was no lock. If someone tried to enter, hopefully it would give him time to sneak off, do what he needed to do and return.

Meanwhile in the back yard, Lora welcomed another visitor while Ashley and Jerry checked on Tara.

'Are you alright girl?' they asked in unison.

'I think so, thanks for asking,' she said, adding a faint smile. With Cameron on her mind, she had wandered off, dreaming that one day they would get married, have a little house in the country and live happily ever after.

As if reading her mind, Ashley said, 'I'm sure he'll be fine in time for the prom.'

'Oh Ashley, you think going to the prom is the answer to everything,' Jerry blurted out.

Ashley realized it wasn't the right thing to say, but she liked getting a dig in whenever she could. 'Shut up. What about you, you think everything in life can be fixed by watching rugby.' She poked her tongue out.

In the kitchen, Jasmin and Karen were busy helping Lora arrange the table.

'I think it's best to let Cameron rest by himself,' Karen said, holding a big platter of fresh cut watermelon, pineapple, and kiwi fruit.

Jasmin nodded. 'Yes, a power nap will do him the world of good. Anyway, I'm so impressed with how you decorated this house. I've been here before you bought it. What a makeover; by just putting the books there and the way you added all the antique ornaments, some potted ferns and the fresh flowers. You've made this place look like a million dollars.'

Jasmin placed a bowl of coleslaw on the polished wooden kitchen table.

'Hmmm yea, but to be honest all of those ornaments were second hand, and the books, when we bought the caravan, those were in it. So, all I did was clean things up and do a little arranging. But, I have to tell you, we are so blessed and I couldn't ask for more. Praise God.'

Well, it certainly looks great. Oh, and if you want my 29-inch TV, you're more than welcome to it as we just bought a plasma TV,' Karen added.

'I won't say no to that, thanks,' Lora said.

At 1:30, Lora and Karen brought the last of the food out. Steven gathered all the visitors. They stood around the table talking and laughing. Everybody could almost taste the mouth-watering aroma of lamb chops, sausages, and steaks, slathered with caramelized onion, as they approached the table. Complementing the meats were bowls of fresh macaroni, Kumara, bean salad and Jasmin's pansit, plus the coleslaw and fruit platter.

'What a lovely spread. I'm hungry,' Ashley blurted out.

Pastor Nick came out onto the patio with a tea towel covered dish. Much more informal than usual, he wore a two tone cream colored striped polo-shirt and khaki, knee-length shorts and a blue sun hat.

Grabbing the dish from him, Lora peeked under the tea towel 'Oh, apple crumble! Thanks!'

'Come in Pastor Nick, your just in time to bless the food,' Steven told him.

'Hi everyone,' he said, taking his sun hat off.

'You know everybody except for Duane Dennet here. He's from New York,' Steven said.

'Pleased to meet you Pastor Nick,' Duane said, offering his hand for a handshake.

'I think we're all starving so, can you please say grace Nick?' Steven asked.

Pastor Nick bowed his head, and everyone else followed. 'Thank you, Lord, for gathering us together to praise you for saving Cameron and for your abundant blessings of the Owens family. And thank Lord for the food we're about to received and blessed are the hands of those who made them. Amen.'

'Okay, everyone stop gawking and talking. What are you waiting for? Dig in,' Steven announced.

Karen sat between Keegan and Liam and shot Liam a look, warning him not to embarrass her, after seeing the overflowing plate he dished up for him-self. As usual, Liam ignored her and, annoy his mom even more, he loaded more food onto the overflowing plate.

Tara and Ashley continued to talk about the prom. Jerry sat between James and Laura and continued to talk about rugby with James.

Duane, in a light blue team signature polo shirt, and dark colored jeans looked around. 'You've got an awesome place here. I'd kill for that BBQ area,' he told Steven.

'So how did you meet Duane?' Pastor Nick asked Steven, as he took a bite of sausage.

'One day, I couldn't start the car after work. Duane came to help but, it took ages to figure out what was wrong with the engine. Long story short, the last thing we thought to look at was the petrol gauge… which was sitting past empty,' Steven explained as everyone laughed.

'

'That's classic,' Karen said, adding a giggle.

'Duane offered to buy some gas in town,' Steven continued.

'So, you're the good Samaritan then,' Pastor Nick asked Duane.

Cameron could hear the clinking of silverware, laughing and talking downstairs as he continued to make a hole in the floor of his wardrobe. He wondered whether he should go down when he finished making a hole.

When everybody was almost finished eating, Lora said, 'Excused me. I'll just go check on Cameron.

As soon as Duane overheard what Lora said, his raced to think of an excuse to see Cameron as well.

It took Cameron a painstaking half an hour to make a hole inside the corner of the wardrobe, pull a floorboard up and hide the notebook. He hid the hole with a pair of shoes he seldom wore. Tired, he placed pictures of him, Hollie and Mitch on the dresser. Staring at the pictures, his heart yearned for her and the wonderful memories the picture reminded him of. Then he reached over and put the leather bracelet on and laid on bed. Exhausted he fell asleep.

Lora knocked on the door. She tried to open the door, but it wouldn't budge. Her thoughts flashed to a recent event when one of a residents had locked himself in his room, then was found dead hanging in the wardrobe.

Freaking out, Lora yelled. 'Cameron open the door! Open the door… please!' Overcome with fear, panic set in and she ran downstairs.

'Help! Cameron's barricaded himself in his room. I couldn't open the door.'

Duane was thrilled. This was the opportunity he was looking for. Without hesitating, he raced to up the stairs.

Right behind him, Lora said, 'This way.' Trembling, she said, 'Oh my God, help please.'

Duane shoved the door open, everybody right behind him, to find Cameron lying on the bed. Cameron woke with a start, looking up and finding a sea of eyes gazing down at him. He sat up then got to his feet 'What's up? Did I miss something?'

As they looked at each other, everyone seemed to understand that what had happened was likely caused by Cameron's condition. Cameron looked over at the dresser sitting in the middle of the room. 'Oh, sorry. I barricaded myself in. I don't know why.

'No need to apologize,' someone said, then added, 'Hi. I'm,-Keegan Tara's Dad. I was going to wait to introduce myself but maybe now's as good a time as any. I'll be your coach. Jerry said that you and James will join the club this rugby season.

'Pleased to meet you sir,' Cameron replied, quickly figuring out that Keegan was not Tara biological dad, he was an African American who look like Denzel Washington, and Liam was a fat teenage version of him.

After seeing that Cameron was fine, Jerry and Ashley scanned Cameron's room. Ashley, hiding her mouth behind her hand, whispered to Jerry, 'Steven didn't have a chance to get to Cameron as Duane raced to save him, and he's not even related.'

'Typical American. They like to be a hero, like in the movies,' Jerry whispered back.

Later, Lora told Cameron how Duane and Steven met and how he had helped his dad.

Nodding, Cameron looked at the door. 'I'm hungry. I can smell the BBQ from here,' he said.

Looking over, Cameron caught Tara's eyes staring at the top of the dresser. He followed her eyes to the picture of Cameron and Hollie, both smiling their arms around each other, eating ice cream at San Diego Zoo. Next to that was a picture of Hollie, Mitch and Cameron together, fishing. Mitch held a single fish, which is their total catch for the day.

Curious about the picture Ashley and Jerry fought hard not to say how beautiful Hollie was and what a lovely couple they made. Staring at Tara, as she glared at the picture, they protected Tara's emotions, by again not saying anything about the picture.

'Are you okay son? Let's get you some food. For everyone else, its pudding time guys,' Steven said, waving at Cameron to follow.

Liam's eyes widened with the array of desert being served.

Karen and Jasmin got the pavlova, apple crumble and crème caramel flan from the bench and hockey pokey ice cream from the freezer.

Cameron sat between Tara and Duane and Ashley was obviously annoyed to see Duane acting like Cameron was his long-lost brother.

'Are you two related?' Ashley asked pointing to Duane and then Cameron.

'No, why?' Duane replied.

'Just asking,' Ashley answered.

Tara tried to paste on a smile, pretending the picture of a happy Cameron and Hollie, didn't hurt her. Instead, she sat quietly while Cameron ate, waiting for him to say something.

'Can we go for a walk later, you and I?' Cameron asked, finishing the last bite on his plate.

Tara's mood changed as soon as Cameron asked. 'Yes, of course,' she said, smiling and hoping it would be sooner, rather than later.

After dessert, everybody followed Pastor Nick inside to bless the house. They went from room to room praying. It was a great opportunity for Duane to figure out his plan and where to put traps and poison. The Lomar's would be pleased that he was moving ahead with his mission to assassinate the Owens.

After blessing all the rooms, everyone had tea and coffee. 'Can I borrow the toilet please?' Pastor Nick asked.

'Oh, I'll use the other toilet upstairs if you are going to use the one down here,' Duane said.

Duane made sure no one had followed him, as he slipped into Cameron's room. No sooner had he eased the door shut when he heard footsteps. His adrenalin spiked as he slipped behind the door and listened carefully.

'Come on, I'll show my room and the view from the balcony. By the way, thanks for the brownies,' he heard James say.

Duane slipped out of Cameron room before James and whoever he was with reached the top of the stairs.

Heading for the stairs, he wiped a bead of sweat from his forehead, as James and Melissa passed him on their way up.

James introduce Duane to Melissa.

'Sorry I'm so late for your party,' Melissa said, as they entered James's room.

Relieved, Duane mumbled to himself, 'Jeez, that was close'. Then he joined the others on the couch as someone offered him a cup of tea, brownies, and carrot cake.

Chapter 35

It was 5.30 pm. The blazing sun had finally cooled with the breeze and the blue sky created a nice afternoon to go for a walk. All the visitors had left except Tara. She texted her mom saying she was staying a bit longer to talk to Cameron. As soon as Tara got a message back that it was ok, Cameron and Tara went for a walk along the beach front.

Walking along barefoot, Cameron said, 'I'm sorry I didn't tell you about Hollie and Mitch.'

'I understand, we've known each other only for a short time and I don't expect you to move on because of me.' Cameron told her about his life with Hollie and Mitch.

Although Tara knew Hollie had died, she hadn't known the details. After he told her about Hollies tragic death, she wanted to give Cameron a hug, but she hesitated, then decided not to. She wasn't sure yet if Cameron wanted her to be a part of his world. And she felt that Cameron wasn't over Hollie. But that didn't change her feelings for Cameron.

As they continued to walk, Cameron couldn't help but notice the pinecones on the ground by the pine trees bordering the beach. Tara didn't notice the pinecones but she did spot a small hedgehog buried among them as he popped his head up. She pick it up and after examining it, she realized the hedgehog wasn't hurt; he was just playing dead, so she let it go.

Looking around, she said, 'How could this be? This is the only pine tree with pinecones on the ground. It's as if the storm singled it out,' She picked up a pinecone and shuffled it in her hands.

Cameron squinted. Were those the pinecones King David had targeted? He wondered. Again, the voice in his head said the word practice.

More importantly, he couldn't help admire Tara for the care she had shown the hedgehog.

'You'll be a wonderful vet nurse one day. That's now a special hedgehog thanks to you.'

Tara felt her heart warm at Cameron's comment. 'It's just that hedgehogs are an endangered species so I hope I made just a little difference. That's why I volunteer at the SPCA. By the way, you might want to pick up those pinecones, they're good to start a fire with and it'll be winter before you know it. Oh, mom just texted me. Let's go back,' she said.

'Ok, I'll come back later to collect the pinecones Will you be at church tomorrow?' he asked.

Tara couldn't help but feel disappointed, still hoping that Cameron was interested in her enough to have asked her out today, or at least talk about the dinner text he'd sent.

'Yes, I will be, you?'

'Yes, I will. See you tomorrow then.'

When they reached the walkway, Karen's Range Rover pulled up beside them.

'Hi Cameron,' Karen said as she turned the ignition off. 'Tara it's time for music practice,' she added.

Not wanting to, Tara walked to the car. 'See you at church tomorrow, bye.'

When Cameron arrive home, Steven and Lora were sitting at the picnic table having iced tea.

'Cameron you got the lawn mowing job at the golf course. My mate told me to tell you.' Steven said.

'I know you like the kids to learn to work hard, like your dad raised you, but with his condition...' Lora paused and let out a sigh of concern.

'That's why I got the second hand Jeep Cherokee for him. It has a good sound motor, and for that price, it was a steal. Plus, Cameron will love it. Right Cameron?' he added.

'It will be safe for me mom, and the check Mr. Hartley gave me should be enough to pay for it,' Cameron said.

'No, I'm paying for it,' Steven said. 'So, that you'll have pocket money Cameron. I'm sure you'll buy that aquarium you've wanted.'

'What are you going to pay it with? Your wages are just enough to pay for the groceries.'

'I know this guy. I did some favours for him and he's leaving for overseas and he wants me to do some work for him.'

All the visitors had left the housewarming party by 6 pm and after the short walk with Tara, Cameron still could not settle the inner voice that kept saying: practice–practice. Like a whirlwind the word practice intensified, flashing in his mind again and again. Finally, Cameron felt compelled to do something about it. He had to make it go away.

He went to the garage to take his mom's car so he could go for a ride, to be alone, to find some way to act on the word and make it stop. His faith told him it was some kind of divine calling. But still, he wrestled with what the doctor said, that he may be hallucinating, seeing and hearing things that weren't really there.

Cameron looked up. 'I have trust in you Lord. If this is what you want me to do you will speak to me in a vision, just like this.'

Steven wondered what Cameron was up to and followed him. 'Where are you going, son?' he asked, when he caught up with him.

Cameron turned around 'I just need to be alone for a little while.'

'Can I drive you somewhere? I got this car for you.' Before Steven could finish, Cameron cut him off.

'Dad leave me alone.'

Lora came up and whispered to Steven, 'Let him be. Remember what the doctor said.'

'I'm okay, I'll see you later.' Cameron told them.

Before Cameron left, he took a bundle of black rubbish bags, which James, sitting on the folding chair nearby, noticed. He didn't question it as he realized, Cameron was having some strange moments, and this was likely one of them.

However, James did notice and ask, 'What's that bracelet for?'

***

After, a long drive, Cameron came to a never-ending line of pine trees along the base of the hills.

He stopped his car, at what looked like a good place to practice, it was isolated and not a house in sight. He made sure he had his EpiPen as he got out of his car.

Looking around for targets, he narrowed his eyes. 300-yard-up the hill he saw a pinecone and a bird's nest, as if he had a telescope. 'Can I really see that far, or am I just hallucinating?' he asked himself. He stopped squinting and the pinecone went out of focus. He squinted again and it came back into focus. Astonished Cameron's heart raced as he thought about when King David had anointed his eyes with oil, when he had been granted his exceptional vision. He smiled as he thought about what else he could do with his vision.

He took his sling shot from its holster, left the backpack on the ground, then turned. His eyes widened in disbelief when King David came out of no-where. Am I just imagining this? he thought.

Like a coach on the side-lines, he directed Cameron. 'Put a stone into the pouch, pull it back then let loose and fire the stone. Uncoordinated at first, he followed the instructions and carried on practicing. After a few goes, he got the hang of it and he was hitting the pinecones and avoiding the bird nest.

Suddenly, he found himself in the middle of an ancient war. Up the hill, he was looking down where there were heavy armoured roman soldiers 300 meters away, marching towards him. With unbelievable accuracy, he hit the soldiers and watched them fall one by one. Blown away by his supernatural talent Cameron was elated, this was almost as good as having an acid trip. At that moment Cameron was certain that the slingshot was better than a 45-automatic pistol.

Suddenly his bracelet buzzed and broke his concentration. In the blink of an eye, King David disappeared. Then the image of a farmer took shape and he watched him coming toward him. He stopped shooting and put the sling-shot back in its holster.

Wearing blue overalls, the farmer yelled 'Hey boy do you know this is private property and you're trespassing?'

It took a few moments for Cameron to answer as he tried to understand why the bracelet had warned him. 'Oh, sorry sir, I was just collecting pine-cones.' To his relief farmer hadn't noticed him shooting stones at them.

'Goodness gracious that's a lot of pinecones,' the farmer told him in a heavy English accent, waving his hand at the pile of pinecones on the ground. 'Since we have a heat pump and don't need the pinecones to fuel the fireplace, I suppose you can have them. What are you going to do with so many young man?'

'I'm going to use some and donate the rest to the church or anyone who needs them.'

'Well, young fella in that case, you can take as many as you like. By the way, what's your name?'

Cameron hadn't forgotten the manners Steven had taught him. To look people in the eye and sincerely offer your hand. So, he did, introducing himself.

'Cameron Owen sir.'

'Are you the grandson of the late Glen Owen from America?'

'Yes sir.'

The farmer was touched by how polite and genuine Cameron seemed. Not many teenagers were this polite nowadays, he thought. 'I'm Winston Perry. I knew your grandad, he helped us settled in NZ years ago,' he said as he shook Cameron hand. 'I'll tell my wife that you'll be out here picking up pinecones, so she won't be alarmed,' he added as he walked off.

Cameron watched as the farmer disappeared. Had the bracelet warned him that someone was coming? Besides his telescopic eyes and the warning from the bracelet, Cameron began to believe that none of this was a hallucination and seeing King David again convinced him that he was real too.

Cameron continued to practice, until almost dark. He gathered more stones to replenish his supply then picked up all of the pinecones, shoving them into black rubbish bags. On his way home he couldn't help but think, how good it felt to have had such a great practice where, toward the end, each time he hit the pinecone target with ease.

As he drove, his mind battled with conflicting thoughts. Why his imagination seemed so real, like when he was hitting the Roman soldiers with the slingshot? And, he knew if he told his parents about King David, they would put him in therapy for counselling. He wondered, was he prepared to go through with the oath he had agreed to with King David? And would anyone believe him? He shook his head as his mind wandered to Tara. Although his feelings for Tara had rekindled when he learned the truth, but still, he held it back thinking of the gang. It made Cameron felt ill thinking of Tara being kidnap. He had to set his feelings for her aside, but for how long?

It was 9 pm. Steven had dropped off the sleep while watching TV. But as soon as he heard the sliding door he woke with a fright. Lora couldn't believe her eyes when Cameron barged in rubbish bags full of pinecones. Lora gave him a strange look. It was in the middle of summer, no one needed pinecones to start a fire. Steven grabbed her hand and gave her a look that said, just be glad he's alive.

Sweaty, and with a t-shirt full of pine needles, Cameron felt a flicker in his heart to see his mom and dad holding each other's hand. 'Here you go mom and dad. Two bags of pinecones for us and another one for the church,' he said as he moved towards the kitchen.

'Oh, wonderful sweetheart. I'm sure Karen and Jasmin could do with those this coming winter,' Lora said, adding a hesitant smile.

Opening the fridge, Cameron rubbed his stomach 'I'm hungry. Hmm left over lamb steak,' he said, pulling a Glad wrapped plate out. Then he dished himself out some, along with a plate of salad.

'Are you not going to take a shower first?' Steven asked.

'Hmmm, okay dad, I guess I'd better. I have church tomorrow, so this way I don't have to wake up early to take a shower. By the way, where is James?'

Lora answered for him. 'He went to the movies with Melissa. Oh and Karen asked us to come for dinner at their place on Monday. I'm excited, it's Tara's birthday and they're having a party just for family and close friends.'

'Before you take a shower, I want to show you something,' Steven said, waving his hand for Cameron to follow as he headed to the garage. Steven opened the garage door and there sat a 2000 Jeep Cherokee, finished in a Silverstone Metallic paint. It looked immaculate. Steven hoped the jeep would help win Cameron's acceptance and trust.

'I bought the Jeep for you. Do you like it?

Cameron's eyes almost popped out of his head as he stared. 'Is the Pope Catholic? Yip. Of course I like it, dad. Thanks, love you dad.'

After his shower and hearing about Tara's birthday party, he thought about taking her out for dinner at Sylvanus café for her birthday, just him and her. He leaned back in his chair as he ate the leftovers. Hesitating, he told his mom, 'It's my first day of the lawn mowing job at the golf course so, I'll be late to the party.' Obsessed with how well his practice had gone, but needing a better target than pinecones, before going to bed, he took some material from the sewing room, drew a target on it and stuffed it into his backpack.

Chapter 36

Monday, 10 March

As soon as Cameron finished his lawn mowing job, he drove his jeep to Mr. Perry's property. Driving along, the word practice remained, then faded with the overwhelming feeling of amazement at having supernatural powers. Afterward, his mind drifted to thinking of Tara. Cameron imagined his upcoming dinner with Tara as it played out like an old classic movie. He was wearing a tux and Tara a silky cream coloured V neckline dress. Dancing cheek to cheek, an orchestra played nana Mollie's favorite song, All the Way by Frank Sinatra in the background. Then he remembered nana Mollie and pop Glen, dancing to this song and he smiled, deciding to get Tara a present on the way.

Cameron placed the fabric-target on one of the pine trees. 150 yards away, he tried several times to hit the bullseye. Finally, after 5 minutes, he began zeroing in on hitting the center of the target one shot after another. He moved another 250 -yards back. Hitting the target, Cameron was impressed that he could still see the target with normal vision. Cameron felt a surge of adrenalin as he thought about how this weapon could save his family from the gang. As, the voice told him to carry on, he focused on the target and was soon lost in the practice. Suddenly, out of nowhere, a swarm of bees, furry, with bright yellow stripes, obscured his face as they tried to sting his nose and ears. Cameron panicked. Letting go off his slingshot, hysterical, he searched for his EpiPen. But in his haste, when he tried to unzip the pocket the pull tab came off, the zipper stuck and Cameron couldn't get the EpiPen out. The bees kept stinging his face but the voice kept saying carry-on, carry-on, focus.

Waving his hands he yelled, 'No, I'm over it I don't want this anymore.' Suddenly, the bees disappeared. Once Cameron ceased struggling, he effortlessly, glided the zipper open and the EpiPen fell into his hand. Starting to feel the effects of the bee stings, he stabbed his thigh with the EpiPen

Cameron sat on the ground hoping the bees wouldn't return when a memory suddenly flashed in his mind. Cameron and Azoma were 6 years old, at the playground, his family a short distance away. While Cameron played with his sling shot, he accidentally hit a beehive. But the swarm of bees chased only him. He ran for his life while Azoma watched, not helping Cameron as he was stung over and over, struggling to breathe, trying to survive. When Azoma saw a man rushing over when he saw what was happening, she pretended to seek help, running toward the man. Next thing Cameron knew, he was in the hospital fighting for his life. While, lying in his hospital bed, he heard the doctor talking to his dad. 'You should be thankful that your niece Azoma ran for help.'

As Cameron recovered, nana Mollie told him in secret not to play with Azoma by himself—Cameron's phobia with bees fogged his judgement. 'Are you testing me with those bees? If so, that's it I'm out, it's over. I'm not doing it—the mission. Hello, I'm over it, this is worse than my nightmare. I can't do it sorry my Lord-- my friend-- King David I can't do it,' Cameron said.

Out of nowhere King David appeared in a light blue long sleeve shirt and white trousers. 'That's it, you're just a voice in my head, a figment of my imagination. I made you like my imaginary friend when I was young. I can stop you if I take Valium,' Cameron said.

King David replied. 'I'm real Cameron if you only believe. Like the Bible says, there will be trials. I'm trying to make sure that no distractions will get you out of focus. But because God gave us a precious gift of free will, I can't force these powers and the mission to you. You only have to ask, and they will be given to you. So long Cameron KEEP THE FAITH.'

Isolation and uncertainty struck Cameron as he walked out to remove the cloth target, full of holes in the center. He narrowed his eyes but his magnifying eye power was gone. So was the voice. Due to his phobia with bees, he struggled to not let his fears and emotions cloud his judgement. But the voice in his head was loud and clear, telling him: 'The only way to end this is to kill yourself. Then the gang cannot hurt you or your love ones'. As he walked closer, staring at his jeep, the voice told him to hop in the car and dive it into the ditch. Next thing he knew, he was in the car, his foot pressing down on the accelerator.

Then out of nowhere, he saw Mr. Winston running, a raging bull chasing him. Cameron's heart raced as he prayed to take back control. 'Oh, please my Lord give me back my powers.' He jammed his foot on the brake and jumped out of the car. He picked up a stone and pulled the sling shot from his bag. Narrowing his eyes, he cast the stone, hitting the bull between the eyes. Letting out a huge wail, the bull fell over, dead. The bulls wail sent a shiver through Cameron. He had never killed an animal before.

Gasping, Mr. Perry ran towards Cameron. 'Good heavens. Thank you… I'm so glad you were around. You killed that beast with one stone. I need to ring animal control and tell them to pick up the bull and how you saved me.'

Killing the bull restored Cameron's faith in King David. In an instant his power had been restored. But now he needed to hide his power. 'Will it be in the local news?' Cameron asked.

'Yes, I want you to receive a bravery award. You saved my life,' Mr. Perry said, wondering Cameron seemed uneasy.

'The thing is, I don't want people to know where I hang out. That's why I'm here, to hide from them. I've already been beaten up'

'Yes, of course, I read about you in the news. You were that boy they found by the beach, unconscious.' He paused. 'Of course, I won't tell anyone about this.'

'Thank you very much Mr. Perry. I've got to go' Cameron said, as relief spread across his face. Cameron realized it was the supernatural of his hand and mind commanding the sling shot. It's what killed the bull.

'Again, thank you very much. Take care. I'd better get rid of this animal now,' Mr. Perry said.

'No worries I've got to get going too,' Cameron said.

'Before you go, I need someone to mow my lawn and weed the garden. Would you be interested?'

In a hurry but thinking of the money for Tara's gift he said, 'Yes.'

***

Noticing it was 7:30 pm on his cell phone, Cameron panicked realizing he was late for Tara's birthday party. Within 15 minutes, he was at the Warehouse, just as the intercom announced they were closing in 10 minutes.

Cameron's thoughts raced trying to think of a special gift. Finally, he headed directly to the jewellery department, remembering that Tara dreamed of being a veterinary nurse. Within minutes he found a silver nurse's watch, which the shop assistance kindly put it in a dainty pink box and tied up with a ribbon and put a bow on.

His phone rang. It was Lora. 'Tara's Birthday party is cancelled. Everyone's got the bug, vomiting and diarrhoea. So, go home. Kirk's parents rang and they'll be here in an hour.'

A few minutes later he was on his way home along the windy road.

Normally it took a day to clean the house, but since the Prestons were coming, 30 minutes and Lora was finished tidying the place. Another 10 minutes and she was showered with make up on, ready for everyone. As she looked outside, she saw Steven rolling something in his hand, which she thought looked like a joint. So, she raced out the door but as she got closer, she saw he was rolling a roll your own tobacco cigarette

Still, she was not pleased. 'What's got into you? How long have you been smoking?'

'I just bought this cigarette kit yesterday. I keep forgetting, this is a small town and word get around, especially at Hartley's.'

'Sorry, I'm just pissed off,' she told him.

'Why?'

'They say Cameron was beaten up because he cheated when he fought Kirk. It's not like Cameron to do that. You know I told the kids to fight fair only fight in self-defence.'

'Don't worry love we'll find out the truth. If Kirk is right why didn't he come to talk to us?'

'Because they're rich. Mr. Preston being a high-flying lawyer and his wife the biggest shareholder of the wineries in Blenheim. Probably they don't want us to lay charges. They'll just buy their way out of it.'

'But it's up to Cameron, right?' He paused. 'Knowing Cameron since he became a Christian, he'll likely just forget it. But will you forget it?' Lora asked.

'Yeah, when I was in my twenties, Mr. Preston's dad was a cop; He let me off after I beat this guy up. He kind of understood that my future was in his hands. Were it not for him I wouldn't have met you...' Their eyes met and a recent event flashed in her mind - when the cop had let Cameron and James go, otherwise, they wouldn't be here in NZ.

Lora rubbed her arms, staring at Steven. 'God is so good to us Steven.'

'Please don't start. It was the cop who forgave me not God. I'm not in the mood for a long discussion about your imaginary friend called Jesus,' he said, rolling his eyes.

Cameron arrived and, as usual, opened the fridge looking for something to eat. When he saw Lora he struggle to look normal, as if nothing happened. He needed to divert her attention. 'Hi mom, you've tidied up. Where did you put the rest of the pinecones,' He asked, noticing the fireplace was clean and the furniture shiny.

'Your mom is not trying to impress anyone but Mrs. Preston is very prim and proper, so your mother made an effort to straighten things up a wee bit.'

Their heads turned as a Mercedes Benz pulled into the driveway.

Chapter 37

Five months later (Aug. 2008). Lora's friendship with Karen and Jasmin deepened. They regularly got together for: prayer meetings, shared tea, flea market excursions and more and soon they became a close-knit circle.

Cameron's feelings for Tara developed into a close friendship, while Brice gained a new recruit in Kirk as he pulled out of the crowd he'd hung with and slowly Cameron forgave him as he gained Cameron's trust.

Cameron accepted Mr. Winton offered to work for him as a handy man. Thinking of Luke, Brice and Anton, he realized that people who are trying to survive on the street and rich people were the same. They are out there to steal your soul if you let them. His fear of the gang rested at the back of his head, and the feeling of being followed remained. But his faith in God was unwavering; trusting God would protect him, and self-assured no one could take his soul but God.

Cameron vowed to practice using his slingshot. Over the next 4 months, even at times when it was almost impossible to stand as the wind was ghastly, and the trees were swaying back and forth. Continuously, he focused hitting the targets in quick succession, scoring direct hits one after another. To Cameron's amazement, he even passed the earthquake test, by seamlessly hitting the mark during one practice when the land shook and trees collapsed around him. Also, he passed the test of another bee attack, as well as scoring while the rats, and cockroaches clambered all over him during practice, but he carried on, focused on hitting his targets.

Believing he was sanctified with supernatural powers, Cameron thought of moving on to boxing and kickboxing. On his way to practice he stopped at the recycling center to look for a punching bag but ended up being talked into some old tires.

On Mr. Winston's property was an old barn. Since they had sold their herds, the barn had gone unused. Curious, Cameron unhooked the catch of the rough wooden door. Hanging on the wall were shovels, hay grapples, pitch forks, sacks and ropes. At once Cameron thought of utilizing the shovels to fill a few sacks for boxing practice. For kicking practice, he could make use of the tires that he bought from the recycling center. Filling the sacks and tying them and the tires to ropes hung from the ceiling, Cameron had his practice area done in no time. During practice the voice in his head told him to maintain his posture and balance. To move his whole body when punching, to kick, harder, stay focused. To use his speed and power. Amazed by his own power, Cameron broke the sack on his first day of practice and found himself making a new sack a day each time he practiced. Soon he was also replacing the damaged tires.

Although his daily practice pleased him, the voices in his head insisted he needed more practice.

During practice one day, a vision appeared and he saw himself kicking at bubbles in the air, bursting each one with his kicks. With his vision in mind, he sought out the tool shed. In the corner was a tennis ball lobbing machine and an old vacuum cleaner. He grabbed the tennis ball machine and placed it in the trunk. Then he went to The Warehouse and bought packs of tennis balls. He turned the machine on and vaulted at each ball; kicking the tennis balls as the machine lobbed each one.

Challenged, he howled in frustration but he didn't stop until his kick broke a ball.

Within three weeks he was shattering balls, one after the other, break- ing them into pieces. While he was practicing one morning, his wrist band vi- brated. A vision of an event formed, and the hourglass timer set itself to ten minutes. It also flashed a message that he would be dead in ten minutes if he didn't meet the challenge.

Nine minutes: Narrowing his eyes, he peeked through the crack of the barn door.

Eight minutes: One hundred meters away, he spotted two men, both wearing ski masks. One carried a gun, and the other, a baseball bat.

Seven minutes: Cameron went to the side door and hid toward the back of the shed. Mentally commanding himself to focus; not to let his emotions take hold of him, he let out a small, slow breath.

Six minutes: Cameron stepped into the doorway, aimed the sling shot at the man holding the gun and fired. A split second later the stone hit the 44-calibre weapon, sending pieces flying and the gunman groaning as he grabbed his smashed hand and fled.

Four minutes: Heart racing, Cameron turned as the guy with the baseball bat swung it at him.

Two minutes: Without thinking, Cameron kicked out, hitting the baseball bat, breaking it in half. Shocked, the man turned and ran as Cameron noticed a pistol tucked into the back of his pants.

One minute: Cameron wondered why the second guy didn't use the gun to kill him.

Cameron's phone rang bringing him back to reality.

'It's me,' his mom said.

'I know mom, you don't need to tell me. You're in my favourites list so it tells me it's you.'

Trying to encourage Cameron to spend more time with her, Lora mentioned she was having tea with his friends. 'We're having fish and chips at Karen's, Jerry and Ashley are joining us. Come over, I'm just ordering the food now.'

Convinced he now possessed supernatural powers, he was sure he could protect Tara and his family. That made him more motivated to see Tara. 'Okay, order me three pieces of fish and a scoop of kumara chips, please.'

'Okay, see you soon… love ya,' she said.

'Love you too mom.'

Cameron felt a warm feeling in his heart and a confidence that he could have a relationship with Tara. He rose and headed to the house and bathroom for a shower. He had to look good for Tara.

He also realized he couldn't hide his feelings for her anymore.

***

Winter - August, Friday 8 pm.

The sweet scent of blooming Daphne flowers monopolized the air along Jasmin's garden. Although it was dark, and cold, the light on the veranda shone along the rows of polyanthus. The array of vibrant flowers lifted Cameron's spirits. He could hear Keegan 's solid voice cheering for the All Blacks. Aching to see Tara he could hardly wait.

As soon as Jasmin opened the door, she said, 'Come in my dear. They left; didn't you get their text? Jerry went out with Ciara,' she added. Pausing and lifting an eyebrow, she sigh then continued. 'Ashley went to her cousins, and Tara went out with Kirk while James and Melissa went to visit a friend in Nelson.'

Instantly, Cameron felt the same feeling as when he was in San Diego; when all his friend had nothing to do with him after his parents' scandal. Self-pity took over, as his heart sank and his face turned pale. Suddenly, he realized he had forgotten to turn his cell phone back on after his practice.

Her eyes glued to the TV, Keegan finished her bottle of ginger beer and stood. 'You can join us, but don't forget about rugby tomorrow,' She turned back to the TV on the wall.

Karen was about to tell Cameron that Tara went with Kirk to help him take the injured hedgehog, that Kirk found in their garden, to the SPCA; where Tara was a volunteer, helping to save endangered species. Suddenly, she realized she didn't have to explain to him, or anyone else, as they were only friends. A message Cameron had sent loud and clear from the very beginning. She did however notice that Cameron seemed particularly well groomed and was carefully dipping his chips into the tomato sauce, making sure not to get any on himself. 'You wash up well, and you look good in that black leather jacket. Are you going out on a date?' Her comment didn't sit well with Cameron. He was already heartsick to find that Tara had gone out with Kirk, who had apparently broken up with Azoma.

Noticing Cameron seemed distressed, she asked him, 'What's the matter Cameron, are you alright?' Her question just added to his already heightened sadness. She gestured for him to sit down with Lora.

Suddenly Cameron felt the strong urge to go back to the barn and kick the crap out of something. His cheeks flashed bright red and he told her, 'I'm fine, thanks. I've got to go.'

At the same time Karen was seated on the sofa sipping an iced tea with Lora. She could see Cameron was upset and she knew why. She also knew Cameron wanted to be alone so, there was no point of asking if she could go home with him. Knowing he would flatly refuse, Lora asked him anyway. 'Do you want me to go home with you?'

'Yes, mom if you'd like. Will Karen and Jasmin be okay?'

'Of course, they'll be fine,' she replied. She stroked Cameron arm. Thinking it may be bad news, Lora felt jittery but at the same time was ecstatic. For the first time she could remember, Cameron wanted to be with someone when he is in one of his distant, broody moods. Maybe there was hope for him after all!

'Absolutely, no worries. Don't forget your Kumara chips and fish in the warmer,' Jasmin reminded her.

'Of course, we'll be alright. See you at rugby tomorrow,' Karen said.

Next minute they were pulling out of the driveway. In the distance, Cameron spotted Kirk and Tara. They were walking, laughing, and chatting, as if they were having a fabulous time. Luckily, they didn't see Cameron and Lora was busy texting. By the time they reached home Cameron realized that it was 8 pm and he was late, as usual. His friends waited long enough, and after reading all their text messages inviting him to various places, his feelings of rejection quickly disappeared. But his feelings about Kirk and Tara remained. Arriving home he put the Kumara chips and fish in the microwave, while Lora turned the wall heater on, then took a jug of orange juice and poured two glasses.

Lora was pleased to see Cameron looking brighter. 'Is there something you want to tell me?' she asked, taking a sip of orange juice.

'I hate this feeling mom. Why am I jealous? Tara is just my friend, but I can't help being jealous.'

'Maybe it's time for you to tell Tara about your feelings for her.'

Lora shared her experience about her first love while Cameron ate.

Afterward, they went to bed and Lora couldn't help feeling delighted that she was gaining the trust of her son.

Cameron laid his head on the pillow and thought of how to tell Tara about his feelings for her.

Chapter 38

Aug 8, Friday 9 pm - A usual gusty night in winter.

Cedrick called an urgent meeting. In the basement, the musty odour of mildew hung in the air. Azoma, Beth, Brice, Cedrick, and Duane sat around the table with a dim light hanging above. Feeling on edge, Duane struggled to regain his composure as they started to question the success of the operation they had assigned him.

Disbelief covered Cedrick's face as he rubbed his eyebrows. 'Give me a good reason why these jobs didn't pan out? Let's start with the van.'

Appearing relaxed and trying to look confident, Duane tapped his foot on the floor under the table.

'Well, Azoma told me they would all be going home in one car, but next thing Cameron is in his car. James and Lora in Melissa's car. I couldn't possibly ditch Cameron with Melissa's car at my back and I couldn't push his car into the pit with a witness behind me. That would have implicated you as the van is registered in your name, Cedrick. Plus, you ask me to run their car into the ditch and make it looked like an accident. That was impossible.'

Beth doubted his alibi. 'Tell me what happen with the poisoning operation, there should have been nothing to that one. Why did that crumble?' she asked.

Duane didn't have to think hard to reply. 'I thought the mincemeat was for their meal but Steven grabbed it before I could stop him and fed it to the stray cat. It died quickly and he realized someone was trying to poison them. I couldn't believe how trusting he was when he told me he put monitors all over the place. Lucky, he didn't take the video to the police. He wants to do his own investigation since he knew something was up. Otherwise the video would have incriminated us for sure,' Duane added.

Frustrated, Beth let out an exaggerated sigh. 'Knowing Steven, he will do his own investigation alright. Lucky for us, he doesn't trust cops after living in the US for so long,' Beth added, throwing her hands up.

Azoma had been itching for her take on things and couldn't longer wait any longer. 'I don't believe Steven would refuse $400 a week rent for a caravan when he's really hard up.'

Duane cocked his head and stared at Azoma. 'They signed a contract with Mr. Hartley that they would have no tenants on the premises. So, they can't have me as tenant.'

Beth became even more suspicious 'Really? Even you've told her no one would know you're renting the place. I know Lora, she's a con artist. She would have taken notice of Mr. Hawley's contract for $400. She's a whore and would sleep with anyone for that kind of money.'

'That's when she was gambling,' Duane said.

'Well thanks for your honesty. Is that why Steven shared Lora's secrets with you?'

You're just so clever! What did you do, help him hide his drinking from Lora?' Beth asked.

'For the record, Steven thought it was the locals who were trying to poison him because of the gossip about him being a paedophile,' Duane said. Then he explained what happened in the barn. 'I watched Cameron take aim. It was over 100 meters away. It was unbelievable, like magic. How could someone hit something with that accuracy, even if he had practiced with his sling shot since he was a toddler?'

Duane wondered why and how Cameron found out they were at the place. He had been spying and following Cameron after school for weeks. He had been sure that no one had seen him, but now he was having doubts. But he kept it to himself. 'Yes, we need to find out if the sling shot has the power we think it does. If it does, we need to steal it,' he said.

'My man you're the one who hesitated to hit Cameron with the baseball bat,' Cedrick said. His eyes narrowed. 'If you'd just done what you were assigned, we'd not be in the position of having to deal with him.'

'It's not my fault, it was the dope he offered me before the operation. We each had a joint before we went,' Duane replied, nervously licking his lips, hoping they would believe him.

'Well how moronic was that?' Beth said. 'Of course your reaction would be slow.'

'From now on, no weed, no booze. When it come to your operations. And this meeting is also to inform you guys we'll have the boys from Auckland charter here to help us. They'll be here soon, they're Satanists as well. Their expertise includes a sharpshooter with a black belt. They also have Satan's super evil power flowing in them. I'm sure that Cameron's ludicrous slingshot will have no bloody power to match theirs.'

'Uh, Cameron won't be unconscious this time. He'll be in the box with the rest of them. If the Owens win their case, we'll be in dire straits,' Cedrick said, avoiding eye contact with Beth.

'They'll only win over my dead body,' Beth said, slamming her fists on the table, then standing up.

'Let's move on. I want to meet with the Auckland members a soon as possible so we can plan our next move immediately,' Brice said. 'I don't think the slingshot can have all that power from 100 meters away. There must be something else we're not aware of that we need to find out about,' he added, making eye contact with Duane.

After going over all the plans to destroy Cameron, the meeting ended.

At the end of the meeting, Beth asked Duane to stay, hoping to gain Duane's trust, and therefore the Owen's. That would give them the best prospect of success for this mission. Duane assumed that Beth wanted to get rid of Cameron first. As Satan's Cult had told her, they intuitively believed that if Cameron was dead, the Owens had no protection.

Beth lined up the plan for Duane to execute, with the help of everyone else. Feeling certain everyone believed his excuses, Duane calmed down. Their new plan for the Owen's ensured no connections to Lomar or the gang. But in their desperation to get rid of the Owens, they were putting their trust in Duane. And, Beth was sure money was the best incentive for Duane to kill Cameron first.

It also solved the problem of concealing the money from their drug operations that she needed to get rid of. So, Beth had offered Duane $50,000 up front and another $100,000 upon completion of the job.

'I want the Owens to disappear from the face of the earth,' Beth told him, handing him an unmarked brown envelope bulging with cash.

'Considered it done,' Duane said, grabbing the envelope. A month later, to gain the gangs trust, Duane joined the Satan cult with the same goal of killing Cameron and his love.

Chapter 39

The northerly wind was moderate with a clear blue sky. The blades of grass were covered with beads of dew, sparkling under the sun's rays. The scent of the newly mown grass hung in the air.

Parents were arriving at 10:00 am for the game as Lora parked the car and turned the ignition off.

Looking sharp and athletic, Cameron wore a red nylon jersey with a Maori design on the shoulder. He sat on the passenger side, still feeling sleepy at 10 am. He had not slept well, thinking of Tara all night while trying to decipher what happen at the barn. 'We're early mom,' he said, his eyebrow furrowed.

Lora empathized with Cameron's being cranky as she noticed he was up and down last night, which kept her awake as well. 'Well by the time we get the drinks and uniforms from the trunk it will be time for the game,' Lora said, as she took the key from the ignition. She tied her hair in a bun and straightened her grey pullover and blue jeans.

'That won't take 30 minutes,' Cameron said as he leaned back and closed his eyes.

'It won't be like this every week. It's just my turn to wash the uniforms since you were the player of the day last week. I wished I'd been there to watch you,' Lora said with regret.

Practicing kick boxing since he was small meant Cameron was incredibly fit. Which was why he'd been chosen as the player of the day. 'I'm sure there will be a next time mom when it's your turn to watch James play.'

'I know, at least your dad was there and he was so proud of you son and I'm so proud of you too,' she said giving Cameron a hug. They made their way to the rugby grounds with the duffel bag of uniforms and cooler full of drinks.

At school last week Kirk had pissed Brice off when he stopped Brice from doing a wet Willy again on Cameron's ear. Since then, Kirk had been banned from Brice's circle of friends. It didn't take long for Brice to replace him with another crony; Archie Brockman who would play on their team today. Archie was not into rugby, he was a black belt in Tae Kwando. But with Brice's evil spell on Archie, his sister Ciara fell under Brice's control and they were initiated into Satanist cult.

Today's game would normally be an equal match between Honi and Saxon High in their red and white striped rugby jerseys. But today they only had 14 players instead of their normal 15.

The key player line-up in Honi High team would be: Brice hooker, Liam forward, Jerry and Cameron wingers; with Kirk on reserve.

Customarily, one player would be asked to play for the other team to make up for their missing player. With Brice as the team captain, he knew Kirk would hate to play for the rival team. So, to torment him, he told him he needed to play for the opponents. To Brice's displeasure Kirk didn't object.

In the grandstands sat parents, family and friends; there to support their team. Wearing sunglasses and thick winter jackets, some had dreadlocks and tattoos. Still others sat on folding chairs passing a flask or cups of coffee. Near them, a St John's ambulance was parked, ready for any emergency.

Normally Marion Preston, Kirk's mom, would have been with Beth's group, along with the wives of lawyers, accountants and rich owners of the town's businesses. But today she was with Karen, Lora, Jasmin, and other parents. Karen wore an All Black rugby jersey with a red stripe, while Jasmin wore a pink Everlast pants tracksuit.

Waiting for the game to start, Karen move away from Marion and Jasmin while they were busy talking.

Karen shot Lora a look, then her mouth twisted. Pointing to Marion she said, 'I know why you're with our group. Speaking of prayers, I'm so thankful. I thought I'd lost Tara.'

'Ah… why?' Lora asked as her eyes focused on Cameron, across the field warming up before the game.

'A year ago, she was so obsessed with Brice, she'd runaway with him. They were smoking weed heavily with her sister Azoma, Kirk and others. One day I told her off because she was bad-mouthing Liam. She hardly calls by his name and degrades him by calling him fatso.' Karen cleared her throat then continued. 'She swore at me and I almost slapped her. The night before I saw you at the market I cried and prayed like I never prayed before. Then I fasted for the whole day. I believed God answered my prayer that day. It was the day she broke up with Brice.' Karen stared across the field at Tara with Ashley and Melissa.

'I can relate to that, but I can't blame Cameron for acting out,' Lora said. as she continued to watch Cameron practicing with Jerry.

'I'm the same actually. I was so busy with the café and Keegan …'

Karen had been about to say more but the whistle blew and the game began.

Totally focused, with adrenalin pumping in their veins, both teams lined-up opposite their rival team, waiting for the ball. Brice threw the ball in to Archie but he dropped it. A Saxon player was about to pick the ball up but Cameron dove in, got the ball and passed it to Jerry. Forward and back, the players ran to and fro supporting their team plays. The referee, in his white and red striped uniform, was running back and forth with them as if watching a race. A Saxon player tried to tackle Jerry, but he side-stepped, then passed the ball to Liam. Liam was tackled and fell, got up and ran forward but the referee stepped in and a ruck was formed, as both teams tried to get the ball. Saxon's forward tried to rip the ball from the ruck, but was not fast enough. As Brice grabbed the ball, he passed it to Archie but the ball slipped from his hand, again.

'Butterfingers!! shouted and giggled a rival team supporter. Saxon's forward was about to grab the ball lying on the ground, but everybody jumped on it, then formed a ruck again. Jerry wriggled out and dragged the ball out from the ruck. The rival team chased him but Honi's players supported Jerry, keeping the ball as he ran, looking for his team mates to pass it to. Suddenly, he dropped-kicked the ball, passing it to Cameron. Cameron ran, saw Liam was ahead waiting for the ball near the finish line, along with another player. Cameron passed it to Liam. Just as two Saxon players were about to tackle Liam, Jerry and Cameron intercepted them. Breathing hard, Liam ran another four meters, with Jerry and Cameron now paralleling him until Liam, finally close enough, dove over the try-line.

The Honi supporters erupted: cheering, screaming, applauding, and whistling. While the Saxon supporters booed.

'Well done son. Let's stay focused and keep the momentum going!' Coach Keegan   yelled from the side-lines.

Proud, sweaty, and panting. Cameron, Jerry, and Liam gave each other knuckle bumps. Tara stared at Cameron with a sweet smile, while Ashley gave him a thumbs up. Up in the stands, Karen and Laura did a little dance and high fived each other.

In the next scrum, Jerry got the ball. He passed it to number 8 just as Saxon's number 7 tackled him and got the ball. Number 7 passed the ball to Kirk as Brice and Archie tackled him. The three of them fell to the ground and another ruck was formed. Everybody was pushing and shoving to get the ball while Kirk lay on the ground covering his ears. Cameron bent down, trying to get hold of the ball, but suddenly, a voice in his head told him to shield Kirks head. Out of nowhere someone kicked Cameron's hand just as he brought it up to protect Kirk's head.

Kirk had no idea whose hand covered his head until he heard Cameron cry out. 'Ouch, that hurt,' as he supported his injured hand.

'Toughen up wimp. Get back in the game,' Brice yelled, waving Cameron to go back onto the field, as he walked to the sideline nursing his hand.

The referee blew his whistle and called an injury time out, seeing Cameron walk to the sideline.

Lora struggled to stay calm as she came out of the bleachers and sat beside Cameron on the team bench. A minute later she was joined by her support group of Tara, Ashley, Karen, Jasmin, all telling Cameron how he'd saved Kirk from serious injury.

'You need to take him to the emergency hospital. It looks like he may have broken his wrist,' the ambulance officer in a white polo shirted uniform told them. Then, he bandaged Cameron's wrist and put his arm in a sling.

'Okay thanks' Lora said, patting Cameron's shoulder.

After a long wait in the hospital, Cameron's insecurity started to overpower him as he wondered how he could protect those he loved with his wrist injured. Surely, using his slingshot was now out of the picture.

Chapter 40

Saturday 8 pm.

It was a cold night when Cameron and Lora came home from the hospital. Both in silence as there was nothing much to talk about after an exhausting day waiting at the hospital. As Cameron felt freezing cold, he lit the fireplace at once with a little difficulty from his broken wrist in its' plaster cast. Yawning, Lora plugged the electric jug in to make a cup of tea, then turned the TV on. Cameron went to his room while Lora kept on watching TV while having a cup of tea, the warmth and scent of burning pinecones filling the air, soothing her.

Cameron laid in bed nursing his broken wrist and a broken heart from jealousy, thinking Tara might be hooking up with Kirk as he'd seen them together at the game and Tara seemed to be quite fond of Kirk. *But I can't stop her we're only friends,* he thought. He was about to cave into a pity party but was distracted when he heard the doorbell ring. Jasmine came in, talking to Lora, her voice sounding distressed. Cameron got up and sat on the stairs to listen.

Lora wrapped her arm around Jasmin and Jasmin let out a stress filled moan. 'Can we pray for Jerry, please. I'm worried about him. I think he is under Satan's spell.'

If Lora had not been a Christian, she would have thought Jasmin a bit weird. As soon as Jasmin was comfortably seated on a dining room chair, Lora squeezed her shoulder. 'What do you mean, what's happening?' she asked, trying to sooth her.

Jasmin's eyes twitched involuntarily. 'He's been hanging around with Ciara, staying overnight, even if I didn't give him permission. I think he's using drugs too, even though he swore to me he wouldn't. He told me he hated me and wished he were never born as a half Asian bastard. The things he said were horrible. And when I pray in tongue, he tells me to shut up, that it's gibberish and a whole a lot of crap. If I tell him to do something, he gives me the finger and tells me f… off. He's not himself at all. He comes home, his eyes all red, like he's been crying and won't tell me what happened. When he leaves, he won't tell me where he's going.'

'I can relate to that. Something must have happened, and I believe it's the work of the devil as well. But what about Ashley? Has she noticed anything different?' Lora asked.

'Ashley is a troubled kid herself. Jerry's behaviour would be normal to her since that's how she grew up. It's Jerry that's kept her on the straight and narrow. I felt sorry for her; going from one foster home to another. But, I think she has a thing for Jerry and now he's going out with Ciara, it must break Ashley's heart, so she stays away and I hardly see her anymore.' After a long prayer, spoken in tongues, Jasmin felt slightly better and left. At 11pm, Lora went to work on the graveyard shift. James was still out with Melissa and Steven wouldn't be home till 4 am.

As soon as Cameron heard their conversation, he headed upstairs and rang Jerry. After several attempts with no answer, Cameron texted him: Hey what's up? Are you alright? Can we hang out tonight? Come over or can we meet.

While waiting for Jerry to text back, he rang Ashley. In the background he heard rowdy voices and rap music as Ashley answered in a slow and giggling voice. 'I don't know. Who cares?'

Ashley was making no sense. 'Are you ok?' he asked.

She hung up. A minute later, he got a text from Jerry. 'I'm swift, cool thanks.'

Exhausted by the day's events, his mind was spinning, with Tara, Jerry, and Ashley, flashing in and out, he couldn't fall asleep.

At 1 am, Cameron woke up from a horrible dream. The dream had kept replaying; too real to ignore.

He raced into his car. The vision in his dream sent him to Jerry's place. It told him he had to warn Jerry and avert a tragic event.

Cameron raced to Jerry's, his backpack with the slingshot and rocks, slung over his shoulder.

***

Ten minutes later, he was at the back of Jerry's house. He turned the torch of his cell phone on, shined it toward the rustling he heard and was shocked to find Jerry, a yellow nylon rope around his neck as he stood on the branch of the plum tree. His hands held onto the branch above, where the rope was tied. Red eyes, filled with tears, rolled down his cheeks and he looked ready to jump.

Cameron emerged from behind a tall red fuchsia bush.

'Jerry please don't do it,' Cameron begged, stunned to see the horrid state Jerry was in. He dialled 111 and the dispatcher advised him to stay on the line. Cameron tried to think of ways to prevent Jerry from jumping. Doubtful he could damage the branch enough with his slingshot to make it break, because of his broken wrist, prayer became his back-up plan. 'God, please stop Jerry. I trust in you Lord.' His heart pounded.

Still, he was ready to pull the slingshot from its' holster and hit the branch, as best he could, in case Jerry jumped.

'What about Ashley, Laura and your dad?' Cameron yelled up to him.

'Tell mom I love her, so much, and tell Ashley I'm sorry that I hurt her... I loved her from the first time I met her. No one is to blame for this.' He snivelled. The branch he was standing on creaked as he moved.

'Just get down please... please we can talk about it.'

Without warning, the branch he was standing on bent, about to snap. Upon hearing the branch pop, Cameron pulled out his slingshot and fired at the branch the nylon rope was tied to, weakening it enough that it snapped as Jerry fell. Jerry landed in the bushes, coughing but unharmed. With perfect timing an ambulance arrived and the EMTs rushed to Jerry's aid.

When they tried to take the rope from Jerry's neck, he resisted, kicking and punching the EMTs, screaming 'Let me die, let me die. You bastards.' Within minutes, the police arrived and restrained him as one of the EMTs gave him shot of risperidone to subdue him.

Cameron felt a vibration on his wrist as a text message came in. The text was from Ashley, asking him to pick her up from a party she was at. He glanced over to make sure Jerry was in safe hands, then rushed to his car to get Ashley.

Chapter 41

0130 Sunday

It was a twenty minute ride to 35 Rosselli Street. The houses along the way were Italian in style. Cameron's backpack hung from his shoulder. It was quiet, the only sound, the tweeting of a bird coming from a line of cabbage trees. There were several expensive cars parked along the street.

After ringing the doorbell several times with no answer, he went around back where he found a marble stairway leading down to the basement. He peeked through the misty glass window and Ciara spotted him. She waved, then indicated to meet her at the door. As soon as the door opened, the smell of weed hit Cameron like a tequila shooter.

As soon as he stepped through the door, Ciara pushed him against the wall, offered him a toke on her cigarette and kiss him.

Most girls at the party wore skimpy clothes and glittery makeup. The boys were in their usual hoodies and branded T-shirt as they swayed along with the loud thumping sound of the bass of rap music. Almost everyone was smoking and drinking. It reminded Cameron of the parties he and Hollie had gone to early in their relationship when he was rebelling.

He watched Ciara's 5 foot 4 inch frame, wrapped in a black halter bodycon, showing off her well-proportioned curves, her dark brown page boy haircut and deep-set green eyes. She looked beyond tempting as the weed intensified her natural beauty and Cameron struggled to keep his guard up and not be tempted by her.

After another passionate kiss, Ciara grabbed his hand and dragged him into another lounge. In the middle of room was a coffee table full of weed, bongs and pipes. Shantell and Brice were necking on the couch while Archie and Azoma were dancing to their own music, like a couple of maniacs, out on the floor. Once Brice saw Cameron, particularly at this moment as Cameron looked fit, perfect nose, and seemed sober, his insecurity surfaced. But Brice had been well verse in hiding his insecurity by intimidating and putting people down. Then he recalled the Kiwi fruit patch where the last time he made himself high so his reaction to deepen his will weaken, but it didn't. So, this time he thought alcohol and weed will do a better job for their plan later.

On the couch, while kissing Brice, Shantel covered his mouth and said to Brice. 'Why can't you just spike his drinks, so he passed out and get what you want from him.'

'We can't ask him where it is when he is unconscious, duh! And Cameron is such a smart ass he would not just keep it where everyone thinks where it would be,' Brice replied.

Cameron could not wait to get Asley out of here. That's all that matter to him at the moment and his fear grew that there was something else going on. He approach Brice without hesitation. 'Where is Ashley? I need to get her out of here.'

'Okay, but sit down and have a drink. For old time sake,' Brice commanded, pushing Cameron onto the couch.

Shantell rose from the couch. 'There is no torture here Cameron like you see in the movies. If there were, you would have a broken nose and finger by now if you didn't do what the torturer asks you to do. I'm sure you can handle one drink. So, drink up before we get the baseball bat, beat you up and put you in the boot of the car,' Shantell said, narrowing her eyes.

Cameron felt lightheaded as his lips moved rapidly trying to say all his word at once. 'I'm driving, sorry, can you please just tell me where Ashley is.'

'Yes,' Archie applauded. 'Bravo, Cameron for pretending you're such a good boy and not drinking, but it looks like you're loaded with other drugs, taken before you came here, so here it is,' Archie said as he forced the shot of vodka into Cameron's mouth with the help of Brice, opening Cameron's mouth. The vodka went straight to his gut.

Determined to get Cameron to fall for her, Caira gave him a spell of lust. As Cameron's faith shrunk due to weed and alcohol, Ciara's spell penetrated partially and she threw herself on to Cameron. This time Cameron did not try to avoid her. 'That wasn't too bad aye, now I can have some fun with you.' Ciara said as she held Cameron's hand, then lead him to an empty bedroom. Once inside the bedroom, Chiara thrust Cameron onto the bed, then took his clothes off. With surging testosterone, fuelled by the weed and alcohol, Ciara's spell wormed it's way in and soon he was having sex with Ciara with her on top of Cameron howling in primeval sexual gratification. Afterward, Ciara took off like an animal, relieved after having feasted on her vulnerable prey.

Riddled with guilt, it took a gigantic effort for Cameron to get up. He made his way to the hallway and found the bathroom. He was unaware Archie and Brice were cautiously tailing him. When he knocked on the door and no one answered, he turned the light on. As he entered the bathroom, Brice bull-dozed him further inside. Archie then held onto Cameron's arms and dragged him to the toilet bowl. With all his might, Brice forced Cameron's head into the toilet bowl, full of faeces and urine. With his guard down Cameron gasped as he struggled to break free. Asphyxiated, Cameron's strength expired. But out of nowhere someone kicked the door open with a huge thump leaving a big dent on it.

Brice and Archie, panicked. Fearing someone had witnessed what they'd done, they let go of Cameron and ran out the door.

Gasping, Cameron rose to his feet and struggled to the sink. After cleaning himself up, he to continued looking for Ashley. Entering a large library, he spotted Ashley; her hands bound with plastic handcuffs and her mouth gagged with a piece of cloth. Cameron's heart pounded.

Seconds later, Brice and Archie came in and shut library door. Cameron still couldn't decipher what was happening. Why would they do this to Ashley? From his back-pocket Brice took out a knife and stuck it against Ashley's jugular. 'Give me your slingshot otherwise, I'll slit her throat.

Without hesitation Cameron handed his backpack to Brice; it was the only choice he had. As soon as Archie and Brice spotted the slingshot, they put the backpack aside but didn't let go of Ashley in exchange. With a black belt move they came in for the kill, surrounding Cameron. Fuelled with Satan's evil spirit, along with Karate-killing chops, Brice's hands collided with Cameron gut and ribs, one after another.

With rage, Ashley tried to wriggle out of her bindings as she watched. Suddenly, she remembered having a lighter in her pocket. She worked it out and scorched the plastic hand cuffs.

Brice with Cameron on the floor, was about to finish him off. Quickly, Cameron rose, shook his head and focused. One swift hovering kick to Brice's head was all it took to knock him out and he landed unresponsive on the floor.

In fear Archie hesitated to counterattack seeing Brice unconscious. He kept moving, from left to right so the strikes won't land while trying to concentrate on hitting Cameron's injured wrist. Archie threw dozens of kicks and punches but Cameron intercepted everyone with force point-accurate blocks. Archie used small head movements to avoid strikes, all the time studying Cameron's style and tactics, trying to get a measure of him. He ducked and weave and tried not to get hit by Cameron.

Cameron reached out, grabbed a thick hard covered book and threw it, hoping to hit Archie in the head, but Archie booted it out of the way. Cameron struggled to ignore the throbbing pain in his wrist. Archie sensing this, took a chance and gave Cameron an upper cut, then kicked his leg, dropping Cameron to the floor.

He was about stomp on him, but Ashley grabbed a nearby chair, and with adrenalin flowing crashed it into Archies head, knocking him to the floor. As Ashley tried to help Cameron, Archie stood and gave her roundhouse kick in her belly. She groaned and curled onto the floor in pain. Seeing his opening, Cameron flew at Archie, his sidekick landing like a spear to his head. Archie staggered away, eyes glazing momentarily, then landing unconscious; but for how long?

Ashley staggered to her feet clutching to her stomach. Cameron grabbed his backpack, 'Lets' get out of here,' Ashley said waving her hand and directing Cameron to the way out.

The party was still raging with the crowd wildly dancing and the guests oblivious to the atrocious smell of faeces from the toilet with its growing queue. All of them obviously having no idea what is going on.

On their way to the carpark, Cameron's bracelet buzzed as he looked back and saw Archie in the distance, running to his car. A future vision emerged in his head. He had to stop Archie so he couldn't run them over. Before reaching for his slingshot, he handed his car keys to Ashley. 'Get in the car.' Without a question, Ashley unlocked the car and got in. Cameron took his slingshot and a rock out, aimed and hit one tire of Archie's car, some 50 meters away. Quickly, he shot out the other three tires. Archie got out and found all the tires shattered to pieces. As dark as it was, Archie had no idea who smashed the tires but couldn't have chased Cameron if he want to.

Cameron watched and had a vision of Archie pulling out a 45-revolver and shooting Cameron in the forehead after a high-speed chase. Cameron smiled, got in his jeep then drove away, thanking God.

Along the way, Cameron explained to Ashley why he was late, and the toilet event with Brice and Archie. Then he painstakingly related Jerry's attempted suicide but didn't mention Jerry's feelings for her. *It's better for Jerry to tell her himself,* he thought. Ashley's eyes filled with tears, then streamed down her cheeks while she listened to him describe Jerry's traumatic event.

Ashley received a text from Tara saying that Jerry was home and tranquilized after his attempted suicide. 'Thank God 'I could still see him. Does he love Chiara?' Ashley asked Cameron, her eyes starting to fill with tears.

Remorse overtook Cameron as he thought of God and Tara. 'No way, he doesn't.' Suddenly regret and worry begun to creep in as he worried if anyone at the party had taken pictures of him and Ciara kissing. If they had, had Tara seen them?

'I don't think we can go to Jerry's with you smelling like this Cameron. Phew!!! Oh, you stink like hell,' Ashley told him. Did you mess yourself stinky poo? Is that what happened,' she joked, wrinkling her nose.

'Yip, it's not just me, I think they put something in the drinks or the punch because everybody at the party was busting to go to the toilet, apart from Brice and his cronies. It must have been a laxative. Maybe whoever busted down the door was dying to go to the toilet, and unintentionally saved your ass,' she said, adding a chuckle.

'Well that makes more than just me smelling like shit, so I don't feel so bad no. Do you think Brice will be fine?'

'Men, that should be the last thing on your mind. And where did you get those bad ass moves? You could be an Olympic champ.'

'Can we keep it a secret… What happen tonight?'

'I certainly won't be a witness as they will torture me. My life will not be worth living if I report them to the police.'

It pleased Cameron to hear what Ashely said. 'I'll take that as they're real criminals huh?'

'You can say that again, like my cousin up north, it was a waste of bloody time reporting it to the cops. They beat him up and he almost died. Beth bought her way out of it. There was justice for Brice and his mates. They escaped jail by saying it was self-defence.' Ashley blew out a quick breath in anger.

'I take it that Beth has connections with the cops, right?'

'For sure, hey we better stop at nanas on our way so we can have a shower and you can change. I'm sure you won't mind my dead grandads' trousers.'

Chapter 42

August 24 9 pm.

They stopped at nana's little Victorian cottage. Moana, Andrew and Ashley's grandma opened the door. She wore a faded purple bath robe. Behind her the lounge had a shiny wooden floor, a camel back sofa sat in the middle of the room, covered with a worn-out multi-coloured fleece blanket. In front of the sofa was a coffee table with a half-full bottle of Sherry and an ashtray full of cigarette butts.

'Hi nana, I'm glad you're still up,' Ashley said, leaning away, conscious of their smell.

Moana's brown eyes averted her for a moment, assuming something terrible had happened. Suddenly, she pinch her nose and said, 'You smell like poo. What's going on? What happened? Didn't you make it to the toilet you two? Did you get the trots? How embarrassing.

I was starting to worry about you, go take a shower, you first Cameron. On your way to the bathroom, in the cupboard, grab yourself some towels. When you change your clothes, there's a plastic bag in there to put them in.'

'Thank you very much Mrs. Andrew.'

'No worries, just call me Moana. There's some shepherd's pie in the warming oven for your tea Ashley. There's enough for you and Cameron if he'd like.'

Ashley's face clouded with concern when she spotted the cigarette butts in the ashtray. 'What is this? I thought you'd quit?' Ashley said, pointing to the ashtray.

'I'll try again next week. I just wanted to finish the pack that someone gave me. But don't change the subject. What happen with you and Cameron?' Moana stared at her, her eyes declaring she was glad they were alive and safe.

'Nana, you promised you'll quit. I'll explain everything to you later, but we've got to get cleaned up and go.'

Suddenly, she bent over and wrapped her arms around her stomach. 'Aww my tummy aches, it must be the punch from the party. Bloody hell.'

'Me too. Actually, can I use the toilette?' Cameron said, clutching his stomach.

'Well, when I have indigestion a little sip of sherry helps, you know that Ashley,' nana said, handing her a glass of sherry.

Ashley took the sherry and drank it down, then took a second shot.

In agonizing pain, Cameron's stomach churned. He threw down the first shot and Ashley refilled it. 'Come on, drink up Cameron, then get in the shower. I'm going to go see Jerry right now.'

Thinking it would fix his stomach, Cameron drank the second glass of sherry. After a quick shower he looked much better, like an actor from an old black and white TV show, with his hair pulled back, in grandpa's loose shirt, and buggy trousers.

Ashley still had on her black jeans and red Nike hoody after her shower. 'Love you, Nana, see you later. Don't wait up for me. I may stay the night at Jerry's.'

'So long as it's okay with Jasmin and how is Jerry? He hasn't been here for a while. He's so good to you, that young man. I hope you didn't do anything that would hurt his feelings,' Moana added, clasping her hand to her chest.

Ashley didn't tell her what had happened to Jerry as Moana was just recovering from a minor heart attack. 'That's why I want to stay the night nana, to see what's going on.'

On their way to Jerry's house, Ashley told Cameron, 'Stop the car. We're being discoed.

'What the heck do you mean by that?'

'You see those red and blue lights flashing behind us like disco lights? That's the cops pulling us over.'

'Damn, you might get breathalysed,' Ashley said, her eyes widening.

Cameron was frantic as he remembered the sherry, and the drink he had at the party. He was pretty sure he would be over the limit if tested. Disgusted with himself, he thought *from hero to zero*. 'I'm in dire straits if I'm over the limit and screwed if I can't drive,' he told her as he pulled over and turned the engine off.

Brett Giles approached the car and motioned for Cameron to open the window. He bent into the window a little, coming face to face with Cameron.

'Please state your name and address,' Brett ordered. Then, upon smelling alcohol, held the Breathalyzer up to Cameron's mouth. Ashley watched, then got out and walked around to speak to the cop before he issued a ticket. Cameron noticed her body language as she seemed to be negotiating with the cop.

He looked again at the alcohol level on the reading. 'Your alcohol level is just before the limit, so you're a lucky boy. But you were driving over the limit. This is 50 km zone and you were at 55. But I'll let you off this time. It's half past nine now so hurry home as you're on a restricted license. Make sure you're home before 10 pm'

Ashley got back in the car as Cameron took a long deep breath of appreciation. His faith was mounting. 'Thank you very much, sir.'

As they drove along, Cameron was amazed how Ashley had persuaded the cop. Sucking in a quick breath, he asked, 'Far out, how did you do that? You're da bomb. Thanks for saving my arse.'

'For sure, you were over the limit. That's just a little thank you for saving me from those creeps. Turns out, Brett is having an affair with my auntie. Me and Jerry saw them, going to it on the kitchen table one day. So, I just told him I might mention it to his wife.'

Untimely, his bracelet created a future vision and he saw fire burning the whole town had fifteen minutes to achieve his mission – stop the fire --- otherwise many people will lose their lives.

Fourteen minutes: 'I'll drop you at the corner as I've got a stumping headache. I've got to go to the dairy to get some headache pills,' Cameron said, rubbing his temple.

'Laura has lots of pills for headaches, just ask her for some,' Ashley said, her eyebrows drawing close.

'Sorry, but It has to be one I'm not allergic to,' Cameron answered, his lips narrowed.

'Okay. See you at Jerry's soon then,' she added, as she stepped out of the car.

Ten minutes: The arsonist was near the public library with a petrol can in one hand, and a cigarette in the other.

Seven minutes: Cameron hid himself along the box hedges, across the road from the library.

Three minutes: It was dark but there was enough light from the lamp-post to just barely make things out. Without hesitating, he aimed the slingshot and fired, hitting the arsonist on the hand, causing him to drop the petrol can. A second later, the cigarette ignited the spilled petrol, enveloping the arsonist in a huge fire ball.

Cameron ran to a phone booth by the library, dialled 111, reported the fire, then left.

Chapter 43

It was cold and dark when Cameron arrived at Jasmin's. Jasmin's circle of friends was there to support Jerry through this critical event. James came to see Cameron and met him along the concrete path near the entrance of Jerry's house. He showed him the picture of him kissing Ciara, then added, 'Just to give you a heads-up. Do you want the good news or the bad news?

'Whatever, just tell me,' Cameron told him, moving toward the veranda.

'Tara may have seen the picture on Facebook. You and Ciara kissing one another. The good news is, Mr. Hartley invited us to go fishing on his flash boat,' James said as he tilted his head to the side.

Before Cameron could reply, they heard the deafening sound of a fire engine's siren. Everybody filed out of the lounge and looked up at a huge pillar of smoke contrasting against the dark sky. Karen was the first one out. 'That must be the arsonist again. It's so close to the library,' she said. It pleased Cameron that he had fulfilled his mission as he looked up and whispered secretly, 'Cheers mate,' to KD.

After a few minutes watching, Lora said, 'It will be in the news tomorrow, let's get back in.' Then Karen and Lora headed to the kitchen. Cameron spotted Tara as she entered the room and sat on the couch.

Ashley had gone to Jerry's bedroom and she sat beside him as he slept. Jasmin stuck her head in then left Ashley to be alone with Jerry. As soon as she entered the lounge, Cameron came in and she raced over and gave him a big hug. 'Thanks for being there,' she said trying to hold back the tears. He had no idea what to say. They both sat in silence, looking off into the distance as Tara joined them. After a few minutes Jasmin rose and went into the kitchen, following the aroma of spicy garlic pansit that hung in the air.

Content, Cameron sat on the couch looking at the aquarium, pondering the last 7 months and thinking about the eel and the flooded lounge that made him smile inwardly and warmed his heart. At the same time, he was astounded at how he had carried out three events with a broken wrist. The fact that he had saved his love ones brought a smile to his face. Finally, he glanced over at Tara and worked up courage to talk to her. He watched her staring at her cell phone; her hair in a bun, with little make up and wearing a yellow hoodie with a US flag on it. He stared, realizing how striking she looked.

He moved closer to her. 'I know you've seen the picture of me and Chiara kissing.'

She stared into his eyes. 'So, what about it?'

'I thought you'd be disgusted.'

'To be honest, why would I care? It would be a different story if you were my boyfriend.'

'Do you think less of me now?'

'No, I know it's just a game Ciara's playing. Look what she's done to Jerry and Ashley. And Brice used her as well to make me jealous. Honestly, I don't want to discuss it,' she added.

Cameron understood this was not the right time or place, but he asked anyway. 'So, would you go out to dinner with me to Silvanus Café on Saturday? That is, as long as you're not seeing Kirk.'

'Kirk? What about him?'

'I thought you liked him.' She felt a flutter in her stomach as she realized Cameron might be jealous of Kirk.

'Kirk? No, he and Azoma just got back together. He even asked her to be his date at the prom. We're friends, that's all. And lately, I've been helping him save the hedge hogs who were sick and injured on their property.'

Thinking of the upcoming prom, he asked her, 'Would you be my date for the prom?'

'Uh, no thank you.' A big smile formed as she added, 'Just kidding. Yes! Yes! I thought you'd never ask.'

He bent forward, about to kiss Tara, just as Karen and the rest of the group came into the lounge offering carrot cake and coffee.

Cameron excused himself and headed for the toilet just as his bracelet vibrated. A new mission called. He snuck out the back door, ensuring no one saw him. The timer told him he had three minutes; three minutes until some-one would try and kill him, again.

As he came around to the car park, a hooded man approached.

Two minutes: Cameron pulled the slingshot out, aimed it and hit the hooded guy in the center of his forehead. Cameron tried to approach the hooded guy who was knock out and lying on the ground, but someone yelled out calling his name before he was able to see if the guy was dead

Cameron turned and went back inside, acting as if nothing had hap-pened. He looked around wondered who yelled his name, but was unsure if the voice was real

He sat back down next to Tara and his thoughts went to the notebook. Maybe now it was time to go back to US and turn the notebook over to the authorities. This would be the perfect time. He would be turning 18 soon, so he would not need his parent's consent to leave the country.

Teaser for The Slingshot Guy- Part 2

Missions Through Visions

September 7

Confident of his bracelet and power, Cameron got ready to meet Tara for their first dinner date at Sylvanus Café. He spent half an hour in the shower, and another half an hour choosing what clothes to wear. He looked at his watch. He still had plenty of time. After trying on some clothes, he ended up wearing a white Rip Curl long sleeved shirt and a black leather jacket. After applying deodorant, he remembered to be sure and take the heart-shaped nurse watch with the glittering studs around it.

After choosing a lavender cowl neck satin dress with a wraparound white woollen jacket, Tara put applied blue eyeliner, which accentuated her blue-gray eyes. She put on perfume that had a sweet spicy scent. Full of anticipation, she drove to Sylvanus Café at the marina.

Cameron stopped for petrol on the way. As he was filling up the tank, the bracelet nudged: He had ten minutes to accomplish the mission. But when he was about to get back in the car, suddenly a guy in a mask grabbed him from behind. Cameron managed to break free. Instantly a blow landed on his eye then another on his mouth. He rushed to get in the car, but he couldn't shut the car door as the masked man pulled him away. But with his adrenalin pumping, he slammed the door shut jamming the masked man's fingers in the door,

'Aww, rat bag ,' the man yelled.

But then three other masked men followed, and one put a gun to his head and ordered for him to get out of the car.

As he stepped out of the car, the gun still pointed to his head, one of the masked men tried to put a sack cloth over his head. Cameron somersaulted, breaking free. In a split second, he kicked the hand of the guy with the gun, and it dropped to the ground. Cameron threw a succession of kicks and punches at each one of them while he blocked their counterattacks, however, some punches landed on his nose which made it bleed. He lost his footing. Nothing seemed to knock them out. Amidst the relentless fight, he heard sirens. The masked men took off in a black Pajero, the police giving chase.

Cameron had two minutes, but he looked up to find a line of cars that looked like a wedding procession, with classic cars decorated with ribbons and he couldn't get through.

By the time he reached his mission there were zero minutes left. When he saw ambulances, cops and spectators, he left. With a fat lip, a black eye, and blood all over his shirt, he decided not to even text Tara. He wanted Tara to hate him as he'd lost all faith in his ability to protect her.

As he listened to the breaking news, they announced three people were dead at the Bella Pub. Two men in their thirties were in custody. Disappointed at not fulfilling his mission, Cameron's doubt grew quickly. He went home and buried his head in his pillow, frozen in shock. This time he had mistrusted his supernatural power, and he thought: *Why was there was no warning of his attackers? His attackers seemed unbeatable. Why had God given him obstacles to achieve in addition to his mission?*

At Sylvanus Café, Tara waited patiently, looking out at the ocean. She had texted Cameron several times, but he hadn't replied. After an hour, Tara left. She was filled with disappointment as she climbed down the stairs with a heavy heart, but she set off to Cameron's house, determined to find out what had happened.

Do you want to know how the story goes? Read *The Slingshot Guy* Part 2 Missions Trough Visions . It will be available in Amazona by September 2020 in Kindle and Paper back please follow this link : amazon.com./author/ligaya

THANK YOU

Thank you so much for your time in reading this book If you enjoyed this book or found it , Can I ask you a favour of reviewing can you please make a quick review as review is so important both readers and author . Your review will be much appreciated. God Bless you.

About the Author

L. J. Parsons has been a Registered Nurse for over 35 years, who believes that reading and writing is a form of psychotherapy to cope with stress, and loss of her loved ones.

This book is her first debut novel. She endeavors to finish part 2 of this book trilogy at the end of 2020.

Originally from the Philippines, L. J. immigrated 35 years ago to New Zealand, where she lives presently. She lives with her husband Terrence and their 2 cats.

In her free time, she loves going for a walk, swimming, playing scrabble, and reading books.

amazon.com/ligaya/ author

www.ljparsons-nz.com

Facebook:

@ligaya.parsons

Twitter: @ligayapink

Instagram:

@ligayaparsons

E-mail   ligayaparsons1

@gamil.com

www.ingramcontent.com/pod-product-compliance
Lightning Source LLC
Chambersburg PA
CBHW032054050726
47590CB00001B/261